ORPHAN'S EGG

A CASTOR'S GROVE YOUNG ADULT
PARANORMAL ROMANCE

A.J. RENWICK

PLOTWORKS PUBLISHING

1

FRANCES

Frances West stood, frozen on the sidewalk, staring at the familiar gray door.

It was the first thing she'd recognized since returning to Castor's Grove three weeks ago. Though she'd been born in the city, Fran's return had felt less like a homecoming than she'd secretly hoped. The streets were easy to navigate with buildings organized in square grids, her temporary apartment on the edge of downtown was clean and conveniently located, and there was nothing lacking in the environment. With the ocean on its south and east borders, forest to the north and west, and dense urban high-rises in its center, Castor's Grove was a city that boasted something for everyone.

But there was nothing special about a city that everyone could enjoy. Fran liked it, but it was in the same way any visitor might. While waiting to hear back from the adoption agency, she'd wandered the streets, avoiding the usual tourist activities, waiting to see something that sparked some long-buried memory or wander into someone who would recognize her.

Now, it was happening.

But instead of the sense of belonging she'd imagined, Fran's chest tightened, and her breath caught. Her anxiety buzzed in her brain.

There was an image of a sword burned into the door. It stretched almost the entire length, its hilt hovering only a few inches above a sunflower welcome mat that looked far too normal in the context. Who lived in this house?

Your foster parents. Fran grappled with her anxiety to take control of her own thoughts. *They're probably into Dungeons and Dragons, or one of the kids they cared for did it.*

Either way, it was nothing to worry about.

Fran took a deep breath and pushed her hands into the pocket of her large black jacket. It wasn't cold, but she wrapped it around her as she walked up the steps. There was no doorbell. She tapped her elbow against the wood.

No response came from within. Fran could've tried again. It had been a light knock.

This is too weird. They might not even live here anymore. What was I thinking just knocking on their door?

She should just leave a message. There was paper in her pocket; she could buy a pen somewhere nearby, write a letter, and slip it into the mailbox.

"Upon my honor."

Fran spun around to see a thin middle-aged woman with olive skin. Short gray hairs frizzed around her temples, narrowly escaping the band that pulled the rest into a black ponytail. She wore an oversized green dress with a canary yellow jacket that matched the shopping bag in her hand.

The woman took a few steps closer, keeping her eyes on Fran. There was a wariness to her expression.

"Um, I was just—"

There was nothing suspicious about knocking on someone's door in broad daylight, but Fran felt suddenly guilty. "Do you know if the Franklins still live here?"

"We do." She narrowed her eyes, glancing between Fran and the door as though she thought the teenager was blocking her path. "Is this a university project? Are you doing a census?"

Fran was tempted to lie, tell Mrs. Franklin yes, and bolt, but she'd made it this far, so she shook her head. "No, I'm not with the university. I'm actually, well I was, one of the kids you fostered. It was like fifteen years ago. You probably don't remember—"

"Frances Buckler."

The sound of her original name rang like a bell in Fran's ears. Her lips mouthed the word *Buckler*, trying to wrap themselves around the harsh first syllable and the slur of the second. She'd whispered it to herself every night since she'd learned it, but it still felt like it belonged to someone else.

"It's Frances West now, actually."

"You've dyed your hair." Mrs. Franklin reached toward her. Fran flinched, but she was too slow to stop the woman from grabbing a clump of black hair. Mrs. Franklin ran her finger over the ends as though testing if the dye would rub off. Then she dropped the hair, pulled a set of keys out from her bag, and turned to the door. "Come inside. You shouldn't be out here."

"Oh." Fran pulled her jacket tight again. Her first instinct was to refuse. Stranger danger and all that. But how did she expect to get information about her parents if she didn't talk to Mrs. Franklin? "Maybe for a minute, but I can't stay long."

The strange yet familiar door led to a normal and therefore relatively forgettable living area. There was a fireplace in the corner with olive green couches and a squat brown coffee table. Paintings of flowers hung on the walls.

Fran's stomach tightened as she stepped in. *Why doesn't it match the door?*

"Sit." Mrs. Franklin instructed, pointing at the couch.

Fran hesitated, but the woman kept smiling and staring. Eventually, she gave in and sat on the edge of one of the chairs. Mrs. Franklin didn't join her.

"You must tell me about your life, dear. What's brought you back to the city?"

"Nothing in particular," Fran said, fingers crumpling stray pieces of paper in her pockets as she tried to guess what Mrs. Franklin's angle was.

There's no angle. She's just a nice older lady who took care of me for six months when I was a toddler. Don't listen to your anxiety.

"Although, I was wondering if you knew anything about my parents," Fran forced the truth out. "I wouldn't bother you about it, but there's no record of them anywhere, no birth certificate on file for me, but you're the one who recorded my last name as Buckler, and my dads said you sent that gift with me, so I just thought, maybe you'd known them?"

Fran held her breath as she waited for Mrs. Franklin's response. This was it. Her former foster parents were her last chance of learning the truth about her birth parents. Who had they been? What had they done? Had they loved her?

The woman before her might have those answers.

Mrs. Franklin's smile faltered. "What gift?"

"You know," Fran said. If the woman had been able to

recognize Frances after fifteen years, she must have remembered it. "The Fabergé egg. It's purple with gold details."

Mrs. Franklin's smile stretched so tight that it looked like her skin would snap. "You still have that?"

"Obviously." Sarcasm leaked into Fran's voice before she could stop it. Did the woman really think she'd have thrown away the only gift she'd ever received from her parents?

"It's here with you? In the city?"

Fran stiffened, feeling her heart thump in her chest. That was a strange question. It wasn't just her paranoia.

"No. I left it back in Lansing."

"Excuse me a moment. I need to make a call." Mrs. Franklin spoke with the smile frozen on her face.

Fran nodded. Her eyes flicked to the front door. It was close, but not so close that the older woman couldn't grab her before she got to it.

Mrs. Franklin didn't leave the room. Eyes trained on Frances, she pulled a phone from her pocket, pressed a button, and raised it to her ear.

Fran struggled to keep her breathing steady as she stared at the woman.

"Dammit." Mrs. Franklin's smile finally dropped as she lowered the phone. She knelt on the carpeted floor before Fran and rested her hands on the teenager's knees.

Fran was small, but the woman before her was frail. She could push her off. But her body was frozen. All she could think about was the fact that she should've hidden her knife in her pocket instead of her boot.

"Listen, Frances, I have the answers you want, okay? But we need to be honest with one another. What's the address of your home in Lansing?"

There was no way Fran was telling her that.

"Never mind. Two dads, West? I'll look it up. Just wait here until I'm back, okay? I'll tell you about your parents then."

Before Fran could fully process what the woman had said, Mrs. Franklin had raced out of her own house. The tension in Fran's body slackened as she realized that she was alone, but her heart continued to quiver. This was all far too weird, and try as she might, Fran couldn't pierce through her anxiety to come up with a logical reason for Mrs. Franklin's actions.

I need to leave.

But Mrs. Franklin knew her parents. Fran could finally learn who they were, who she was.

The longing burned within her, begged her to stay, just as her anxiety screamed at her to run. The result was that Fran sat on the olive chair for a lot longer than most sane people would have. And she might have remained there until Mrs. Franklin returned were it not for the noise.

A loud twang shook the floor beneath Fran's chair.

That settled it. She leaped up and grabbed the door handle without hesitation. But it wouldn't budge. Mrs. Franklin had locked her in.

Crap.

Trustworthy people didn't lock teenagers in their houses. Whatever claims Mrs. Franklin made about her parents could easily be false. She couldn't stick around.

But how could she escape?

The Franklins' house had only one entry, and there were bars on all their windows. Except for the ones in the basement.

It was the design of all the houses in this area. Fran had noticed it while walking through the neighborhood. But the strange noise had come from the basement.

Fran reached into her boot and pulled out her knife. Fingers trembling, she managed to get the blade free. She held it before her, afraid to breathe as she searched for the basement door.

It didn't take her long to find it in the kitchen.

Cold sweat trickled down Fran's back as she stared down a long flight of steps. There was no sound now save Fran's own pounding heart.

Maybe the noise she'd heard was a cat. People owned those. They knocked things over. At least, they did in television shows.

And I think I'm too smart to die in a horror movie? This is the dumbest thing I've ever done.

But waiting for Mrs. Franklin would've been just as foolish. So Fran tiptoed down the stairs, knuckles white around her knife.

A stream of light from a high window illuminated the bottom of the staircase. The tension eased from Fran's body. It was too high for her to climb through, but there might be a ladder or something she could stand on down below. Maybe she wasn't about to die.

"Dust!" a boy's voice exclaimed.

Or maybe she was.

"Couldn't you at least give me a few minutes to try to escape? Maybe we could make a trade?"

Fran's legs turned into metal rods, anchored to the ground, unable to move. Her heart did its best to escape them. It took all her effort to turn her head toward the voice.

Her mouth dropped open. The only thing that stopped her from gasping was that her chest was too tight to let the breath escape.

Trapped underneath a silver net was a boy about her

own age with a mass of red curls. But it wasn't the net or the color of his hair that made Fran feel as though she were about to faint.

He had wings.

2

IVAN

Ivan's eyes flicked to the silver badge glittering on the edge of the table. He could just make out the edge of the sword's blade engraved in the metal. The badge was his ticket to success. The entire reason he'd broken in. And it was just a few feet away.

But it didn't matter how close it was. With the stupid net on him, Ivan couldn't move. And now, someone was here.

Dust it all. This was precisely why it was pointless making plans. They always went to shit.

Of course, Daisy would tell him that spending two days watching the Franklins didn't count as planning. But that was because his sister wouldn't factor in the twenty-four hours he'd spent searching for a knight's house, or all the effort he'd put into rushing the week prior. Gaining acceptance to the Phi Eta Gentlemen wasn't all partying and drinking. They were the most exclusive fraternity at Castor's Grove University and pledges had to pass a series of dangerous tests to prove their worth.

Getting a knight's badge was the final one.

And it should have been so easy. Ivan was a fairy. With the Franklins gone, all he had to do was fly through the basement window, grab the badge, then fly back out.

But he hadn't anticipated the anti-magic net. Despite its name, the weapon was itself enchanted. Most knights wouldn't touch it with a ten-foot pole. All the planning in the world wouldn't have saved Ivan.

Still, the net was a minor issue. He might've been trapped, but like all enchanted items, his current prison had a weakness. Ivan just needed a few minutes to figure out what that was, and presto, he'd be free.

But now someone had come into the basement.

Howard and Bethany Franklin lived alone. They didn't have children. So either the sudden intruder was a visiting cousin, one of the knights, or another burglar.

Given that his wings were out, Ivan was really hoping for the last option. He didn't think any knight or relation of the Franklins would be very sympathetic to a fairy.

Ivan shuffled the net before him so that the strings didn't obscure his vision. He got a clear glimpse of the person before him, and his eyebrows rose. "You're a girl."

In profile, her black hair had blended into her oversized jacket, but now he could see her face, the statement seemed obvious. She had a small chin, dark eyes, and trembling cupid bow lips that she'd painted black.

"Yes." She licked her lips. The makeup stayed on. "What are you?"

Ivan breathed a sigh of relief. A knight would have recognized a pair of fairy wings. This was just a normal human girl. And that meant, he still had a decent chance of making it out of here with his wings intact.

"I'm a boy. Actually, nineteen is probably too old to be called a boy, isn't it? I suppose I'm a very young man." Ivan gave her his most charming smile. "I love your lipstick. Very empowering."

The girl stared at him, lips still parted. Ivan wondered if his compliment had left her speechless. Normally, he had to do a bit more work, but he had been told he was irresistibly charming many times, and at least once by a woman other than his mother.

"I don't have time for this." She stepped away from Ivan slowly, almost as though she was concerned he would jump at her, despite the very obvious net holding him in position. Something glinted in her hand.

She had a knife. It was so small Ivan almost hadn't noticed it.

Forget about finding a clever way to free himself from the net. It was mostly string. "Can you cut me free?"

The girl didn't answer. One eye still on Ivan, she approached the table with the knight's badge. The silver must've caught her eye. She picked it up, staring at it for a few seconds as though she'd been teleported to another world.

"Hey, maybe we got off on the wrong foot. I'm Ivan. What's your name?"

She jumped at the sound of his voice, almost as though she'd forgotten he was there. Her fingers closed around the badge, and she slipped it into her pocket. The knife trembled in her other hand.

Perfect. Now she has both the things I need.

"Would you believe me if I told you I was your fairy godfather?" Ivan tried.

She snorted. "No."

Great. But at least she'd responded. That was an improvement.

"I'll grant you three wishes if you free me." It was a lie, but once Ivan was free, he wasn't planning to let the girl remember the encounter anyway.

"That's what a leprechaun would say." The girl turned away from him, focusing her attention on the table where the badge had been. She rested her hands on one side, bent over, and grunted as she began to push.

"I could help you if you let me out."

"Don't. Need. Help."

Ivan opened his mouth to argue, but the girl's stubbornness paid off as the heavy metal legs finally inched along the floor. The corners scraped the wallpaper with a *screek* like an out-of-tune violin.

He covered his ears until the girl finally stopped. She'd positioned the table underneath the window.

"Hey come on. For real, it's not cool to just leave me like this. I mean, you're obviously not supposed to be here either. Just help me out. There's loyalty among thieves or something? That's a code, right?"

Clearly not one the girl followed. She jumped up and managed to grab the corner of the window with her hands.

She's seriously stealing the badge and leaving me here? What kind of sociopath is she?

"At least toss me the knife?"

The girl kicked her legs against the wall, trying to use her feet to help her climb.

It didn't work. She lost her grip and slipped back onto the table.

A smile spread across Ivan's face. She didn't have the upper body strength to pull herself out.

"Ready to make a deal now?"

The girl turned toward him. She climbed down from the table and approached, stopping only a few inches shy of Ivan. Her shoulders rose with unsteady breaths. She pulled the knife out of her pocket. "How do I know if I can trust you?"

Ivan laughed before he realized that she was serious. What did she think he was going to do? He was a fairy, not a creature humans typically associated with danger.

"You don't know. That's how trust works. You kind of have to offer it blindly." His wise, philosophical words didn't move the knife any closer to the net. Ivan groaned. "And I don't see what other choice you have here if you want to escape. I need you, and you need me. That's a brilliant foundation for trust."

As if to accentuate Ivan's point, Mrs. Franklin chose that moment to return. The front door creaked open, and they heard her call out, "Frances, where are you?"

Standing in front of me, I presume.

Frances grabbed the net and pressed the knife to it. Still, she didn't start sawing. Instead, she turned her dark eyes to Ivan. "If I free you, I don't just want help escaping. I want answers. Agreed?"

"Yes," Ivan hissed. "Just hurry up."

Mrs. Franklin's footsteps thumped against the basement ceiling. Ivan's blood pumped in his ears, fingers itching. Frances needed to work faster.

There was a click as the basement door opened. The hole in the net was almost big enough.

"Frances, are you down here? Your mother is on her way."

The girl froze.

"What are you doing? Don't stop now." But Ivan's words didn't affect her.

Frances' head turned toward the stairs.

Dust! So much for all her concern about trust. She was the one betraying him! Frances was giving up when they were seconds away from escape.

Which meant Ivan was going to lose his wings if he didn't take matters into his own hands.

3
FRANCES

My mother is coming here?

The room around Fran vanished, swimming into a blur of grays. The only sound was her heart pounding in her chest.

She'd spent years imagining her mother. Now, she was on the cusp of meeting her.

Ivan swiped the knife from her hand, reminding Fran of her present situation. He hacked at the strong strings of the net then wriggled through a hole, folding the shimmering blue and red wings on his back so that he fit.

Is he really a fairy?

"Come on." Ivan grabbed her wrist and pulled Fran toward the window. He pushed his hands under her armpits. "Dust, you're heavy."

Fran's feet lifted from the ground. Ivan was flying them up toward the window.

Holy crap. He is a fairy.

Ivan shoved her through the window first.

"No, wait." Fran realized what was happening too late. "I want to stay!"

There was a shout from inside. It sounded like Mrs. Franklin. She must've made it to the bottom of the steps.

"Too bad." Ivan pushed her onto the grass beneath then flew out after her. "I promised you answers, remember? Have to keep a promise."

"But my mum—" Fran began to object, but the sunlight landed on Ivan's wings at that moment. The bright blues and reds glittered as if hundreds of fireflies had landed on them. His red curls shone like fire on his head.

Was she really about to say no to a fairy? Because a very suspicious woman claimed her mother was on her way?

Ivan grabbed her hands and pulled Fran off the grass. "We gotta go. Now."

Mrs. Franklin was already out of her house. The middle-aged woman was surprisingly spry. They heard the door swing shut. She shouted Frances' name.

"Time to trust me."

Ivan laced his fingers through Fran's. Everything in her vision blurred except the red-headed fairy. She expected him to drag her, running through the rows of houses to escape Mrs. Franklin. Instead, he put a finger to his lips and guided them toward the sidewalk.

Was he insane?

Mrs. Franklin ran straight past them. She was so focused on getting to the window around the back of her house that she didn't notice as they went past.

It was... *impossible.*

Unless... Fran turned her head, examining the strange blur in the air around her as Ivan guided her down the street. No one looked at them. Almost as if... *we're invisible.*

———

Ivan led her east along Falmouth Street before turning north on 60th. A few blocks further, he dipped between two buildings and folded his wings. As soon as he did, the blur in the air vanished, and Fran was able to see everything clearly once more.

"I doubt she'll look for us in here." Ivan tapped the side of the building, a big grin on his face. "Come."

Fran had little choice. He was still holding her hand.

She followed the fairy through two sliding glass doors into a cafe. Before Fran could notice much else about it, something leaped onto her head.

Too panicked to scream, Fran squeaked. She shouldn't have trusted Ivan just because he was a fairy. He'd led her into a trap.

Ivan clamped his mouth shut, cheeks swelling as he tried to swallow a laugh. The noise sputtered out anyway.

"I'm so sorry." A blonde girl with her hair pulled back into a ponytail stepped forward and grabbed the something off Fran. "Halo's just a baby, and he's still playful."

Fran looked down at the purring white kitten in the girl's hands. The blonde gave her an apologetic smile before running back to the table in the corner where an older boy, her brother judging from their almost identical features, was sitting. She released the tiny creature, and it rushed toward a tower where a large gray cat was snoozing.

They weren't the only felines in the room. As Fran looked around, she spotted two tabbies prowling on a platform that swung over one of the tables. A calico licked its paws beside a woman drinking coffee, and a tuxedo cat lay belly up on the counter with one yellow eye surveying everyone as they entered. A sign on the wall behind it read **Nine Lives Cat Cafe** with black cat heads as the dots in the *i*'s.

"Take a seat." Ivan grinned as he nudged her. "I'll order for us."

Is it a magical cat cafe? Fran's head spun with thoughts about witches and familiars as she took a seat near the door. She pushed her hands into her pockets. There was something round within.

What was that?

Fran pulled out the shiny silver badge. The ever-familiar sword was engraved in bronze on one side, the word *honor* arced above its pommel. But it was what was on the back that had made her grab it. It was four letters: *O.O.T.E.* Fran had no idea what they meant, but somehow, seeing them had been like seeing her own name engraved on the badge. Her hand had grabbed it of its own accord.

"Here we go." Ivan grinned as he rested two large mugs on the table before them. "You drink coffee, right? I mean it's a latte anyway, so it's mostly milk and sugar. Try some."

Fran glanced down at the drink. She loved coffee, but she made it a rule not to accept drinks from strangers. Even ones with pretty wings.

The thought made her realize something else. She raised the mug but didn't bring it to her lips. "I can't see your wings anymore."

"Because they're hidden," Ivan said as if it were the most obvious thing. "We couldn't let you all live in our city if we couldn't hide them, could we?"

Fran's eyes narrowed. "Your city?"

"Castor's Grove is the magical capital of the country." Ivan swept his hand around, almost knocking over a scratching post. "Home to every creature you can imagine: fairies, elves, nymphs, vampires, werewolves. You name it, we've got it."

Fran had to put both hands on her mug for a moment to

keep it from dropping. Silly response really. She'd seen Ivan's wings. He'd flown her and turned her invisible. What he'd said shouldn't come as a shock.

But hearing it aloud somehow felt more significant.

Fran shook her head slowly, fighting the smile that threatened to spread across her face. "Magic is real."

"Yes, which I know is a huge discovery for a Grover such as yourself. That's what we call humans. Us magical beings are Castors. Anyway, you must have a hundred questions." He glanced down at his phone and a grimace passed over his face for a split second before the large grin returned. Ivan reached across the table and grabbed Fran's hand. "And we're not leaving here until I've answered all of them. Think of me as your own personal tutor, happy to tell you everything about the magic in Castor's Grove."

Fran's lips parted to respond, but she couldn't find words. This was too incredible to be real. She stared at Ivan, studying his features properly for the first time since they'd met. With his red curls, high cheekbones, and a smile that took up half his face, he was undeniably attractive.

A cute boy is offering to teach me all about magic.

The thought made Fran freeze. Her chest grew tight. When things sounded too good to be true, it was normally because they were.

Suddenly aware of the warmth of Ivan's fingers against hers, Fran's face grew hot. She glanced down at their hands. Was he flirting with her?

Ivan followed her gaze. He smiled and winked.

That was definitely flirty.

And definitely suspicious.

Fran flinched her hand away.

"Anyone ever tell you you're cute when you blush?"

"No, because I don't blush." Fran took a sip of the latte,

trying to hide her face with the mug. She tasted vanilla before realizing what she'd done and spat it back into the cup.

Ivan was studying her with far too much interest.

Was this a thing fairies did? Flirt with unsuspecting humans and then steal their souls or something? Maybe Fran had been too quick to assume he was the good guy.

"You're not my type," she said, crossing her arms and staring straight at the redhead.

Ivan pressed his hand to his heart and bowed his head. "I'm wounded." He glanced up at her, pale green eyes staring at her under a pair of sparse red brows. "Let me advise you anyway? It's the least I could do given you rescued me."

Fran bit her lip. The fairy looked so earnest it made her feel guilty for insulting him. Maybe the suspicion was just her anxiety getting the best of her.

And she did have questions.

"Who are the Franklins? Are they magical too?"

"Definitely not." Ivan snorted. "They're knights. Opposite of magical."

"Nights?" Fran leaned back and took a sip of her latte. She didn't spit it out this time.

The Order of the Knights, as Ivan explained, was a group of humans dedicated to eradicating magic. They claimed to trace their roots back to the Middle Ages, but they'd probably invented that history to sound more legitimate. More than likely, the Knights had come into existence alongside the city.

Castor's Grove had been founded three and a half centuries ago by a group of magical creatures that had fled from Europe. They'd designed it to be a safe haven, free of humans. But given the sheer number of regular people in comparison to magical ones, the dream was short-lived. The creatures inevitably made contact with humans, who gradually made their way into the city.

In the early days, the laws weren't so strict or well-enforced. Magical creatures were reckless in more ways than one. Some still believed in the dream of an isolated city. They treated the humans as lesser beings at best and prey at worst. Others were kinder to the humans, but less careful with their own abilities.

It was no mystery then, how The Knights were born. The overlap of humans who discovered magic and witnessed the atrocities that could be carried out in its name sought to protect themselves and their fellows. They banded together, creating an organization with noble intentions and questionable methods.

"I mean, it's not really self-defense if you go on the offensive, is it?" Ivan pointed at the plate in front of Fran. "You going to eat that?"

Fran glanced at the vegetable wrap in front of her. A waitress had brought over one for each of them, but Fran hadn't touched hers. She couldn't process everything and eat at the same time.

In contrast, Ivan had no difficulty eating and talking. He'd devoured his own wrap without breaking the flow of his story.

Fran pushed her plate toward him, and Ivan grabbed the food without hesitation.

As he took a bite, Fran took the split second of silence to jump in. "But what do the knights do now? And why were you at the Franklins' house?"

"Excellent question." The beets turned Ivan's teeth pink. "I actually went to the house because—oh, that was faster than expected."

Fran turned her head, following Ivan's gaze to the door. Two girls with auburn hair were charging toward them. The taller of the two had her hair tied into a short ponytail that stuck through the top of a visor hat with a purple juice store logo. A matching apron covered her white t-shirt and jeans, and she carried a large brown purse. The second girl looked about thirteen with long awkward limbs, an oversized pink hoodie, and a neon blue scrunchie tying her curls in a bun.

There was something about the appearance of both girls that told Fran who they were without needing to ask. *Ivan's sisters.*

"Why'd you bring Poppy?" Ivan pointed at the thirteen-year-old.

His younger sister, assumedly Poppy, stuck out her tongue. Fran caught a flash of silver braces on her teeth.

The taller one scoffed, but it was the only indication she'd heard the question. She slammed her purse on the table and reached into it. "You are an absolute moron. Do you realize that? Amnesiac powder is expensive, Ivan. I can't keep bailing you out every time you make a mistake."

Wait. Fran's grasp on magic was admittedly less than elementary, but she understood the word *amnesia*. And *mistake*.

What was it that Ivan had told her in his story? There were strict laws in place now to ensure that magical beings weren't reckless. That included revealing themselves to humans, didn't it?

Just as Fran's brain registered that she needed to stand up and run, a hand pressed against her shoulder, holding her down. She struggled against it, but the person was strong.

"Look, just let me go. Please, I'm not going to tell anyone," Fran said.

The hand didn't budge.

She looked at Ivan. He was sprinkling a sheen of glittering white sand out of a velvet pouch and onto his palm.

"You said I could trust you," Fran reminded him. "Please, I can't forget all this. It's the closest I've gotten to finding my birth parents. Please, don't do this."

Ivan's eyebrows rose. She hadn't told him about her own mission or why she'd been at the Franklins. If she had the chance to explain now, maybe he'd understand and let her keep her memories.

But the fairies didn't give her the opportunity.

"Sorry," Ivan said, eyes wincing as though he meant it. "But I promised you answers, not that you could keep them."

Before Fran could say another word, he pursed his lips and blew the crystal sand toward her.

And just like that, Fran knew. She was about to have her memory wiped.

4

IVAN

The powder settled on Fran's cheeks, added a glittery sheen to the black paint on her lips, and slipped past her lashes to twinkle in her eyes.

Ivan felt only the slightest hint of guilt. *What was she saying about her parents?*

"You're welcome." Daisy slapped the back of his head. She grabbed her purse. His older sister never stuck around to see what happened with the powder after it was applied.

"Wait." Poppy pushed between the two of them, trying to get a better look at Fran. "Isn't it supposed to sink in?"

"It is," Ivan said, trying to push the thirteen-year-old away. "See?"

He turned back to Fran.

The powder remained flickering on her features. She stared ahead wide-eyed.

Ivan's breath caught. That was weird. Normally, it would have vanished from sight by now, seeping through pores and then journeying up to the brain where the magic would cast a fog over the human girl's memories of the past few hours.

Fran blinked and shook her head. The powder shifted, sprinkling onto the table like a hundred iridescent stars.

"Dust," Ivan cursed. He grabbed a napkin and leaned across the table, trying to gather the fallen powder.

Fran chose that precise moment to stop hesitating. She bent over and blew, spreading the powder to the far corners of the room.

Ivan closed his eyes and blocked his head, managing to avoid getting any on himself.

"It didn't work," Poppy said, stating the obvious. When Ivan peeped his eye open, he saw that his thirteen-year-old sister was gaping at Fran, forgetting to hide her braces like she normally did. "Maybe she's a werewolf."

"She's not a werewolf," Ivan objected. He turned to Fran. "Are you?"

"I don't think so." Fran pressed her hands to her face, running her fingers over the skin where the powder had rested. The edges of her lips quivered, occasionally expanding as though she were about to smile before she pulled them back.

It was cute. Ivan held back a smile of his own. *She's excited and trying to hide it.*

"Well you must be something," Daisy said. Unlike the rest of them, she did not sound pleased about the discovery. Instead, she was glaring at Ivan. "You could've figured that out before wasting the last of our powder. Do you have any idea how expensive that stuff is?"

"Whoa." Ivan held up his hands. "I couldn't have known she wasn't a human. She didn't even know."

It seemed like an excellent excuse to Ivan, but his older sister's scowl deepened. "A few minutes of conversation or thought might have uncovered it." She grabbed his arm and pulled him a few steps away from the table so that they were standing beside one of the many cat towers that littered the cafe. "Where did you even find her?"

"Heh." Ivan scratched the back of his head, studying the tower's fluffy white platforms with sudden interest. "In a knight's house?"

Daisy's hands curled into fists. Her jaw clenched. "Ivan Dream, what were you doing in a knight's house? Are you trying to get killed?"

If she was angry now, she was definitely going to be furious if he told her the truth. Ivan tried, and failed, to think of a lie that would soothe his sister.

"I needed something for pledge week," he mumbled the response under his breath, staring at the ceiling.

"Say that again."

"I was trying to steal a badge," he admitted, a bit more loudly this time. A few of the cafe's patrons glance at him. He grinned and waved at an annoyed looking old woman with square glasses. She chuckled in response, which was a lot better than the glower on Daisy's face. "Look, I need a knight's badge to get into the Phi Eta Gentlemen, okay? So I flew in, and I found her in the basement."

Daisy snorted, shaking her head. She glanced at where Fran was sitting at the table. Poppy was leaning beside her, whispering something.

"I'm going to have to bribe her not to rat me out to mom and dad." Not that there was much his parents could do if Ivan made it into the fraternity and moved onto the university's campus.

"Maybe don't call me to bail you out when I'm babysitting then. You do remember that Mom and Dad were going out for their anniversary dinner tonight?"

"Yes," Ivan lied. "But it's not close to being night."

Daisy rolled her eyes. It looked like she might scold him,

but then her eyes landed on Fran again. Her eyebrows pulled low, and she sucked her lips into her mouth the way she did whenever she was thinking.

"She's cute."

"I didn't think she'd be your type."

"She's not. And she shouldn't be yours either if you're smart," Daisy said, lowering her voice to a whisper. "Immune to powder? Found in a knight's house? Everything about that spells danger."

"Eh, what's life without a little danger?"

"I'm serious, Ivan. We're leaving, and you need to come too. I want us away from whatever the heck she is as soon as possible."

Ivan would've laughed, but he knew better than to piss his sister off, even if she was being overly paranoid. Plus, even he could admit there was some truth to what Daisy said. Fran's presence in the basement had been unusual. And even if she was cute, it wasn't like she had any interest in him. So why stress his sister out by insisting on befriending the mysterious stranger?

"Yeah, of course," he said, resting a reassuring arm on his sister's shoulder. "Just let me say goodbye quickly, and I'll meet you and Poppy outside."

Daisy's eyes narrowed with suspicion, but she sighed and nodded. She grabbed the thirteen-year-old and dragged her off despite Poppy's protests. As they left, Daisy held up a finger and mouthed *one minute* to her brother.

Ivan gave her a thumbs up. What he needed to do shouldn't take more than a minute anyway.

He turned to Fran. She stared up at him, black lips closed tight into an annoyed line.

"So, in exchange for saving you, I was thinking you

might be able to give me something?" Ivan said, leaning on the table and giving her his most charming smile.

Fran's eyebrows rose. They were the only part of her that betrayed the fact that she should've been blonde. "I saved you. You're the one who owes me, remember?"

"Well, I'd say we saved each other." It wasn't like she could've gotten out of the basement if he hadn't flown her. Plus, she'd frozen at the end. "So, let's trade. I gave you a ton of information. You can give me something I want too." He glanced down at her pocket where she'd slipped the knight's badge.

"No way. You just tried to erase my memory. You double owe me now."

That wasn't a thing. "So, what do you want? More answers? Cause I can give them to you tomorrow, okay? I just need something first."

"I know what you want. This." Fran's hand whipped out of her pocket. The silver badge with its dark sword flickered at Ivan. He reached out, trying to grab it from her, but the girl was faster than he'd expected. She shoved it down her shirt.

Ivan froze, his hand hovering near her neck. It wasn't like he *couldn't* put his hand down her shirt and try to find it. In fact, it was pretty damn bold of her to assume that he was the kind of guy who wouldn't.

"And here I thought you weren't into me," Ivan said, keeping his hand in position even though he made no movement.

"Try anything, and I'll scream. And I won't leave out the fact that you're a fairy. Just in case there's someone around that might care that a human knows that." Her black lips quirked into an annoyingly smug smile.

She had him there though Ivan hated to admit it.

He forced a chuckle and withdrew his hand, shaking a finger at her in a scolding manner. "You know I can just turn invisible, follow you home, and take it, right?"

In fact, Ivan could not do that because Daisy would be appearing any second now to drag him off by his ears.

"Or we could make a deal," Fran said, folding her hands on the table. "I need your help with something too."

Ivan's eyebrows rose. As much as he wanted to be annoyed with her for manipulating him, his curiosity was piqued. "What?"

"Stone's Throw Apartments. Ten a.m. Be there if you want your badge."

5
FRANCES

Fran rolled the sleeves of her jacket up as she hurried down the stairs from the second-floor apartment she'd rented for the month. She clutched her white backpack in her arms. It was full of the normal things she'd thought she might need for the day: laptop, pencils, paper, cash. And zipped carefully in a padded compartment near the top was the Fabergé egg.

It was already ten. Fran was running behind schedule. It was her own fault. She shouldn't have spent so much time agonizing over the pros and cons of bringing the egg.

Mrs. Franklin had seemed very interested in the item. Fran had tried to remember everything her former foster mother had said while lying in bed last night, her fingers tracing the golden details of the egg. The conversation with Ivan had played in her mind as well.

Magic was real, but Fran's anxiety wouldn't let her enjoy the possibility that her birth parents might secretly be magical themselves. Instead, she'd spent the whole time worrying about the fact that she'd told Ivan to meet her outside her building.

What if he followed her there to try to steal the badge like he'd threatened? And what if he saw the egg and decided to steal that too?

She couldn't leave either unattended. They'd be safer on her person.

"Boo!" Ivan stepped in front of her as soon as she walked out the door.

Fran didn't stop in time. She ended up colliding into him. Ivan wasn't tall, but he towered over her by almost half a foot, so her face buried itself in his chest. It was firm, mostly muscle.

Bet he looks good with his shirt off.

The thought crossed her mind before she could stop it, and Fran felt her face grow hot.

"Damn you have bad reflexes." Ivan stepped back, looking down at her with a massive grin on his face. "Most people scream or run. If you hadn't kept your backpack between us, I might think you were trying something."

He had the audacity to wink.

Stupid, smug fairy. Fran hated that she was almost definitely blushing as she looked up at him. She couldn't believe she'd just thought about his muscles.

"I wondered if you'd show," Fran said, changing the topic as she slid her hands through the straps of her backpack. The thought of being unable to see the zippers made her nervous, so she kept it in front of her, covering the bag with her jacket as much as possible so that from the side, it almost looked as though she were pregnant.

Ivan raised his eyebrow. "Well, I might not stick around if you're going out in public like that."

So he was one of those people who cared about what everyone thought. Fran had gone to school with plenty of teenagers like that back in Lansing. She rolled her eyes. "Guess you don't want the badge then?"

Ivan's grin returned as though he knew that she'd gotten him there. As Fran walked away from the building, he fell into step alongside her.

"Do I get to know what it is I'm helping with?"

"I'm trying to find my birth parents," Fran admitted. "The women at the Records Center say that there's nothing there. But you can turn invisible. You could break in and find it."

Ivan stopped walking.

Fran turned. "What? Don't tell me you're offended by the request. I literally caught you breaking into someone's house."

"You checked the Castor's Grove official city records, right?"

"No, I checked the unofficial ones." Honestly, what a ridiculous question.

"You know, you might want to check that sarcasm because the unofficial ones are exactly where the information might be."

———

Less than an hour later, Fran stood outside a large Romanesque building in the heart of downtown Castor's Grove.

She stared up past the white marble pillars to the temple roof above. There were panels carved with images of fantastic creatures. A griffin and its rider flew through clouds, a foxlike creature sat with nine tails spread behind it, and in the middle of them all, the face of a dragon, mouth open to reveal wolf-like canines, stared down at anyone brave enough to enter.

There was no name on the building, but Ivan had called it The Archive of Legends.

But the creatures it's showing aren't just make-believe.

"Stop gaping." Ivan reached over and pressed his palm under Fran's jaw, pushing her mouth closed. "You're trying to blend in, remember?"

"I wasn't gaping," Fran objected, pulling her eyes away from the incredible artwork to glare at Ivan. "It's just bizarre to me that you all have this building out here in the open for everyone to see. I mean, people must ask about it all the time. It doesn't exactly blend in."

"Do any of the buildings in Castor's Grove blend in?"

Fran pursed her lips. He had a point there. Unlike the classic New England look expected in East Coast cities, Castor's Grove's architecture was a bizarre mismatch of different periods and styles. You could walk past a gothic mansion, modern skyscraper, and bohemian house all on the same street.

But the Archive of Legends still felt spectacular. "What do most people think it is?"

"You mean Grovers?" Ivan shrugged. "A well protected government building, I assume. They're not allowed inside. Which is why I'm going to be going in alone."

He sprinted up the steps. Fran hurried after him. She'd never been athletic, but she was extra wobbly with the backpack in front of her stomach. "That's not fair. You don't even know what to look for."

"True." Ivan stopped, spinning around to face her at the top of the long marble steps. He was grinning. Again.

Fran clenched her jaw. The constant smiling was getting annoying fast.

"So, what's the name? What am I supposed to be looking for?"

"Why are you trying to ditch me?" Fran was already imagining a scenario where Ivan used the information he found to blackmail her somehow.

Ivan laughed. "Dust, you're suspicious. I'm doing you a favor, okay? Grovers can't go into The Archives. They're enchanted."

Fran glanced at the large doors. They were made of the same white marble as the rest of the building, polished smooth to blend in with the rest of the design. She'd never wanted to see behind a pair of doors so badly in her entire life.

The thought of coming so close to something incredible, only to wait outside while Ivan went in without her was unbearable.

It made her give voice to a secret hope she'd been harboring for the past twenty-four hours, something so insane and brilliant she was afraid to consider it, terrified to admit even as she said it aloud. "Maybe I'm not human."

Fran stood, heart pounding in her chest as she looked up at the always grinning fairy. She waited for him to burst into laughter.

He didn't.

"You might not be, but do you want to risk it? Because if a human tries to enter this building, they wind up on the opposite side of the city, with a week's worth of memory wiped. And the enchantment's not like amnesiac powder. It's not the kind of thing that would malfunction."

Fran sighed. Her eyes glanced wistfully toward the doors, but she shook her head. "It's too big a risk."

"Right." Ivan nodded as though he'd expected the

response. "So, are you going to tell me the name I'm looking for?"

"Buckler," Fran admitted, saying the name to another person for the first time. "At least, that's what it used to be."

Ivan's brow furrowed. He seemed to mull over the name for a moment before his grin returned. "Alright then, Bucky. I'll be back in five. Wait for me."

He winked before turning and pulling the door open.

Fran tried to peer inside as he went in. Something flashed, like the reflection of the sun on a mirror. It was too bright to see beyond. Her eyes squeezed shut.

When she opened them, Ivan was gone, and Fran was stuck outside, staring at the magical doors and wondering what lay beyond.

6

IVAN

Ivan coughed as he stepped inside, a cloud of book dust slapping into his face. The Archive of Legends, for all the elaborate architecture displayed on its exterior, was just a library. And not a well-organized one at that.

Finding a book or an article should've been an easy process. Ivan should've been able to raise his hand, say the word *Buckler* and have all the relevant pieces of information fly toward him. He'd heard stories about witches that had designed rooms like that.

But whoever had created the Archive clearly didn't have Ivan's innate librarian genius. Holding up your hand and trying to summon a book would've just made you look like a moron. Ivan knew. He'd drawn a lot of snickers from university students the last time he'd come here.

That had been almost ten years ago. Ivan wasn't exactly a fan of libraries. They had far too many books. Couldn't the witches have found a way to condense all the information into easy-to-watch videos instead?

And the books in The Archives were the worst kind. *Legends* referred to the street where the main entry was located, not the content within. There was nothing legendary or epic to be found in the dusty tombs. It was all facts: dull histories, reference material for different potion ingredients, dictionaries with archaic language that had fallen out of fashion.

And of course, there was the genealogical information. Ivan reckoned that more than half the books in the massive room were family trees. No one kept records of their ancestors quite like magical beings. There was nothing they seemed to enjoy half as much as finding an oil portrait of some great-great-great-great-great granduncle from hundreds of years ago and parading it around, informing everyone they were descended from a former Duke.

A single match and it would all go up in flames.

The image of The Archives burning delighted Ivan more than it should have. If he did something that stupid, he'd be arrested and exiled so fast that Daisy wouldn't even have a chance to scream at him. And it would probably be for nothing anyway. The books in The Archives would be fireproof.

Get the badge. Once you're in the Gentlemen, you can get your own oil portrait.

Ivan spotted a pair of The Archives' record keepers flying in the aisle across from him. One was a fairy, the other a nymph. But both were old women. It was a prerequisite for working in any type of library, Ivan assumed.

The fairy was arranging books about ten feet in the air, yellow wings fluttering to keep her aloft. Her companion stood below shouting numbers up at her.

Ivan was tempted to make a joke about being quiet in a library, but his jokes never seemed to land with librarians.

"Excuse me, ma'am. I'm looking for the genealogical records. There's a specific name, B—"

The nymph glared at him from the corner of her eye. It was a bright yellow that she must have hidden with lenses when among humans.

"Over there," she said, cutting him off before he'd even provided the name. She crooked her thumb toward an aisle behind her. "It's got a sign. Big letters. Can't miss it."

There was something in her tone that made Ivan suspect that he was not the first person to ask her that question today.

She probably assumed he was some member of the nobility.

Ivan didn't bother setting her straight. Instead, he grinned, inclined his head, and took her hand. He pressed his lips to the back of it. "You have my deepest gratitude, ma'am."

The old nymph snorted and pulled her hand away. "I'm not finding it for you. It's all alphabetical. You can fly up and grab it yourself."

That he could.

Ivan wandered down the rows until he spotted the sign. It was indeed unmissable. The term *Family Trees* was spelled out in suspended lights that flickered like fireflies just above his eye level.

"Not pretentious at all," he muttered to himself as he walked underneath it.

The sooner he could get in and out of here the better.

He stared down the aisle at the thirty-foot-high shelves full of genealogical records. It stretched so far, he couldn't see the wall on the opposite side.

Please tell me I'm standing by A.

"Am I dreaming?" There was a strange, deep laugh from above him. A moment later, a boy darted from the sky to hover before him. He had dark brown hair, cut short around a square face. Large scaled white wings spread behind him, a taut fleshy pink skin stretching between their tendons. A long matching tail swept across the floor. "What are you doing in the genealogy section?"

Ivan forced a smile as he looked up at the dragon. Chase Hagen would've made the top ten in a list of people Ivan didn't want to run into in The Archives. But Chase was a Phi Eta Gentleman, and not an insignificant one given his family's fortune. If Ivan wanted in, he needed to be on Chase's good side.

"Me? What about you? Thought you had tapestries dedicated to this sort of thing hanging in your family's manor."

Had a hint of jealousy crept into Ivan's voice?

No, it was fine. Chase laughed and touched his nose as though letting Ivan in on a secret. "There are some family members even we won't hang on tapestries. You have that badge yet?"

"Working on it."

"Hmm, well, I wouldn't judge you if you couldn't get one," Chase said. "Not exactly a cheap purchase."

"You bought your knight's badge?" Ivan didn't know why the information surprised him.

"Of course. You're not thinking of actually trying to steal one, are you? That would be madness."

"Eh, I'm not afraid of the knights." Ivan waved his hand, only half feigning nonchalance. "They're all dust and no magic."

Chase swooped a bit lower, though it didn't escape Ivan's notice that the dragon still kept his feet off the floor. "I wouldn't be so sure. Rumor has it, they're on the rise again. There were a lot of thefts years ago that they tied to the Knights. Police think there was a split in their ranks, and a new order is on the rise."

Ivan hadn't heard anything like that. But then, he didn't have Chase's connections. He hadn't gone to a fancy private school dedicated to magical beings, and Ivan's parents owned a flower shop. They didn't have connections to the police.

Uncertain if the dragon was joking or being serious, Ivan settled on a response he figured worked either way. "Is that your offer to sell me your knight's badge?"

"Don't think you could afford it somehow." Chase laughed and tapped Ivan's shoulder.

Yeah, I didn't inherit hundreds of years of wealth likely built off of human exploitation. Hilarious.

Still, Ivan forced a chuckle. "Yeah, you're probably right. So if you'll excuse me, I've got my own information to find."

With a thought, he called his wings. They fluttered through his shirt, slipping through the fabric as though they were made of air. Ivan took off, shooting into the sky with as much speed as he could muster.

Ivan flitted up and down the aisle, searching for the letter B. There were far too many last names starting with A.

It might not have taken so long if each surname had been restricted to a single tome. But some names were clearly too incredible to confine in such a manner. He counted over a hundred titles with Blackwell written underneath. The Bloods and their many offshoots had so many that they ought to have made their own library.

Buchart, Buche, Buckley.

Wait.

Ivan stopped and scanned the shelf more closely. Aha! There it was. Buckler.

The entry for it was so small, it was no surprise he'd almost missed it. There was only a single beige folder, slotted between books on the Buche and Buckley family trees. Buckler was written on a red tab that stuck out from the top. Ivan slipped it free.

Weird. Most genealogical records dated back years, but this looked modern.

Ivan's fingers flicked along the edge before he flipped it open.

There were only two pages within. One was a family tree with no sign of anyone named Fran. The other was typed.

Ivan scanned it, and a lump rose in his throat.

If this really was Fran's family, then Daisy had been right. Fran spelled trouble.

7
FRANCES

Do it. Just go inside.

Fran stood with her hand on the smooth curve of the door handle, daring herself to pull it open. All she had to do was step into the Archive of Legends, and she would know the truth.

But was it worth it to risk losing all knowledge of magic?

Maybe.

Do I even want to know it's real if I'm just a regular human? It would only depress her to discover an entirely secret world and then not be part of it. *And it would be just my luck too.*

Damn it. She was doing it. It wasn't like she had anything to lose.

Fran pulled the door open just as another boy stepped outside. He was about Ivan's height with short dark hair and thick eyebrows. His thin lips pulled in at the sight of her. His nose wrinkled in a sniff. His pupils narrowed, growing into long slits like a cat's.

Her slow reflexes reliably failed her, so that instead of flinching away from the peculiar sight, she found herself staring at him instead.

The boy's eyes scanned her, hovering over the backpack that was still in front of her chest. His lips curled. "Going in?"

"Um." She was about to, wasn't she? "I'm just waiting for someone actually."

He leaned forward, and his nose wrinkled again.

Fran's stomach turned. He was smelling her.

What is he? Some sort of vampire?

And she was probably just a regular human. Alone with him.

Oh my God. This is how I die, isn't it?

"It's nicer inside. I insist." The boy put his hand on Fran's back.

She tried to object, but he was strong. He pushed her into the enchanted building.

Fran closed her eyes as the bright light consumed her. This was it. She could kiss all her knowledge of magic and fairies goodbye.

"Huh. What are you?"

Fran cracked an eye open. The boy had followed her inside and now stood, openly sniffing the air around her. Very creepy.

But for once, she was too amazed to let her anxiety take control.

Fran turned away from the boy and stared at the room before her. With Ivan not there to judge her, she let her mouth fall open. The Archive of Legends was incredible.

Rows of books stretched so far that Fran couldn't see any of the walls other than the one behind her. The ceiling was at least fifty feet high, painted with more depictions of enchanted creatures. But even more amazing than that were the people in the room.

Creatures with wings flew through the aisles. There were wings with scales, and ones with stretched black skin, and ones that were almost translucent, shimming as though there was sunlight trapped within, just like Ivan's did.

And I'm in here with them. What did that make Fran?

An excited squeak slipped out of her mouth. She slapped her hand over it, but she couldn't do much to contain the growing smile. She was magical. She was a Castor.

"Ivan," she shouted his name without thought, forgetting how large the room was. She got a few odd glances, but no one shushed her. Fran was certain they thought she looked strange, dressed in all black, squealing like a child, and practically shaking with excitement. But she didn't care. "I'm inside."

"You're with Ivan Dream?" The boy raised his dark brows. He scanned her again, and his thin lips rose in an amused smirk. "Seriously? He's not dating you, is he?"

Fran crossed her arms. It probably didn't look threatening over her backpack, but sometimes the dark makeup counteracted that. She scowled at the strange sniffing boy. "He's looking for something for me. You know where he is?"

"For you?" He scoffed in disbelief and shook his head. But as he studied Fran again, his eyebrows pulled together, creating deep furrows in his forehead before he wiped his face flat. He smiled. "Shall I show you where Ivan is?"

Fran pressed her lips together. She definitely didn't trust this guy. But there were plenty of people in the room, and she wasn't likely to find Ivan on her own. "Sure."

The boy offered his arm for Fran to take. She snorted and stepped to the side of him.

If he was offended by the refusal, he didn't show it. Instead, he walked with his body far too close to hers, head bent so that she could feel his breath in the center of her scalp where her hair was parted. Every so often, the scent would waft to her nose. It was like meat.

"I'm Chase Hagen," he informed her, pausing after he said it. Fran got the impression that he was waiting for a reaction.

"Cool." Fran supposed he expected her details too. She was tempted to give a fake name, but it wasn't like he was a creepy guy trying to get her number. "Frances West."

"West." It was a fairly basic surname, but his mouth moved slowly around it as though he were making the motions with his lips for the first time. "Is that a witching family? You'll have to forgive me. I'm not familiar with it."

He guided her down an aisle that had floating lights identifying that it held family trees. Fran's heart skipped a beat. Had Ivan found anything on her?

"West will be far to the back," Chase informed her. "So we'll just—wait, I'm sorry. Ivan appears not to have made it past B."

For Buckler.

Fran hugged her backpack in excitement. She thanked Chase quickly before running down the aisle toward where Ivan hovered. Beautiful books, bound in colorful leathers, winked at the corners of her vision. Ornate letters stamped surnames on their covers and labeled old scrolls, which had been tied with expensive ribbons.

The truth about her own family might be in one of those.

Ivan's head turned toward her. His eyes widened, and

he forced a small beige folder into a space between two books.

"Fran. How're you in here?" Ivan flew down to the floor, landing in front of her. Instead of happy, he sounded shocked. "Do you remember everything?"

The reaction stung Fran. Which was silly. It wasn't like she and the fairy were friends. Why should he care to discover that she was something more than just a regular human?

"If I did, I could tell you what I ate for breakfast five weeks ago." Fran rolled her eyes. "So, did you find anything?"

"Uh..." Ivan stared at her, sounds that weren't words spluttering from his mouth. Finally, he shook his head. "No, sorry, I didn't. How committed are you really to this whole finding your birth parents thing?"

Fran clenched her jaw. "Pretty committed."

"And you really don't know who they are? I mean, no ideas?"

"This was the idea," Fran pointed out. "Did you really not find anything?"

He shook his head, but there was something strange about it. Was it Fran's anxiety thinking or had he hesitated? And there was something else.

Ivan wasn't smiling.

"I should check too," Fran said. "Just in case, right?"

She watched to see if the fairy would object. That would be a clear sign of guilt. But Ivan just shrugged and nodded.

Great. Then there was no conflict.

However, Fran did have one problem. She didn't have wings. How was she supposed to access all the material that was so high up?

"I can lift you," Ivan offered, catching Fran off guard. He

pointed up to the area where he'd come from. "If you want to see for yourself."

Fran ground her teeth. She recalled what her fathers had said when she'd told them she was traveling to Castor's Grove alone. They'd had no confidence in her ability to take care of herself.

But this wasn't exactly the same as proving that she could feed herself and manage in a strange city. Short of scaling the shelves, which would almost definitely get her in trouble (and was also probably beyond what she was capable of achieving), Fran didn't see how she could see higher without Ivan's help.

Plus, maybe he was bluffing, hoping she'd say no so that she'd never discover that he was lying to her.

"Okay," Fran agreed.

"Take your backpack off then."

"Why? Because it looks silly to you. I told you I don't care."

Ivan snorted. "I can't lift you high enough with it. Not sure if you've noticed, but my wings aren't exactly load bearing." He flapped his wings, and the sparkling blue light arced around him like a rainbow, the red swirls lit up like fire.

The fairy was right. His wings were too pretty to be functional.

Fran glanced around. There was no sign of Chase or anyone else in the aisle now. Much as she hated to put it down, her backpack should be safe.

Her chest tightened all the same as she pulled the straps off. "Let's be quick."

She stepped toward Ivan, holding her arms out so that he could reach under her armpits to lift her.

The fairy moved closer. Instead of reaching for Fran,

however, he stepped around her in a single swift motion.
She realized what he was doing a moment too late.

Ivan was stealing her backpack.

8

IVAN

As soon as he had the backpack, Ivan fluttered his wings in the correct motions to turn himself invisible. Two quick circles clockwise on the top, and counterclockwise on the bottom.

There was no need to take to the sky after that. Ivan had always been faster on the ground, and with the additional weight from Fran's backpack, he trusted his legs more than his wings. Because dust, it was heavy.

What the hell does she have in here?

And how was she in the Archives? It didn't make sense. The Bucklers may have been knights, but they were still humans. The enchantments should have wiped her memory and teleported her elsewhere.

Unless she wasn't related to the Bucklers in that file. Ivan could pray.

"Stop! Thief!" Ivan heard Fran's voice shout behind him. It was a delayed response. He was already a few feet away.

Ivan turned to look at the girl behind him. To his surprise, Fran was running straight toward him.

Almost like she could still see him.

Dust!

Ivan sprinted away from Fran. Unless he wanted to fly, there was no way to go but further down the aisle.

He was faster, but he could hear Fran's footsteps, pounding against the floor behind him, and whenever he risked looking over his shoulder, her eyes were trained on him.

But how? Was she tracking him by his footsteps or scent?

No. Neither of those would be possible if Fran was a human. Unless...

Could she be something else?

His curiosity made Ivan forget his purpose for a moment. He ran in a zigzag, looking over his shoulder to test if Fran's eyes followed. It took the strap of the backpack slapping into his cheek to remind him why he'd stolen it in the first place.

Who cares about the girl? Get the badge.

With Fran still coming toward him, Ivan had no choice but to take to the air. He pushed himself off, using his legs to get as high as he could before flapping. There was something heavy in the backpack. He was about to find out what.

Fran stopped running right underneath him. She screamed up at him.

Ivan did his best to ignore her objections to him rifling through her bag as he unzipped it. Invasion of privacy, blah, blah. It wasn't like he cared about her stuff. He just wanted the badge.

The main source of the weight was easy to determine. There was a laptop, two large notebooks, a pencil case full of pens, and a pack of square paper. Ivan couldn't imagine what Fran had been thinking when she'd packed it. Was she planning on going to school when they finished?

"Give it back, and I'll give you the badge. Swear. Please." Fran was growing desperate beneath him. Her eyes were wide, and her lips quivered. She looked genuinely distressed.

Or she's the best actress I've ever met.

Ivan's wings were getting tired as he shoved the many unnecessary objects back into the pack. It was a struggle to keep himself high enough in the air to avoid Fran's reach. Maybe he should offer to trade the bag for the badge after all. It was possible she'd hidden it in her pocket or something instead.

His fingers brushed a large lump in the back of the backpack. What was that?

Whatever it was, it had been hidden in the lining of the backpack. Highly suspicious.

Ivan felt around within and found a zipper leading to the hidden compartment. He pushed his hand inside. It was hot within. *Why?*

The answer became obvious as his arm pressed against the lump he had originally noticed. Whatever it was had been wrapped in cloth, but it wasn't thick enough to trap the item's heat. Instead, it had created a small sauna in the bag.

Miracle her laptop didn't burst into flame.

Near the bottom of the secret compartment, Ivan found precisely what he was searching for. His fingers tightened around the flat, circular metal of the badge.

He just needed to grab it, drop the bag, and leave The Archives before Fran caught him.

That would've been the smart thing to do. After all, he wanted no part in Fran's quest to find her birth parents.

Yet, after Ivan had pocketed the badge, his hand slipped back into the backpack. He just wanted a quick glance at the item in question.

Struggling to support the backpack in one arm with his wings still beating as fast as they could, Ivan used his teeth to pull the cloth away.

He glimpsed something purple with gold details. *An egg?*

As he tried to examine it more closely, Ivan's finger brushed against its surface. It was like touching fire.

Ivan yelped and recoiled.

The object fell from his hand, spiraling toward the floor as Fran screamed.

9

FRANCES

That asshole had just dropped her egg.

Fran saw the flash of gold as it fell toward the floor. Her mouth opened in a scream. It was going to break.

She stepped forward, right arm extending as if on instinct.

Fran had never been good at catching.

But the Fabergé egg landed right on her palm. Her fingers curled up, securing the base, while her left hand steadied the top. The gold spirals winked at her from the deep purple sheen.

The egg was safe.

Fran breathed a sigh of relief and hugged it to her chest.

"That doesn't burn you?" Ivan flew down. The asshole still had her backpack in one hand, the zipper undone. Her laptop case was right on the edge, threatening to fall.

But losing that would've been insignificant compared to the egg. "What the hell is wrong with you?" she shouted at the fairy.

Ivan slapped his hand over her mouth. "Would you be quiet? We're not the only ones in here."

Fran didn't care. She licked the fairy's palm, trying to force him to move it, but apparently having two sisters meant he didn't care about slobber on his fingers. Fran tried kicking at him instead.

"Ow." That worked. He took a step back, glaring at her as though she were the one in the wrong.

"You almost broke the only thing I have from my parents," Fran shouted. "Why? Because of your stupid badge? Do you realize how messed up that is?"

Ivan's eyebrows rose. "Your parents gave you that egg?"

"Yes." Not that it was any of his business, but Fran wanted him to understand just how much of a jerk he'd been. "And you almost dropped it and broke it."

Where Fran's voice was raised, Ivan continued to whisper. "Is it what I think it is?"

She scowled at him. How the hell was she supposed to know what he thought it was? "It's a Fabergé egg. Or a knockoff of one probably."

Ivan licked his lips. He glanced at the egg in her hands, a nervous expression on his face. "Look, you've been telling me the truth about looking for your birth parents this whole time, haven't you?"

"Why would I lie about that?"

"Okay, then I think you need to give up and give me that egg. Okay? I'll put it back and no one ever needs to know how I got it."

"What? Are you absolutely insane?"

"No, I'm trying to help you, honest. Just. Ah shit." He stopped talking, staring at something over her shoulder.

Fran turned to see two little old ladies coming toward them. One of them was a fairy with fluttering yellow wings.

The other looked normal until she got closer, and Fran noticed the color of her eyes. They were bright orange. Her ears looked pointier than average too.

Ivan flung the cloth back over the Fabergé egg in her arms and rested her backpack onto the floor.

"Name, please," the yellow-winged fairy inquired, lips pulled straight in an unamused expression.

"Um. May I ask why?"

"You're creating a commotion. It needs to be recorded."

"No, I'm not creating anything," Fran objected. "He's the one who stole my bag."

She pointed at Ivan.

The two women stared at the air around him. The one with orange eyes clicked her tongue. "Suppose your thief just gave back the object?"

Fran glanced down at the bag. "Well, yes, he did."

"Uh huh. Name?"

Fran glanced at Ivan as she picked up her backpack. He shrugged his shoulders and looked away, indicating that she was on her own. Fran scowled at him. It wasn't fair. Why weren't these women asking him any questions? They were acting like he wasn't even there.

The fairy and her orange-eyed companion were staring at Fran, waiting for a response.

"Frances West," she admitted.

The two exchanged a glance. She got the impression they didn't believe her.

"I think it's time you left The Archives," orange-eyes informed her. "Best not to make us get Dorcy."

Fran shook her head. She had no idea who Dorcy was, but she suspected that she didn't want to find out.

Head low, she followed the two old women out of the

beautiful, enchanted building. She glanced behind her, expecting to see Ivan following.

He hadn't moved.

Fran's ribs tightened, and her breath hitched. Ivan averted his gaze, staring up at the shelves of texts.

Asshole.

Fran snapped her neck forward, jaw tightening. She didn't know why she was surprised that Ivan wasn't coming. He'd gotten his badge. Of course, he wasn't going to keep helping her.

And Fran didn't care. She didn't want him to.

Despite what her fathers thought, Fran was perfectly capable. She would find her parents on her own.

10

IVAN

Not my problem, not my problem, not my problem.

Ivan repeated the phrase in his head like a mantra. He had the badge. That was all he wanted. There was absolutely no benefit getting caught up in whatever was going on with Fran. Bizarre as it was.

A knight's descendant with a dragon egg.

And that was just the beginning. She'd gotten into The Archives without being teleported, and she'd seen him. The entire time he'd been invisible, Fran had kept talking to him as though nothing were different.

That wasn't normal.

How could Ivan not be curious?

Still, Daisy's warnings from the day before echoed in his mind. And as annoying as his older sister could be, she was seldom wrong. If Frances was a knight, then what happened when she found her parents? They weren't going to be offering rewards to the kind fairies who helped reunite them.

The safest course of option was to forget about Fran and hope she did the same with him.

Ivan had his own life to focus on.

Once she was gone and the record-keepers were distracted with whatever boring tasks occupied most of their time, Ivan dropped his invisibility. He pushed his hand into the pocket of his gray hoodie and retrieved the badge.

He grinned at the sight of the burnished sword. This thing was his ticket into high society. After all, the Phi Eta Gentlemen were more than just a fraternity. They were a social club that extended well after university. Once he was one of them, Ivan would be able to gain entry into every exclusive pocket of the magical world guarded by the nobles and mercantile oligarchs alike.

The thought of himself, dressed in a fancy suit at some fancy ball, flirting with some gorgeous, wealthy heiress made him grin. He flipped the badge into the air.

Something swooped out of the sky and snatched it.

Shit.

Chase landed on the ground before him, a thin smug smile on his face. He held the badge between his middle finger and thumb so that the sword was obvious to Ivan. The dragon's wings expanded behind him, their span stretching almost the width of the aisle.

It didn't seem fair that he could have such large, powerful wings and still manage to maneuver in the small space.

"Good one." Ivan tried to keep the jealousy off his face. He held out his hand, waiting for the dragon to return the badge.

Instead, Chase squinted at something on the back. "This is a new one. It's got her order on the back."

Ivan's brow pulled together. "Whose order?"

"Your new friend's, of course." Chase's lips curled in a

snarl. "Your methods are questionable, but I'll admit, I admire your commitment."

He tossed the badge back. Only once Ivan had it safely in his hands again did he notice the other thing that the dragon was holding. It was a beige folder.

Dust.

Ivan glanced down at the badge. The initials *O.O.T.E.* were engraved in the center of the silver, on the other side from the sword.

The initials meant nothing to Ivan. *Only one to engrave? Out of the elves?* He guessed at words that might fit. None seemed likely.

Wait.

He glanced at the folder in Chase's hands. The Bucklers had created their own branch of the knights. It had been in the file.

Order of the Egg.

Was it really just coincidence that Fran had picked up a badge belonging to an order that her family had created? She must have known the truth. Maybe she was just lying to Ivan.

But if that's true, then what did she expect we'd find in The Archives? And why did she risk coming inside?

Even more bizarre. *How did she get in?*

Knights were the most human of humans.

Ivan ran his hand through his hair. His brain felt like it would spin around until it twisted off of him like a bottle cap.

"Do you know where she's staying?" asked Chase.

The question snapped Ivan back to his current situation. His eyes traveled from the badge to Chase, and the hairs rose on the back of his neck. The dragon's pupils had tightened into slits. It felt almost threatening.

"Who? Fran?" Ivan asked, playing dumb. "Why would you care? Think she's cute?"

Chase laughed. "I'd sooner slit my wrists than touch a knight. No, let's just say, her family has something belonging to mine."

The egg. Suddenly the name of the order was making a lot of sense. "What?"

"Perhaps I'll tell you if you provide me with her address."

"Sorry, can't help you there." He held out his arms and shrugged. "If girls gave me their addresses that easily, I wouldn't need to join the Gentlemen."

Chase didn't laugh this time. Instead, he pressed his lips together, making a strange throaty sound that was somewhere between a groan and a purr. "Never mind. She's using the alias Frances West. I'm certain it won't take long to find her."

Nothing took long when you had the kind of money Chase did.

"Well, great. Good luck with that." Ivan waved in farewell. This was the perfect place to end the conversation. Fran wasn't his friend. He didn't owe her anything. She might even have been lying to him about being a knight.

Ivan took a few steps down the aisle, then turned around. "Not that I care, but what happens when you find her?"

Chase's tongue flickered out of his mouth just enough that Ivan could see the fork at the tip. "You know the Hagen motto?"

"Of course." Ivan had no idea. The ancient families of Castor's Grove delighted in having sigils and mottos and crests and every other pompous marker they could attach to their surnames. It would've been a massive waste of time trying to memorize them all.

But he didn't dare admit that to Chase Hagen.

Instead, Ivan hoped the dragon might just tell him his family's motto anyway.

Chase didn't. The corners of his lips twitched upward as though they'd just shared a secret, and he cracked his knuckles. "Precisely."

Ivan forced himself to return the smile. His stomach felt tight. That was a very ominous response.

As soon as Chase walked off, Ivan jumped into the air and flew toward the H's. The Hagens had a massive collection of books, stretching almost a mile on the top half of the shelves. Ivan scanned them until he found what he was looking for, an old leather-bound beast with stained paper that threatened to disintegrate if it ever felt wind.

The Hagen family motto was stamped near the front: an eye for an eye.

Ivan's palms felt suddenly sweaty. He shoved the book back on the shelf, trying and failing not to think about what that would mean in this situation.

The Bucklers had stolen a dragon egg, a member of the family as far as the Hagens were concerned. That meant Chase could only have intended one thing.

A child for a child.

Fran was in serious danger. And Ivan was the only one who might be able to help her.

11

FRANCES

Determined as she was to find her parents on her own, Fran had no idea how to navigate the magical half of Castor's Grove.

As far as she could tell, she had two main avenues that she could still explore. She could return to Mrs. Franklin and inquire about her mother. But Fran wasn't sure about the strange woman who'd locked her in a house. It was probably best to keep that as a backup plan.

Her other option was to return to The Archives tomorrow and hope that the two women who'd kicked her out weren't there, or at least that they wouldn't recognize her. After all, it wasn't like there was security standing guard. She should be able to sneak in and find whatever information there was on the Bucklers.

The only issue was how to get to that level.

But Fran would figure that out when the time came.

She grabbed a couple burgers from a nearby place. One she shoved in her backpack for later. The other she munched on as she strolled around downtown. Fran had no route in mind, and so walked aimlessly, keeping her eye peeled for any more Romanesque architecture that might suggest a magical building.

A few blocks east of The Archives, she spotted the tall spires of the Castor's Grove Castle. It was a curious building in the heart of downtown and a popular spot for tourists. Fran had avoided it so far for that reason. Officially, she'd read that it was a government building. But what if that was just a front?

Fran made her way south toward Lincoln Street where the back of the castle stretched. A man in a large gray trench coat followed a few feet behind. He wore dark sunglasses over his face.

When she stopped by the large fence, the man did too, staring up at the spires only a few feet to her left.

Fran's chest tightened.

He's probably just a tourist.

She pushed her anxiety away as much as she could and began strolling the perimeter of the castle. The man did likewise.

But he wasn't the only one. There were crowds of people walking around, pointing at the building, and stopping to take pictures.

Yet, try as she might, Fran couldn't shake the feeling that she was being followed.

I wish Ivan was here. The fairy could've turned them invisible.

Fran shook her head and tightened her grip on her bag. She didn't miss Ivan, and she certainly didn't wish he was there. She could escape this man herself.

Especially since he probably wasn't following her.

Only, as Fran turned away from the castle, she became

less certain. Every time she thought he'd turned down a different street, he appeared a block later.

Maybe she wasn't just being paranoid.

Stay calm. You can get away from him. Just need to be smart.

Fran tried to think what someone in a movie would do. Change their outfit probably, but it wasn't like she had any other clothes. Although, maybe that wasn't necessary.

When the strange man was out of sight, Fran ducked into a cafe. She bought a black coffee and went into the bathroom.

Fran removed her large black coat, folded it, and stuffed it into her backpack. She splashed water on her face; rubbed off her eyeliner and lipstick. It took a few minutes of scrubbing, but soon, the face staring back at her was quite different. Now there was just her hair.

Should've traveled with a wig.

She did the best she could without one, pulling her hair up into as high a ponytail as she could. Fran didn't have a hair tie, but there was a rubber band in her bag. She used that instead.

Perfect.

The only part of her that someone might recognize was the backpack itself, but even that should've been mostly obscured before. There was no coat to hide it now, however.

As much as she liked the security of having it before her, she slipped it onto her back. Her fingers squeezed the straps as she exited the bathroom, leaving her untouched coffee cup beside the sink.

There was no sign of the man in the trench coat when she got outside. Either she'd lost him, or she really had imagined the whole thing.

Either way, Fran'd had enough of downtown for the

day. She needed to go back to her apartment and collect her thoughts. The extra burger was still in her bag. She could have dinner and watch a movie in solitude before calling her dads for their scheduled nightly check-in.

Those were stressful enough as was. It was the same thing every time. They'd start with a hundred questions on how she was coping with her anxiety, then end by begging her to come home. And underneath it all, she could hear what they weren't saying. *We're your parents. Why do you need anyone else?*

Fran wished she could explain it to them, but her dads would interpret it as a personal failure of theirs if she admitted that she'd spent all her life feeling like she didn't belong. Finding her birth parents was her opportunity to finally fit somewhere.

At least today, when her dads started fretting over whether she could handle herself alone in a city, Fran could inform them that she'd avoided a stalker. Although that might panic them more than soothe them.

Fran crossed the intersection at King and 81st, heading west toward her apartment. She passed by a set of stores.

Something reached out and grabbed her. It covered her mouth, blocking her scream. Fran froze in panic as it pulled her into a narrow alleyway.

So much for bragging about escaping her stalker. At least when her dads learned she'd been stabbed and mugged in the city, they could comfort themselves with the fact that they were right about her inability to care for herself.

Fran's eyes looked up, expecting to see the man in the sunglasses.

Instead, Ivan grinned down at her. "Almost didn't

recognize you. Who knew you were so small under that coat?"

Fran clenched her jaw. No longer afraid, she managed to move her limbs again, shaking free of the fairy. He released her quite willingly.

"Why are you here?" Fran asked, putting her hands on her hips. "You have your badge. I can't give you another."

"Excellent question." Ivan ran his hand through his hair. The muscles in his arm flexed as he raised it.

Fran forced herself not to look at them.

"Listen, Castor's Grove isn't safe for you. You need to forget about finding your birth parents and all that and go home. Preferably without that egg."

"Wow." Fran shook her head in disbelief. "So first, you steal my egg and almost break it, and now you're trying to convince me to give it to you and go home. Do you think just because I don't have wings it means I'm stupid?"

She turned to leave the alley, but the fairy grabbed her wrist.

"Look, that egg was stolen from some very powerful people. And they're out for blood. Give it to me or don't, but you need to get rid of it and leave the city before they find you."

Fran's breath caught in her throat. Another time, she'd have been tempted to assume that Ivan was lying to trick her out of the Fabergé egg. Her fathers had always theorized it could be worth a decent sum. But given the man in the trench coat earlier, Fran wasn't as quick to dismiss the fairy.

Still, that didn't mean she was going to blindly believe him either.

"How would anyone know about the egg besides you?"

Ivan hesitated. His eyes flicked to his feet before he answered. "They saw it. When it fell in The Archives."

Fran's eyes narrowed. He was lying. No one else had been around then.

"Okay, well, thanks for telling me." She pulled her wrist free.

"I'm serious, Fran. I'm trying to save you. You're in way over your head here."

And now he sounded like her fathers.

"You'll save me? What kind of patriarchal bullshit is that? I don't need you to save me."

"I didn't mean—" Ivan tried to argue, but Fran didn't care.

She raised her middle fingers holding them above her head as she walked away from the fairy. "Fuck you, Ivan. I'm more capable than you think."

"Fran," he shouted her name behind her.

She didn't respond. And though part of her secretly hoped Ivan would follow her anyway, she was mostly pleased with the interaction. She felt tough and strong walking away.

Although her confidence was wavering by the time she reached her building.

Maybe she should've taken Ivan's threats more seriously. There were magical creatures in this city. What hope did she have against any of them?

There was no way Fran was giving away her egg, but maybe she should go back to Lansing and lay low for a while. She could always return to the city, and the women at The Archives would definitely have forgotten about her in a month. Fran could come back incognito.

Her dads would buy her a ticket home the moment she asked. For all she knew, they already had one on standby.

But what about my mother? I was so close.

Fran clung to the straps of her backpack as she went into the Stone's Throw Apartments lobby. She rounded the corner to go up the stairs and froze.

"Hello, Frances."

It was the man in the gray trench coat and sunglasses. He was waiting for her.

12

FRANCES

Fran managed to stumble a few steps backward before her body locked with fear. Her grip around the straps of her backpack was so tight that her nails drew blood. Still, she couldn't release it.

Her chest tightened. Fran could feel her breath sticking in her throat. She wanted to gasp for air.

Not now. This was the worst time for a panic attack.

The man's head tilted to the side. She couldn't see his eyes, but she got the impression he was studying her behind his shades. He pushed a hand into the pocket of his coat, but his feet remained planted on the stairs.

"Do you know why I'm here?"

All Fran could muster was a squeak and a twitch of her head.

"You're in possession of something exceptionally dangerous. We need to dispose of it quickly before something terrible happens."

It was only because of Ivan's warning that Fran realized the stranger was referring to her egg.

She took a step back, pressing her backpack against the

wall. "No. My parents wanted me to have it—" *for a reason.* Fran couldn't finish the sentence. The air locked in her throat.

I can't breathe.

"Only your mother." The man's voice was garbled, like Fran was hearing him from underwater.

The room started shaking, or maybe that was just Fran. She gasped, trying to suck in as much air as she could. But it was too much. It clogged her throat, so only the smallest fraction could reach her lungs. Spots swam across her vision.

Through the blur, Fran saw the man step toward her. He was pulling something out of his pocket. It looked like a shotgun.

She needed to run.

Instead, her legs gave way beneath her, and she collapsed to the floor.

This was it. Her dads were right. She couldn't take care of herself.

The realization did nothing to soothe her anxiety. Her body curled into a ball, shoulders trembling as they slumped. Toes going numb in her boots.

She lowered her head, tucking it into her folded arms like an ostrich might bury its head in the sand. Her eyes closed, and she gasped into the darkness.

13
IVAN

After her unceremonious rejection of his offer to help, Ivan should have left Fran with a guilt-free conscience. But he'd barely gotten a block away before turning around.

The Hagens wanted to kill her. Frances might've been difficult, but she didn't deserve death. And Ivan wasn't so useless that he'd give up trying to save her after only one failed attempt.

So it was a strong moral compulsion that had drawn him back toward Stone's Throw Apartments. Because, despite what Daisy claimed, Ivan didn't make all his decisions due to a reckless desire to insert himself into every situation that looked remotely dangerous. And despite the questions burning in his mind now when he thought about Fran, he could easily have walked away and never had any of them answered.

Once Ivan arrived at the apartment building, however, he stopped worrying about why he'd turned around and just became grateful that he had. The Hagens had moved faster than he'd expected. Fran was on the floor shaking before an unknown assailant.

Ivan's initial assumption was that it must have been a vampire who'd injected the girl with poisoned blood.

He'd had to think fast. Fairies weren't adapted to fighting like some of the other magical beings. But there was a reason that Castor's Grove was ruled by a *fairy* king. What they lacked in brute strength, they made up for in magic and cunning.

Ivan's invisibility meant that the man never noticed him. He was able to get close before pulling a powder blue crystal out of his pocket. It was his mother's sleep medication. A tiny piece ensured a good night's rest.

Let's see how he likes the whole dose.

Ivan got his hand around the man's mouth before he could react. He forced the crystal past the stranger's lips as deep into the back of the throat as he could get it. Teeth tightened around his wrist and fists battered up to strike at him, but Ivan kept the man from spitting the crystal free.

Finally, the crystal slipped down the man's esophagus. The strength relaxed from his jaw. His hands slid to his sides.

Ivan pulled his hand free and stepped away.

The man collapsed to the floor, chest rising and falling in the slow steady rhythm of sleep.

Ivan winced as he flicked his wrist. The man's teeth had imprinted onto his skin. There was no sign of fangs.

Not a vampire.

So what was wrong with Fran?

14
FRANCES

Fran barely registered the loud thud against the floor. It was nothing compared to her own choked breaths or the rapid pounding of her heart. They pulsed within her ears with a strange arrhythmic beat.

"Hey, come on. He won't stay asleep for long. We have to go."

That voice.

It wasn't the man. Even in the haze of her panic, Fran knew that. Trembling, she forced herself to look up and saw Ivan kneeling before her. The man in the trench coat was on the floor.

Did he kill him?

Fran's chest constricted at the thought, squeezing her heart so tight she thought it might explode.

It took another few seconds for her to register that Ivan had said he was asleep.

Right, hence why we need to run. But I can't. My body won't move.

It wasn't funny, but Fran started to laugh. Only with her lungs still struggling for air, it sounded more like a wheeze.

Her body shook from the force of it, but refused to cooperate otherwise. It was so pathetic. She'd seriously thought she could survive on her own when she couldn't even convince her own legs to stand?

"Hey. You're okay." Ivan grabbed her hands, holding them steady with his. "He didn't hurt you. You're okay."

Why was he being so nice instead of yelling at her to run? Whenever Fran had panic attacks most people rolled their eyes or muttered under their breath that she was overreacting. The other response was worse. Some people, like her dads, would loudly inform everyone what was happening and make grand displays of empathy and support. Intentional or not, it felt like they used Fran's anxiety as an opportunity to hear themselves speak.

But Ivan wasn't giving her a long speech trying to guide her through her own emotions.

Breath still ragged, Fran's eyes moved from where his fingers were wrapped around her hands up to his face. His expression was soft, steady in a way that she hadn't expected. Their eyes met, and there was no sign of impatience or even concern. He was simply there, with her, in that moment.

Fran didn't fight him as Ivan pressed her own hand against the center of her chest. He kept his fingers on top of hers. Their eyes never broke contact.

Other than the occasional whisper of reassurance that she was okay, Ivan didn't speak. He didn't remind her to breathe or think positively or close her eyes and imagine she was on a beach. Instead, he slowed his own breathing. The pressure of his hand on hers mimicked the rise and fall of his chest.

Fran's heart calmed, matching his rhythm. The air returned to her lungs.

From the edge of her vision, she could see his lips, parted as he breathed. *They look soft.*

Fran leaned forward, wondering if to test the hypothesis for a second before she snapped her head away. Her cheeks grew hot. Clearly, she'd become too relaxed.

If Ivan had noticed her lips moving closer, he didn't have a chance to comment. There was a ding as the elevator arrived on the bottom floor.

Ivan pulled her to her feet before the doors opened. The air blurred around them. Fran's landlord stepped off the elevator. Edgar Kole was a tall man with a prominent nose and a receding hairline that he didn't know how to style. He owned three apartments in the building, two for temporary rentals and one where he lived. He was talking to someone on the phone.

"Yeah, I might have information. What's it worth to you?" Edgar stopped, staring at the body on the floor before him as though he'd only just seen it. He pushed the man's leg with the tip of his shoe. "Ah, shit. Look, can I call you back? ... No, it's not that. There's just, look, give me five minutes, please? I promise, it'll be worth your time. I know exactly how to find Frances West."

Fran's body went rigid once more. She and Ivan exchanged a look.

Okay, you were right. Fran didn't dare say it aloud, but she hoped her expression conveyed the apology to the fairy. *This is serious. I do need your help.*

15
IVAN

The man from the elevator seemed to have decided, based on virtually no evidence, that the man on the floor had overdosed. Instead of calling an ambulance, however, he'd called the building supervisor. The two were arguing over whose responsibility it was to deal with the situation.

Curious as Ivan was to see which asshole won, he was more concerned with getting out of the building. He turned to Fran. Without the dark makeup and black coat, she seemed strangely exposed. He could see the dark circles under her eyes were from lack of sleep, and there was a crack near the corner of her lips that looked old and fresh at the same time, as though she kept picking at it and refusing to let it heal.

He'd liked how she looked in the black, cool, collected. But she was just as pretty like this, just softer, more vulnerable.

She'd probably curse me to the underworld and back if I said that.

Ivan nudged Fran and flicked his gaze toward the door.

She nodded, and together, they slipped out of the apartments unseen.

There were many different magics a fairy might possess, but the majority had only one. Ivan had often longed to be one of the elite few with two talents, but as they hurried along King Street, he was grateful for the one he had. Invisibility didn't allow him to bend nature to his will or heal the wounded, but dust if it wasn't useful!

Once they were a safe distance away, however, Ivan figured it would be safer to drop it. It was the exception, but there were beings that his magic wouldn't work on.

He was walking with one of them.

Only Fran was a descendant of knights, a regular human. Her magical resistance made no sense.

Ivan slipped down an alley, releasing Fran's hand as he did. He kept his wings out and his invisibility in place as he turned her. "You can still see me."

Fran frowned. "Should I not be able to?"

No. Just like she shouldn't have been able to get into The Archives.

What are you, Frances West?

Ivan shrugged and grinned, playing off the anomaly as no big deal. He rotated the tips of his wings and put them away.

Fran blinked as they vanished, but she didn't comment. Instead, she chewed on her lip, teeth finding their way into the groove of her cut. Her fingers twisted around each other. "If I promise to leave the city like you want, will you tell me the truth about what you found in my file?"

Ivan hesitated. "Who said I wanted you out of the city?"

"You did. Like less than an hour ago. And we're walking west." Fran raised her eyebrows as though this were significant. "You're taking me to the station?"

Outside of driving, the only way into Castor's Grove was by train. The station was in the southwest corner of the city, where the surrounding forest stopped. The train left twice a day at six. If she caught it out of the city, Fran could be at an airport before nine.

But in his hurry to get Fran away from her apartment, the thought of taking her to the station hadn't crossed Ivan's mind. And even now that she was presenting it as an option, he dismissed it.

Not because he wanted Fran to stick around. And even if there was a part of him that did, it was only because he wanted to figure out what was going on with her.

The fact was that now the Hagens had found Fran, putting her on the train right away was too big of a risk. They'd expect her to flee.

Ivan shook his head. "They've probably already got someone at the train station waiting. You need to lay low for a while."

"Okay." Fran seemed surprised but not upset by the answer. She chewed her lip again. "So where do I go?"

Ivan ran his hand through his hair. Where could she stay so that the Hagens wouldn't go looking for her? Somewhere she could go without giving her name or identity?

There was one place he knew.

Ivan slapped his hand to his forehead, his eyes turning west. They were already heading in the right direction. Was it just his feet finding their way home or had he subconsciously planned this?

"You'll see when we get there," the fairy assured her before taking off again. He held back a laugh for the rest of their walks. His sisters were right. Ivan had to be insane.

Why else would he take a knight right into the Western Woodlands?

16

FRANCES

Fran knew that Castor's Grove was surrounded by forest to the north and most of the west. But she hadn't imagined that there was a pocket of woods like this in the middle of the city.

Officially, the Western Woodlands was a protected wildlife park, stretching across twenty-one blocks in the heart of a middle-class neighborhood. Murals of flora and fauna, painted on wooden panels protected its perimeter. Ivan stopped at a depiction of a beautiful creature with tawny fur and large brown eyes. Fran thought it was a deer before she noticed the tusks protruding from its jaw. And the antlers on its head were closer to the horns of a goat.

Ivan glanced around. There were people further down the street, but no one nearby. He walked through the painting of the deer-like creature, as though it wasn't even there.

Magic. Fran smiled and followed him.

Even without knowing the blockade's weak point, people must have gotten curious and wandered in. But not for long. The woods were yet another enchanted area, nestled into the city. Any human who walked in would soon find themself anxious to return home.

Fran had never felt calmer in her life as she walked through the trees. She'd never have called herself a nature person. That was the sort of title reserved for people who loved hiking or meditating under trees. But she did find the green of the leaves and the curious cries of unfamiliar animals oddly soothing.

The creatures in the Western Woodlands were unafraid of them as they walked through. There was no shuffling of leaves or bushes. Instead, squirrels and rabbits ran up and sniffed, even joining them for brief parts of their journey before growing bored. The air in the woods was rich with the scent of bread baking and the sounds of children's laughter floated with the wind. There were people living deeper in the forest: fairies, nymphs, elves.

But Fran wouldn't get to see them.

Ivan kept close to the perimeter. They walked almost the entire length of the Western Woodlands, maybe six blocks, before they reached their destination.

It was a tree house.

The wooden structure was high in a large tree with a thick trunk, higher in the branches than most parents would allow their children to climb. It was comprised of three rectangular walls with the trunk acting as the fourth. Two holes had been cut out for windows in the longest one. Judging from the blue curtains hanging behind them, someone had taken the care to decorate the place.

"Give me a minute," Ivan said. He'd pulled his wings out once they were in the forest. Now, they fluttered behind him, lifting him up toward the house. He disappeared through an opening in the base of the floor.

A moment later an old rope ladder tumbled down.

Fran bit her lip. Was she really expected to climb that?

"It's stronger than it looks," Ivan's voice reassured her.

Good thing I'm not afraid of heights.

Still, she hoped the ladder was enchanted to stop climbers from falling as she ascended to the tree house.

As Fran had suspected, the inside was decorated. There was a blue rug on the floor that matched the curtains. A mattress with white sheets already made lay in the corner of the room, another, unmade, leaned upright against the wall beside it. The trunk of the tree had been carved to make holes for cabinets.

Ivan pulled a pack of almonds down from one of the shelves. "Afraid most of the food is snacks. Daisy used to have a vegetable garden growing up here, but Poppy's picky."

"This is your sisters' treehouse?"

"And mine," Ivan said, glancing at her as he grabbed an assortment of snacks from the holes in the trunk. "Don't worry, they won't find you here. Daisy never comes out anymore, and Poppy just uses it to hide all this crap from Mom and Dad, and they're on a surprise anniversary trip, so you should be safe for the week."

Fran rested her bag in the corner and pulled out the few things she'd packed. She found her eyeliner and lipstick. There was no mirror, but she applied it all the same while Ivan put together something.

"Dinner," he announced. There were two plates that consisted of dried, hardened leaves that had been glued together. On each one was an assortment of nuts, dried apples, potato chips, cheese triangles, crackers, and chocolates.

Fran put her fingers over her mouth to stop from

giggling. It wasn't what she'd call dinner, but it was still sweet that Ivan was trying to feed her.

"I have a burger in my backpack," she said, but not wanting to sound ungrateful, she added, "We could cut it in two and add it to your selection."

"Oh." Ivan's nose wrinkled in distaste for a moment. "Thanks, but fairies don't eat meat. None of the creatures in the Western Woodlands do. But you should feel free to have it."

That explained the incredibly friendly rodents they'd passed.

Fran thought of one of the little gray bunnies who'd stood on his hind legs and twitched his nose as they walked by. The burger suddenly didn't seem so appealing.

"Nah. When in fairyland do as the fairies, right?"

"You'd piss off a lot of people calling Castor's Grove *fairy*land," Ivan told her, grinning.

He rested the two plates of snacks on the mattress and took a seat. Fran joined him, and for an awkward few minutes, they chewed in silence. Normally, Fran would enjoy the quiet. But not now. There was something she needed to say, difficult as it would be.

"Thank you for saving me!" She blurted it out while pinching a piece of cheese between her fingers. "And for being so nice to me. Most people aren't so understanding when I'm having a panic attack."

"No biggie. Poppy gets them sometimes," Ivan said, tossing a peanut into the air and catching it in his mouth.

That explains why he was so calm.

But he was wrong. It was a huge deal. At least to Fran.

"You can make fun of me for it, you know. I mean, I just told you how capable I was and then you found me trembling against a wall, gasping for air."

Ivan lowered the dried apple slice he was holding. "There was a creepy dude attacking you. When you said you were capable, I didn't think you meant you were some warrior ready to karate chop a dude."

Fran stared at the snacks before her. The man in the trench coat hadn't attacked her. Fran had thought he was reaching for a gun, but if there was one in his pocket, it seemed strange he never fired it.

Ivan's hand reached out and touched hers, forcing Fran to look up and meet his gaze. He raised an eyebrow. "You're embarrassed I saw you like that."

"Obviously."

"Is that why you wear all the black?"

Fran's cheeks grew hot. She felt his green eyes studying her. Ivan with his easy smile and reckless charm was more thoughtful than she'd realized. No one had ever come right out and asked her that before.

"Probably," she admitted.

Ivan nodded and moved his hand, leaning back on one arm as he nibbled on a triangle of cheese.

Fran crossed her arms around her. Giving him an honest answer left her feeling strangely exposed. She'd basically just admitted that her entire look was a disguise. He must have been judging her, thinking she was fake and pathetic.

"Look, it's not that I care what people think," she said, trying to explain herself. "But everyone always saw me as so fragile, but I don't feel fragile. Or I don't want to. And when I look in the mirror and I see myself with black lips and cat eyes, I feel like I can actually do shit, not just burst into tears, shaking because of some stupid little thing that most people don't even care about."

Ivan was still reclining, but he hadn't taken any more

food while she spoke. He studied her for a moment before he smiled and sat back up. He leaned forward. "Well, I know you don't care, but I like your aesthetic too. You're cute. With or without it."

The compliment caught Fran off guard. She blinked in surprise, trying to figure out what to say.

Ivan leaned back again, tossed a few almonds into his mouth. Fran glanced down. He'd stolen them from her plate.

Was that why he'd complimented her? To distract her?

Fran rolled her eyes and grabbed one of her chocolates. "You're right. I don't." She popped it in her mouth.

"Of course not." Ivan grinned. "No one with any consideration for social standing would wear her backpack on her chest." He grabbed an apple slice from her plate, but paused, holding it in his hand almost contemplatively. "That's not a bad thing though."

"Wearing your bag so you can see the zipper? Agreed. The number of thefts it could potentially stop—"

Ivan's laughter cut her off. "Wow, you really do have anxiety, don't you? Not the backpack. I mean not caring what other people think."

Fran took her apple slice back from his hand, holding back a smile as he stared down in indignation.

"Do you care?" she asked as she bit down on it.

His smile disappeared. "Constantly."

"So stop." She meant it as a joke. Even if Fran knew it wasn't that easy.

But Ivan didn't laugh. He stared at his plate, mouth pulled tight in an unsettlingly serious expression. "I'm trying. Because if anyone ever discovers that I've helped you, I'm going to be lower than dirt."

"So why are you helping me?" Fran was almost afraid to

ask, yet it slipped from her lips before she could obsess over it. "I mean, you have the badge you wanted. You could've just let me get attacked."

"Killed," Ivan corrected her. "And I might want into the Gentlemen, but even I can recognize that wanting some rich kids to accept me in their social circle is a much smaller issue than someone's life."

The fact that he was sacrificing something he wanted to help her still made Fran feel strangely guilty. "Who are the Gentlemen?"

There were so many names and concepts she'd been introduced to in the past forty-eight hours, she was losing track. But she didn't think Ivan had said anything about this group before.

"The Phi Eta Gentlemen. They're a university fraternity. I needed the badge to get accepted," he explained. "But one of their members is the dragon you met in The Archives. Chase Hagen. He's the one who wants to kill you."

"Oh." That was a lot. Fran blinked as she tried to process it. Then, she took a page from Ivan and forced a smile. "Well, at least I don't have to feel bad. If I stop you from getting into a fraternity, I'm doing you a favor. Have you never watched a teen movie? They're full of horrible people."

"Can't argue with that given the circumstances." Ivan laughed. It was deep and full, from his stomach.

And genuine.

Fran realized just then how much she liked it.

Unfortunately, Ivan's cheer didn't last.

"Listen, Fran," he said, mouth tight again and eyes heavy with thought as he stared at her over their plates. "We need to talk about that egg."

17

IVAN

An hour later, Ivan and Fran were still sitting on the mattress, but instead of plates between them, there was a purple dragon egg. The moon had risen in the sky. The egg reflected its light in an eerie hypnotic way, casting a pattern into the air around it and taking on an unearthly glow. Even keeping his distance, Ivan could feel the heat radiating from it.

Fran ran her fingers over the gold spirals on its shell, somehow immune to the fire within that burned Ivan when he tried. He didn't understand how. It was like the powder and the enchantment at the Archives. Did Fran have some sort of special ability?

Ivan had never taken The Knights seriously, but one with magical immunity? Who could go places that a regular human couldn't?

The thought sent a shiver through his spine.

"So, this dragon *isn't* like the one who's trying to kill me," Fran said, pulling Ivan out of his worries and back to the current moment.

"No, this is a great dragon," Ivan wanted that to be clear

though he suspected it was hypothetical. He had already explained dragons to her when discussing the egg. There were two main kinds. The bipedal dragons and the great dragons. Chase was the former, able to pass for a human as easily as a fairy. Bipedal dragons had massive, scaled wings and tails that they hid whenever they were out in the human areas of the city.

The great dragons were entirely different beasts. Unlike their bipedal cousins, they were large reptilian creatures with four legs and a pair of wings. They couldn't hide as easily amongst the humans and as a result, they'd been hunted almost to extinction. Castor's Grove was one of the few places that was rumored to still have a wild colony; the rest had been domesticated.

"Like pets?" Fran had asked.

"Sort of," Ivan had said. "If you can have a pet that's just as clever as you."

But even that was a gross oversimplification of the matter, as he tried to explain. They were family to the bipedal dragons who cared for them. As different as the two species might have been, they shared a common ancestor. And ancestry mattered to the magical inhabitants of Castor's Grove.

"Seems confusing to give both the same name," Fran noted, staring at the egg before her. She'd barely taken her eyes off of it since she'd removed it from her bag.

Ivan shrugged. Most people, even magical ones, lived their whole lives barely interacting with any great dragons. "You can normally figure it out from context." *And the bipedal dragons would be furious if anyone suggested they lost their right to the name.*

"Is there another type of fairy too? Like a small one that wears flower petals and waves a magic wand?"

Ivan laughed, fairly certain that Fran was joking. "You're thinking of pixies. But they don't have wands."

Fran smiled, but her eyes weren't on Ivan. Instead, the glow of the egg reflected in her eyes. She stared at it, mesmerized.

In the strange dark light, Fran looked striking, beautiful but dangerous.

"You're avoiding answering my question," Ivan said, staring at her with the same intensity with which she studied the egg. "Will you let me return it to the Hagens?"

"Why would my parents steal a dragon egg and send me away with it?"

The first part, Ivan could guess. But he held his tongue.

"Mrs. Franklin seemed surprised I hadn't destroyed it."

Ivan's eyebrows rose. Fran was too focused on the egg to notice the change in his expression. But he felt like he'd just figured out the answer to the second part of her question. Dragon eggs weren't easy to destroy. They were protected by magic. But that shouldn't have mattered to Fran.

Of course, it still doesn't explain why Fran is different.

Ivan shook his head. Fran had once again managed to deflect. "If we return it to the Hagens, they might stop trying to kill you."

"I know." Fran's voice was a squeak. Her eyes squeezed shut; the light caught on the tears that leaked through the corner, trailing down her cheek. She took a few deep breaths before speaking. "Obviously, returning it is the smart thing, and the right thing. But I—it's all I've ever had from my parents." Her hands fluttered before her face, trying to catch the tears before they rolled down her cheeks. "I've always thought that it was my birthright, somehow. Like, it held the answers to where I belonged. But—"

Her voice cut off as she choked on a sob.

Ivan fought past the egg's heat to cross to the other side of the mattress. He wrapped his arm around her. He half-expected her to push him away. Instead, she buried her face into the crook of his shoulder, and he held her.

Minutes passed.

Finally, Fran looked up. Her lips hovered only a few inches from his, eyes glistening as they stared at him.

Ivan's heart stopped for a moment as he looked at her. He forgot about the fact she was descended from the knights, or that she had a dragon egg, or mysterious abilities. She was just a girl, who was alone and scared and being asked to give up the only object that connected her to her past.

"I need you to tell me the truth, Ivan. Did you find anything about my family in The Archives? Please, even if it's something bad. I can handle it."

And just like that, the spell broke, and Ivan remembered everything about Fran once more. The weight of all her secrets filled the air around them, chilling the sweat on his skin.

"I just want to know who I am. I want to know where I belong." He could hear the longing trembling in her voice.

"I'm sorry, Fran." Ivan's stomach turned. He pulled her close again and rested his chin on her head. He couldn't bear to keep looking into her eyes. Otherwise, he might forget again just how dangerous she could be. "There was nothing in The Archives. I swear."

18

FRANCES

Fran had never had a problem occupying her time when she was alone, but she hated feeling like a prisoner. The Western Woodlands, with its lack of meat-eating creatures, was probably the safest forest in the world, but Fran didn't dare explore too far beyond the base of the treehouse. It wasn't the animals, but the other inhabitants. She'd gone for a walk and heard voices. Ivan hadn't specifically said that she shouldn't be seen but, given that there was a powerful magical family of dragons looking to murder her, keeping her location secret seemed prudent.

Confined to the treehouse, Fran had spent the rest of her morning folding paper cranes, trying to keep her mind calm by distracting her hands. But she'd only had so much paper in her backpack, and sixty-three cranes later, her thoughts began spiraling again.

The egg remained on the mattress, laying on the pillow. Fran had cuddled it tight to her chest all through the night.

Without anything to distract her, Fran's eyes kept wandering to the egg. Her chest grew tight whenever she saw it. Her most precious possession, the one item that she'd always imagined held the key to her identity, and it wasn't even hers.

Why did my parents steal it?

Could her parents have worked for the Hagens and grown angry with them? Maybe their desire to murder her made Fran biased, but she doubted the Hagens would've been kind employers. Perhaps her parents had stolen the egg to teach them a lesson and then shipped it and Fran away for safety.

Which meant that unless the Hagens had gotten them too, her birth parents might still be alive somewhere in Castor's Grove. Fran should be focused on finding them, not worried about the egg. After all, her parents were the real answer to where she belonged.

I need to find them.

Reminding herself of her purpose in the city helped steady Fran's nerves. The Archives had been a dead end, but what about Mrs. Franklin? She'd known something about Fran's family and the egg.

The battery in Fran's phone was almost dead, but it was enough for a call.

She looked through her pictures and found the one she'd taken with her adoption information. The Franklins' details were all there, complete with a telephone number. Fran had been too afraid to call it before. Besides, this was from over a decade ago. What were the chances it was still in use?

Fingers trembling, Fran entered the number. It began to ring.

"What's done in honor," a woman's voice said on the other end.

It sounded like she was expecting a specific response. Fran didn't know it. "Mrs. Franklin?"

"Who is this?"

That was definitely her voice. Fran's stomach tightened.

Was calling the woman who'd trapped her in a house really a good idea? From what Ivan had told her, the Knights weren't fond of magic, and whatever Fran was, she had to be something special. Otherwise, how would she have gotten into The Archives?

Still, she'd come this far. And she was in an enchanted forest that humans couldn't enter. There couldn't be a safer place for her to make the call, right?

"Frances Buckler."

Silence. Then a frantic voice. "Where are you?"

"What do you know about my parents?"

"I'll tell you in person. I can pick you up if you tell me where you are."

That was a trap if ever Fran heard one. "You know about the egg. Why did you think I would've destroyed it?"

"Because of the letter." Fran's lack of response must have made her confusion clear because, after a moment, Mrs. Franklin continued. "Didn't your adopted parents give it to you? It was from your mother instructing you to destroy the egg."

Fran's chest grew tight. Her mother had left her a letter? But she'd never seen one. Had it gotten lost or—

They kept it from me. Water filled Fran's eyes at the realization. Her dads had read the letter, seen what it said, and kept it from her. They probably thought she'd break down learning that her birth mother wanted her to destroy the thing she cherished most.

"Thank you." Fran hung up on Mrs. Franklin.

She sat trembling for a moment, staring at the phone in her hand. She should call her fathers to confirm Mrs. Franklin's story, but she didn't need to. She knew the woman was telling the truth. She could feel it in her bones.

Fran crossed the small open room, falling onto her knees on the mattress. The gold spirals on the deep purple shell shone before her. The egg seemed to have absorbed the moonlight from the previous night, a glowing aura settling around it.

My mum wanted me to destroy it.

Just the thought of it made her feel anxious. Her chest tightened, and her breath grew fast. She sensed a panic attack coming on.

Which was probably precisely why her fathers had kept the letter secret. They knew how attached she was to the egg, how she'd kissed it every night before she went to bed. They didn't think she could handle knowing that her birth mother wanted her to destroy it.

Fran pressed her hand against her chest. She took a few deep, steady breaths.

Her fathers were wrong. She was stronger than they thought.

Fran recalled her agreement with Ivan the previous night. She'd agreed to return the egg to save her life. But her birth mother had made *one* request of her. Even if she didn't understand, Fran owed it to her to do it.

Didn't she?

19
IVAN

I van wandered from his dorm room in the center of campus toward the periphery where the University's Greek houses were established. Phi Eta was the furthest from the others, a tall Victorian-style mansion with large wrought iron fencing around it.

There were many CGU students who whispered about how pretentious and old the building was. Most of those were people who'd been rejected from the Gentlemen's ranks.

Ivan was close to joining that large and unimpressive group. Mostly, it was made up of humans who'd tried to pledge the fraternity only to be rejected after the meet and greet of the first round. But there were plenty of Castors who'd been deemed too insignificant or worthless to qualify for membership.

Just going up to the building without an invitation might have been enough to ensure Ivan's own rejection, even with the knight's badge still tucked in his pocket. But he didn't know how else he could find Chase Hagen.

The mansion itself was enchanted to ensure nonmembers couldn't enter, but the external wrought iron gate had no such protection. Humans were willing to dismiss many things, but even they might have noticed if they couldn't walk through an open gate.

Ivan strolled up the long walkway. Bright autumn blooms exploded in color on either side. There were enough fairies and nymphs among the Gentlemen that the plants were prioritized.

Trying to hide his nerves, Ivan shoved a hand into the pocket of his blue hoodie and leaned against the pillar of the veranda. There was no point in knocking. He was certain someone had spotted him the moment he walked in.

And he was right.

A moment later, the large white door opened and a tall boy with blond hair pulled in a ponytail behind his head stepped out.

Ivan tried to hide the surprise from his face. Silvan Pemberley was the leader of the Gentlemen and, even more notable, despite being less impressive as it was an inherited position, he was the fairy king's nephew.

"Awfully bold for a pledge," Silvan said, smiling at Ivan as though they were two friends sharing a joke. "But you'll have to wait. We don't accept badges early."

"How do you—"

"Chase mentioned you'd shown it to him."

Shown wasn't the word Ivan would have used, but he should've guessed the dragon would have told the rest of the Gentlemen. "Is he here? I need to speak with him."

Silvan raised an eyebrow. His eyes flicked over Ivan. Then his smile returned. "He's upstairs. I'll fetch him."

The idea of Silvan Pemberley *fetching* anything like a

dog seemed absurd, but Ivan wasn't stupid enough to laugh at the idea. He nodded in thanks.

"Come inside. You can wait in the foyer."

It was an order, not a request. Ivan pushed himself away from the pillar and walked through the large white doors into a massive entrance room. It made him think of the places people were always dancing in the period dramas that his sisters enjoyed. There were two massive staircases that formed an arch at the far end, leading to an upper level full of doors and more stairs. Gold vases with heraldic images decorated the perimeter of the room, and bright woven tapestries hung from the upper banisters. He didn't recognize the families attached to most of the symbols in the room, but there was a large bird with snowy plumage and large opalescent eyes. Its wings stretched the span of its tapestry. There was an olive branch in its beak.

The Fairy King's sigil.

Ivan didn't care about nobility or titles, yet his breath caught as he stared up at the magnificent bird. A feeling of awe and longing washed over him. The king himself had been a Gentleman during his time at the university. If Ivan was accepted, he'd be joining the same ranks.

It sent a thrill through him.

But is that because it makes me feel good or because I'll enjoy telling people and seeing their reactions?

Ivan wasn't certain.

"Pretty, isn't it?" Silvan followed Ivan's gaze over his shoulder. "It's custom-made. Pure silk."

Which meant it probably cost as much as everything Ivan owned. He forced a smile and looked away from the tapestry. "I thought pledges weren't allowed inside."

"I've made an exception. But don't get too bold and try

to explore." Silvan released his wings and flew up to a room on the second floor.

Ivan stood, frozen in place as he tried not to notice the splendor of the room. But the more he tried to ignore it, the more the questions spun in his head. What material was the rug? Were the vases pure gold? Did the king ever visit the fraternity?

"It seems Silvan's taken a liking to you." Chase Hagen swooped down with shocking speed. He folded his large, scaled wings, though he kept them visible so that the spikes on the edges curved around his shoulders like some strangely designed collar. He folded his arms, thick brows rising as he waited for Ivan to speak.

Ivan cleared his throat. Now that the dragon was before him, he suddenly wasn't certain how best to bring up the topic. *Hey, hypothetically speaking, if I give you back your family's egg, will you stop trying to kill my friend?*

Wait, friend? Even in his thoughts, the word caught him off guard. But how else would he describe Fran? The cute goth? No. Definitely not that. Maybe *the random girl I'm risking my ass to try to help*?

Luckily, Ivan was saved from having to find the correct description because Chase did it for him.

"Is this about that Buckler girl you were with?" The dragon gave him a small, tight-lipped smile. "Let me guess? You want me to keep your association with any knights a secret."

"No that's—" Ivan cut himself off. "Actually, yes." That just wasn't why he'd come. "But I wanted to talk to you about something else too. You said her family stole something from yours."

"I already told you," Chase's pupils narrowed as he

stared at Ivan. A soft hiss whistled through his teeth as he spoke. "That's a private, family matter."

Well, this is off to a great start.

"I already know it's a dragon egg," Ivan said. Then before Chase could inquire where he got that information, Ivan crossed his arms and grinned, feigning confidence. "Anyone with a half a brain cell could guess. I mean, why else would the Bucklers have named themselves the Order of the Egg?"

The smile twitched on Ivan's face as he waited to see if Chase would call him out. It wasn't a conclusion he would've arrived at on his own. Dozens of creatures laid eggs, and the Hagens were insanely wealthy. Ivan was certain they had any number of prized possessions, strange eggs included.

"The egg of my beloved cousin, Starsong." Chase's mouth twisted in fury. "The grief of its loss killed her."

Dust. That's not going to incline him to forgive a vendetta. Still, Ivan pushed forward. "What if I could get it back for you?"

The dark expression vanished from Chase's expression. He stared at Ivan with wide eyes.

Maybe this will work after all.

Chase threw back his head, his mouth opening to reveal sharp canines as he let loose a loud cackle. He slapped his hand on Ivan's shoulder. "Oh, you are bold. But also foolish."

Ivan clenched his jaw to stop himself from firing off his own insult.

"The egg is worthless now. It will have died after being separated from its mother for so long." Chase's tone grew patronizing as he continued to pat Ivan's shoulder. "I suppose they didn't teach you that at, well, where was it you went to school?"

Westfield County.

But the name would mean nothing to Chase. All he wanted was to remind Ivan that he'd attended a human high school and not one of the magical private facilities that existed for the elite of Castor's Grove. Ivan didn't take the bait.

"I saw the egg," he said, stepping backward to stop himself from shoving Chase's hand away from him. "It didn't look dead."

The news didn't seem to surprise Chase. The dragon snorted and a wisp of smoke came from his nostrils. "What do you know of the difference between a living egg and a dead one? They last for years after the embryos die until one day, they overheat and disintegrate."

Ivan recalled the heat radiating from the egg between him and Fran last night. *Dust!* That meant the egg didn't have long left. Fran was going to be devastated if it crumpled to nothingness.

"There is something you might offer that's of interest to me though." Chase stepped once more. His eyes burned with an unnerving intensity, and his mouth opened in a smile just large enough to reveal his canines. "The Buckler girl's location. You obviously know where she is. And I want vengeance for my cousin."

He sounded certain.

A lump rose in Ivan's throat. He couldn't say no to Chase Hagen. Not here where the rest of the Gentlemen would rush to his defense.

"I do," Ivan said. He couldn't force his usual smile, but at least he'd found his voice. "Stone's Throw Apartments. They're just outside of downtown."

"Really?" Chase's lips curled upward, his smile extending higher instead of wider on his face. "Hmm. Perhaps you'll make a fine Gentleman after all, Dream."

He raised his hand to pat Ivan's shoulder but stopped himself this time. Chase inclined his head instead, a nod of gratitude.

But that didn't make sense. Chase had already known Fran was staying there. Why did he seem pleased?

The hair rose on the back of Ivan's neck.

There were only two possibilities here. Either Chase was an incredible actor, or someone else had sent the man in the trench coat to attack Fran.

20

FRANCES

Fran rested her fingers on either side of the shell, pressing into it with all her strength. Sixty-three white paper cranes watched from their perches on the shelves.

The egg trembled in her hands. There was a sharp crack, and a piece of the shell dropped to the floor. A sudden burst of heat erupted from within.

Fran's eyes filled with tears, but she didn't stop. She pressed harder, feeling the shell begin to disintegrate.

She couldn't bear to watch. Fran closed her eyes tight so that she wouldn't see the thing she loved most in all the world destroyed by her own hands.

I'm so stupid. The Hagens are going to kill me now and all for what? The approval of a mother I've never even met?

A piece of the shattered egg landed on Fran's leg. The edges scratched her skin.

She moved her hand to brush it off, and her fingers hit against something small and scaled. It mewled like a kitten.

Fran's eyes burst open.

Crouched on her leg was a tiny creature with large eyes like liquid gold. It had a neck that was comparatively long for its frame, four stout legs, a tail, and a pair of wings, all covered in deep purple scales that glowed with moonlight. It opened its mouth, revealing small sharp teeth, and mewled once more.

Fran's jaw dropped. There was a dragon on her lap.

What did one do when there was a dragon on their lap?

Uncertain whether to shout with excitement or panic and run, Fran reached toward the little creature. It turned its glowing eyes toward her palm, then nestled against it with the top of its head. A soft purr rumbled in its chest.

Oh my God. My parents didn't give me an egg. They gave me a dragon.

The baby dragon walked up her leg, its claws scraping her skin. It leaned against her stomach before curling itself there. She felt its warmth radiating through her clothes. The dragon stretched its long neck up, resting its head on her in such a way that it could stare up at her with its large eyes.

Fran stroked its spine with her fingers, tickling between its wings. The dragon wiggled its tail with pleasure, drawing even closer. A smile spread across her face.

She had a dragon.

The creature's stomach growled, and it opened its mouth hissing in sudden displeasure. Fran withdrew her hand, worried she'd touched somewhere sensitive.

There was another gurgle, and the dragon opened its mouth, yelping up at her, trails of smoke rising from its mouth.

Fran froze, suddenly panicked.

She had a dragon.

Dragons breathed fire. Fire burned things. Things like paper cranes, and trees. Both of which surrounded them.

Ivan had said that dragons were as intelligent as people. Maybe she could reason with hers.

"Please, don't do that," Fran said, scooping the little creature up with her hands and holding it in the air before her. "We're going to be in a lot of trouble if you burn this place down."

The dragon hissed at her, more smoke escaping its jaw.

Okay, clearly reasonable negotiation was failing. Fran tried another approach.

"No." She maneuvered her left hand so that two of her fingers formed a loop around the baby dragon's mouth, holding it closed. "No smoking."

The dragon's nostrils twitched in surprise.

"Good," Fran said. She'd never had a pet, but she'd seen her friends talk to their dogs like this. "Good dragon."

She released its jaw.

The dragon opened it at once and sent a small jet of flame toward her.

Fran squeaked and dropped it, raising her hands to protect her face from the fire. Though she felt the warmth of the flame, the harsh sting of a burn never came.

Meanwhile, the little dragon flapped its wings, breaking its short fall onto the mattress. Its stumpy little legs moved faster than they should have, and it scurried across the bed. Before Fran had a chance to realize what it was doing, the creature was halfway into her backpack.

If it breathed fire in there, it was going to destroy the few things she'd managed to take with her from her apartment.

"Stop, please!" Fran shouted as she scrambled across

the mattress, reaching for her backpack. She grabbed onto the open front pouch and pulled it toward her. As she did, it fell, and the baby dragon scrambled out carrying something proudly in its jaw.

Fran's heart leaped with panic for a moment before she realized what it was.

The burger from yesterday. She'd never eaten it.

The small creature swerved between the paper cranes before stopping in the middle of the wooden floor. Using its short stubby front legs to hold the white paper bag steady, it wormed its long neck through the opening at the top. A satisfied purr rumbled from its stomach, and a moment later its head popped out. It waved the ground beef patty before it, gold eyes twinkling at Fran.

The burger was almost as large as its entire body. Twice the size of its head. Yet the little dragon opened its jaw impossibly wide and inhaled the entire thing.

Fran's eyes widened in shock. She crept closer to the creature. "You were just hungry, weren't you?"

In response, the little dragon opened its mouth and burped. With it came a small wisp of flame.

"Oh no." Fran followed the fire with her eyes as it lighted on one of the cranes in the far corner of the room. The paper went up in flames.

Unbothered, the creature curled itself into a ball and promptly fell asleep in the center of the floor.

Fran hurried toward the burning crane. She stomped on it a few times with her foot, managing to put out the flames before they spread.

The wooden floor was blackened where the fire had touched, but that wasn't so bad. At least nothing serious had happened.

A relieved smile spread over Fran's face. She laughed and looked up toward the window. Her laugh turned into a sharp squeak.

Fluttering before her was an auburn haired thirteen-year-old with a massive metal grin.

21

IVAN

When Ivan returned to the treehouse that evening, he was hoping to find Fran still there. In some ways, her running off would've made things easier for him, but beyond his curiosity about her abilities, he'd also found himself missing her that day.

Which was silly given he barely knew her.

Still, he smiled when he saw her standing near the base of the tree. She was dressed in her usual black coat and dark makeup, a large bucket of fried chicken in her hands.

The sight of it made him freeze for a moment. It meant she'd left the safety of the Western Woodlands and ventured out into the city. She couldn't risk that. There were too many people looking for her. What if something happened? How would he find her again?

A knight's descendant, and I'm worried about losing contact. I really must be an idiot.

Ivan forced a laugh, trying to hide the strange mixture of relief, excitement, and worry that seemed to battle within him at the site of the girl with her cute nose and parted black lips. "Couldn't survive another minute without meat?"

Fran turned to him, eyes wide with apprehension. Did she think he was going to be angry? Just because fairies were vegetarian didn't mean they couldn't respect other peoples' diets.

"Hey, stop!" The shout came suddenly from the treehouse.

Poppy?

Ivan looked up toward the hatch expecting his sister to come flying out.

The creature that emerged, however, was not a fairy.

It was small and covered in deep purple scales that shone with a strange, dark glow. Two tiny gold nubs that would be horns one day poked through near the top of its head. A large pair of round gold eyes twinkled from deep within its skull.

Ivan's jaw dropped as he registered what he was seeing.

Chase was wrong. The egg wasn't dead. *It had hatched.*

The creature flashed out of Ivan's sight as it dove head-first into the bucket in Fran's hands. Pieces of fried chicken exploded out of it in a sudden tidal wave as the dragon displaced them.

"Sorry. He doesn't really listen," Poppy apologized, flying down the hatch a moment later.

Under regular circumstances, Ivan would have addressed the issue of his sister's sudden appearance straight away. For now, however, the dragon took precedence.

He took a step forward, put a hand on the edge of the bucket, and peered into it, half wondering if he'd imagined the entire thing.

Sure enough, there was a dragon in there. The creature flicked its large gold eyes up to Ivan, and his breath caught.

In all his nineteen years of life, Ivan had never seen a great dragon. There was something incredible about the creature, an aura of magic that clung to its very being. He recalled the many tales that existed of the great dragons from before the humans had hunted them almost to extinction. This was a creature capable of great and terrible things.

The little dragon opened its mouth and swallowed a drumstick whole, bone and all. It shuffled its wings, making delighted purring sounds, then burped.

A little piece of flame jumped onto the bucket.

Fran crushed it with her thumb an instant later. Her eyes flicked to Ivan. "So my egg—"

"Hatched," he finished for her.

"Right. And your sister—"

"Found you."

"Yes, and I'm—" She paused, eyes on Ivan as if waiting for him to finish this sentence as well.

Cute? Fascinating? A knight?

All true, but Ivan couldn't guess any of them. So he tried something else based on her tone. "Sorry?"

"No. Well, maybe a little actually." Fran bit her lip, but her hands tightened around the bucket, squeezing it and the dragon within closer to her chest. "Because I'm keeping him."

22

IVAN

Keeping the baby dragon was insane for a number of reasons. One, the Hagens might stop hunting her if they returned a live hatchling instead of a dead egg. Two, the Western Woodlands were not a suitable habitat for a meat-eating beast. And three, Daisy was going to kill them all, dragon included, should she ever discover the truth.

But Fran was so certain in her decision. Within the first few minutes of listening to her explain, Ivan had known that nothing he could say, no amount of logical objection, would change her mind. Her mother had wanted her to have the dragon. She'd left the instructions to break the egg to free it. This must have been her plan all along.

Ivan's hand went to his pocket. The knight's badge was still in there with *O.O.T.E* engraved on the back. His thumb traced the inscription as Fran spoke.

Had this really been what the knights wanted? To steal and hatch a dragon?

Like everything with Fran, it didn't make sense. The

knights were against magic. And what was more magical than a great dragon?

"This is what I'm meant to do, Ivan. Whether you let me stay here or not, I'm keeping the dragon." Fran stared up at him, eyes glistening with tears that she refused to shed. "I can feel it. I belong with him."

Ivan could hear the longing in her voice as she spoke that last sentence. If he'd intended to argue, that would have silenced him.

That's what she came here for really, isn't it? A sense of belonging?

"Say they can stay with us?" Poppy clasped her hands together, pouting her lower lip and making her eyes look big and desperate. "Please?"

Ivan sighed. When had the two of them found time to become friends? Though it didn't surprise him that his younger sister wanted to keep the hatchling. She'd always had a fondness for strange pets.

"Dust it!" Ivan threw his hands into the air. "The Hagens might keep trying to kill you whether we return the dragon or not, and I'm not going to let you wander out and get yourself killed in the city. You haven't the faintest clue how to take care of a dragon."

None of them did.

This fact became increasingly obvious in the week that followed. There were nine incidents where items in the treehouse caught on fire, five cases of non-edible items being chewed to pieces, and one very unfortunate occurrence where a plastic bottle was eaten and they ended up spending an entire afternoon scrubbing dragon poop out of the rug.

Even so, Ivan didn't regret his decision.

The little dragon, with its big gold eyes and curious

manner of purring, made Ivan laugh more often than curse. He had to cover his mouth to keep quiet when the creature tried pouncing on insects instead of frying them with its flame, and they'd made a game of trying to test just how wide it could open its jaw. And even Ivan thought it was cute when the dragon curled up on his lap.

Most importantly, having the dragon in the treehouse also meant that Fran was there.

Ivan had come to appreciate the strange juxtaposition of her tough, sarcastic mask and the anxious, vulnerable core that it hid. Sometimes, when she grew stressed or tired, the mask would crack, and he'd see hints of her beneath. She'd admit something, then grow embarrassed and over-explain until he reassured her that having feelings was perfectly normal.

And beyond that Fran was interesting. She had an opinion about almost every topic. Some of them were undoubtedly wrong opinions, but Ivan still found it entertaining listening to her reasoning.

"You love horror movies?" Ivan dropped a pile of carrots in an overdramatic fashion. He'd been rearranging the shelves, barricading the bottles of water behind a pile of fresh vegetables. They seemed to be the only thing that repelled the dragon as Poppy had discovered.

"They're the best genre."

Ivan snorted. It was yet another example of an undeniably wrong opinion. He raised an eyebrow and turned toward Fran. She was curled up on the mattress, under strings of paper cranes that she and Poppy had hung from the ceiling. Her black coat covered her like a blanket.

The dragon was curled in a ball on her lap, purple scales rising and falling in a soft, steady rhythm. Without being near, Ivan knew that there was a stream of hot air blowing from its nostrils straight against Fran's thigh. It would've made the fairy uncomfortable, but somehow, the human never seemed to notice.

Fran's laptop was on the pillow before her, luckily out of the trajectory of the dragon's snores. She had asked Poppy to charge it at the house for her, and the thirteen-year-old had agreed. Ivan supposed their parents, who were back from their vacation now, hadn't noticed.

"What? You don't like horror movies?" The corner of Fran's lip quirked upward in amusement. It seemed extra taunting whenever she had her lipstick on.

Ivan scoffed. He absolutely did not. Horrifying monsters? Evil humans with knives? "They're literally the stuff of nightmares."

"Aw. You get scared?"

Ivan's eyes narrowed. He did not like that tone. It was the kind Fran used when the dragon farted. Instead of answering the question honestly, he changed the topic. "Don't you suffer from panic attacks? How do you enjoy having weird things jump out at you?"

Fran turned away, the smile suddenly gone from her face.

Ivan felt a stab of guilt in his chest. He had only been teasing, but Fran was unusually sensitive about the fact that she suffered from anxiety.

"I'm just saying, it's very impressive," Ivan said, turning back toward the vegetables. His barricade was already indestructible, he hoped, but he adjusted a bunch of turnip leaves to try to look busy. "For someone not to get scared during something that freaks most people out."

That at least got a giggle. "I knew you got scared."

"Yeah, well, anyone with a half-decent imagination would."

Fran laughed again. It was a rare sound, higher than expected, soft and short, like she cut herself off before it could get out of control. Ivan was desperate to hear what it would be like if she did. "I get scared too. That's why I like them."

"Ah, you're a masochist. Makes sense now." Ivan turned to her with a grin. "You always did strike me as such."

Fran rolled her eyes, but she couldn't hide that she was smiling. "No, I mean, because I'm panicked, but with good reason. And I'm not the only one, you know. Like, it sounds stupid, but it's comforting to know that other people are having the same reaction. Like, I'm not the only one who's freaked out."

"That doesn't sound stupid." Ivan glanced out the window. The sun had set a few hours ago. It was getting late. He should get back to campus. The same assignment had been sitting on the desk in his dorm for the past three days. Instead, he kept fiddling with the vegetables. "You've always wanted to be part of a group. You're very concerned with fitting in like that."

"Oh, ha, ha." Fran stuck her tongue out. "I want to belong somewhere, and I do now. I have the dragon and I have—"

She cut herself off.

Ivan's eyes flicked toward her. Her cheeks had turned pink, and she was staring at the computer screen. *What was she going to say?*

"Do you think it's weird that I still don't know his name?"

That hadn't been it. Ivan stared at her for a moment, taking longer than it should have for him to realize that Fran was talking about the dragon.

"Nah, he's only a week," Ivan reassured her, shrugging

his shoulders. "He probably doesn't even know his own name yet."

Fran's finger stroked the length of the dragon's head and neck where small gold spikes had begun rising along the ridge. He'd already doubled in size since Ivan had first seen him. Soon, he'd be too big to hide in buckets of chicken. "Maybe I'm overthinking it."

"Guaranteed. But that's kind of your thing." When the joke failed to receive a laugh, Ivan crouched on the floor beside the mattress. He leaned over to scratch between the dragon's eyes, and the creature purred in response. "His mother was Starsong. Maybe he's Sunpoem or Cloudprose."

Fran raised her eyebrows. "Are you being serious?"

"Of course not. Those are ridiculous names."

"Well, I don't know." She leaned her head back against the wall, eyes staring at the cranes overhead. "What does it say about me if I can't even tell good dragon names from bad ones?"

"That you're human?"

Fran's neck snapped toward him. "I'm not though. Poppy and I discussed it. I'm obviously something. Maybe a witch. He wouldn't have hatched for me otherwise."

Ivan shrugged. He'd love to know where his little sister heard that humans couldn't hatch dragons. Poppy's knowledge of dragon lore should have been as lacking as his own.

Of course, Chase Hagen should've had a good sense of it, and he'd thought the egg would be dead.

"You're definitely something special," Ivan said, staring at the paper cranes Fran had folded. He only realized what he'd said after it was out his mouth.

Fran's cheeks turned pink.

Dust, that had sounded flirtier than he'd intended. Ah well.

Ivan pretended it was intentional and grinned.

She rolled her eyes.

Good reminder that she's not interested. Fran had made that clear from the very first day. It hadn't bothered Ivan too much then. So why did it upset him to see her look away now?

"I, uh, should get going. I'm becoming a Phi Eta Gentleman tomorrow." Ivan tapped the badge in his pocket as he pushed himself up from the floor.

"Ick." Fran stuck her tongue out and made a face. "You know we can't stay friends after you're in a fraternity. It's the principle of the thing."

"But you admit we're friends now?"

"Of course. Though I don't know what it says about you that you're friends with a girl who wears her backpack backwards"

"Oof, yeah, we need to work on that, or I can't be seen in public with you."

Of course, they couldn't be seen together by anyone, no matter how Fran wore her backpack. The realization seemed to settle on both of them at the same time. The smiles disappeared from their faces.

Ivan felt like an idiot for saying anything. He cleared his throat, trying to think what might make it better. "You know, once I'm a Gentleman, I'll have more pull. I might actually be able to help you somehow."

"By convincing the rich sociopath not to kill me and let me just keep the dragon he thinks was stolen from him? You have a very high opinion of your persuasive abilities."

"Well, I'm very talented." Ivan played the comment off as a joke, but it wasn't an impossibility. Not that he had any great skill, but people like Chase were more likely to listen to their peers. Ivan Dream, son of two florists who lived in the Western Woodlands, was far from that now. But maybe, Ivan Dream, Phi Eta Gentleman, would have a chance. "Worst case scenario, I could get the resources for a better house for you to hide in."

"I don't mind this one. The forest is growing on me. Especially now that I have Poppy to charge all my devices." She smiled and tapped her laptop. "Honestly, becoming a hermit might be in my future."

Ouch. Wouldn't she miss him?

Ivan laughed. "Nah. Poppy likes you too much. She'd find you so she could keep talking your ear off. She's very chatty."

"Family trait, you think?"

"Okay, okay. I can take a hint." Ivan ran his hand through his hair and went for his own bag, which he'd dropped by the window when he flew in. "I'll get you more meat tomorrow."

"Wait."

Ivan did.

"Do you want to watch a scary movie with me before you go?"

A smile spread across his face. He got it under control before turning around. "I thought you were becoming a hermit."

"Yeah, well, I want to see how scared you get before I commit myself to solitude."

Ivan laughed. He should go. It was getting late, and he needed to be at the Phi Eta Gentleman's house before sunrise. And he didn't even like horror movies.

"Yeah, fine. Might be interesting to see what kind of weird shit you like, Bucky."

Fran rolled her eyes at the nickname, but she inched over. Ivan climbed onto the mattress beside her, acutely aware of her arm brushing against his as they huddled together to share the computer screen.

The little dragon's tail swept onto Ivan's leg, and its back legs scooched back so that it was laying over both of them. Its limbs pulled their thighs closer, somehow spreading the jacket so that it was over both teens.

At some point in the movie, Fran's hand found its way into Ivan's. Their fingers interlaced, squeezing together. They didn't let go, even after the movie ended.

23
FRANCES

The past few days, Fran had been woken by the dragon chewing on her hair or pawing at her chest, not realizing that its claws were sharp. This morning, however, it was a noise that was noticeably undragonlike. It was high and girlish.

Like a giggle.

Fran didn't want to wake up. She buried her face deeper into Ivan's shoulder, feeling the muscles in his chest as her body pressed closer to his. Did he spend all his time when he wasn't around working out? Or were fairies just naturally ripped?

Wait. Why was she in bed with Ivan?

Fran's eyes flew open.

Thanks to the twinkling blue lights from Poppy's wings, Fran could just make out Ivan's younger sister standing over them. The thirteen-year-old had a guilty, close-lipped smile on her face, but she wasn't looking away. She'd taken the dragon off of them and was now cradling him in her arms. The creature had settled there with a peaceful look on its face.

More peaceful than he looks with me?

"Poppy?" Ivan pushed himself up groggily. The white shirt he'd been wearing before clung to his skin. Fran's eyes trailed down his chest to where it had risen, revealing a line of visible abdominal muscles just above his pelvis. "What're you doing here so early?"

The thirteen-year-old giggled again.

Fran felt her face grow hot, and she turned her head up to the ceiling. Surely, in the darkness, Poppy couldn't have noticed Fran staring at her brother's abs.

"Making sure little Purple Scales doesn't go flying around the woods by himself to pee," she said. "I come every morning just before sunrise."

And I never noticed? Fran wrapped her arms around herself, trying to think back to all the other days this past week. It was always mid-morning already by the time the dragon woke her. But it fell asleep much earlier than she did at night. Had she really been so naive to think that it was sleeping for twelve hours?

"Dust!" Ivan flew off the mattress, wings popping out behind him as soon as he was up. The blue and red glittered, adding their light to Poppy's. He turned around the room, grabbed his bag, and tossed the strap over his shoulder.

"Wait, don't run off," Poppy said. "I need to talk to you about Daisy. She's—"

"I can't now," Ivan cut his sister off. "Tonight, okay? I'll be back then." He addressed the last part to Fran as well before flying out the window.

Fran bit her lip, curling her body tighter as she watched him disappear. His sudden departure stung more than it should have.

I'm being ridiculous. We're just friends who happened to fall

*asleep on the same mattress. He doesn't owe me breakfast or
some long goodbye.*

Still, it felt a bit like he was choosing his strange fraternity over her.

"Did you guys hook up?"

Fran's face grew hot.

"Don't be silly. We watched a movie and fell asleep." She pushed herself up from the mattress and went over to where Poppy was cradling the now stirring dragon. "I can take him."

"Oh, it's fine. I like having the chance to spend time with him." The thirteen-year-old grinned, forgetting to hide her braces. She often did when she was with the dragon. Her excitement for the creature outweighed her hatred for her braces.

Fran crossed her arms, trying not to feel resentful as she watched the dragon's tongue flick out and lick Poppy's chin. The dragon was her gift from her parents. It had hatched from the egg she'd cherished all her life. They belonged together. Fran could feel their connection whenever the dragon curled on her lap.

But what if she was just fooling herself?

Fran loved the dragon, but she wasn't certain that she understood it. Poppy was the one who'd discovered how much it hated vegetables, and who'd realized that beef was its favorite, and who'd been waking up early to take it outside.

Even Ivan had been the first to realize when the dragon had eaten a plastic bottle and gotten itself sick.

And every time the two fairies realized something that Fran didn't, her chest grew tight. Was she supposed to be with the dragon? What if it was all a mistake, and she wasn't magical at all? Maybe the dragon belonged here with the fairies, and she belonged somewhere else.

"Do you know his name?" Fran asked, struggling to keep her tone neutral. Her chest was already tightening in anticipation of the answer.

Great dragons weren't pets, Poppy had explained. You couldn't make up a name for them the way you could a cat or a dog. They would tell you their name when they were ready.

The thirteen-year-old shook her head. "Hopefully he tells one of us soon. Although I think Cutie Pie works until then."

The dragon licked her again as though in approval before flapping its wings and taking off through one of the windows. Poppy followed it.

Fran's heart clenched at the sight of them flying together. And what was that lick? What if that was the dragon choosing his name and Fran couldn't even realize it?

He's a baby, Ivan's voice reassured her. *He probably doesn't even know his name yet.*

She tried to focus on that thought as she grabbed her pocketknife from under her pillow. Fran slipped it into the waistband of the jeans she'd fallen asleep in and climbed down the ladder.

The grass felt cool beneath her feet. She wrapped her arms around herself, wishing she'd grabbed her jacket from upstairs.

Poppy's wings provided just enough light for Fran to make out the dragon. He was on his feet, leaping between the large roots of the trunk, likely hunting a beetle. It seemed to be one of his favorite pastimes.

Fran smiled at the sight of him.

"So, you totally avoided my question." Poppy leaned

closer to her. "Did something happen between you and my brother?"

Fran felt her cheeks heat up again. She really thought they'd moved off of that topic.

"It totally did, right? Do you like him? Are you guys together?"

Dear God, that was far too many questions.

Fran crossed her arms and pushed a few strands of hair off her face. "We fell asleep watching a movie. It wasn't a big deal."

"And spent the whole night cuddling?" Poppy squealed as if this was just as exciting.

"I don't think we were cuddling," Fran said, turning away from the thirteen-year-old and focusing on the dragon once again. He was crouching low, tail up in the air as he tracked a trail of ants climbing up the trunk of the tree.

"Do you like him? I swear I won't tell him if you do."

"Of course not. What is he doing?" Fran pointed at the dragon who was now attempting to climb the tree to chase the ants.

The little creature was using its claws instead of its wings for some reason and had stopped about four feet up. It whimpered.

"He's gotten himself stuck." Fran hurried toward the dragon.

It waited until she was about to grab it before turning to her. The creature opened its mouth in a large toothy grin, shot a tiny ember toward her, and dropped down on its own.

Fran managed to grab the spark and squash it in her hand before it spread.

She sighed, looking down at the dragon, who was

finally peeing right by her feet. *Guess you didn't need me after all.*

"That's too bad," Poppy said. "Because I think he likes you."

She wasn't talking about the dragon.

"Ivan?" Fran's head turned toward the thirteen-year-old faster than it should have. Her voice sounded too excited, didn't it? Fran took a deep breath, relaxing her stance and trying to keep her tone as unbothered as possible. "What makes you say that?"

"I don't know. He seems really happy and relaxed around you?"

Fran rolled her eyes. That hardly seemed like proof. "Isn't he always?"

"Not with his other girlfriends. He was always kind of fake around them. Like he was trying too hard to impress them."

That just sounds like he cares what everyone thinks other than me.

"Ivan dated a lot of girls?"

Poppy raised her hands, muttering to herself as she counted on her fingers.

"Never mind." That was definitely a yes, and Fran, despite all logic, felt herself getting annoyed by that answer.

Which was so silly. What did she care if Ivan had dated a ton of girls before she met him?

Because it means he has options. But Fran should've known that anyway. Ivan was sweet, and he had abs worth drooling over. Obviously, he was popular. And Fran knew herself well enough to know that she wasn't destined to end up with anyone popular.

And she'd always been happy about that.

Until now.

"He never let any of them come to the treehouse," Poppy said. "You're the first girl he's ever invited."

Fran smiled, though she hated herself for the fact that hearing that made her happy. She turned away from the thirteen-year-old, trying to hide her expression, and Fran's eyes landed on the roots of the tree.

"Hey, where did he go?"

"Ivan? I think he was pledging today. Wasn't he?"

"No, I mean, the dragon." Fran's head spun to either side, chest growing tight.

"Oh. Uh." Poppy sounded just as panicked as Fran felt. She fluttered a few feet in the air, and did a lap of the large trunk, calling out to the dragon. A moment later, she landed in front of Fran. The thirteen-year-old's eyes were wide, and she was trembling. "I don't know. He's never run off before."

But he chose the exact moment that Fran was there to make an escape.

If that wasn't a sign that she wasn't cut out to take care of a dragon, Fran didn't know what was.

Her chest felt tight, and breathing was getting difficult, but as she looked at Poppy, Fran realized that the thirteen-year-old was even closer to breaking down than she was. As the adult in the situation, Fran didn't have that luxury.

"He can't have gone far," Fran said, putting a hand on Poppy's shoulder to steady her, and faking a confidence that she definitely didn't feel. "I'll find him. Wait here in case he comes back."

The thirteen-year-old nodded, and Fran turned. She chose a direction at random and started running, praying that luck was on her side for a change.

Otherwise, any dreams she had of staying in the Western Woodlands were going to go up in flames.

24

IVAN

There was no time to catch a bus to get back to campus, so Ivan broke all the protocols and more than a couple of laws, human and magical.

In his defense, his wings were technically hidden. All of him was. The rule about fairies not using magic in human spaces shouldn't have applied to ones with Ivan's ability. Because there was no chance of any human spotting him.

Which was why he didn't feel so terrible about riding on the tops of the buses. Was it breaking a law? Of course. But if no one ever found out, were you really doing something illegal?

Obviously, yes. He'd asked that question before and received that response from Daisy. His sister had also pointed out that he was bound to be spotted by someone. Just because he could turn invisible didn't mean he should get over-confident. There were always enchantments that could break past his ability.

But anyone wearing some magical amulet allowing them to see the unseen was probably up to no good themselves in Ivan's opinion. They weren't likely to rat him out to any authorities.

So Ivan used his foolproof method for fast travel, alternating between flying when traffic stopped and hitching a ride on cars when it flowed, giving his wings a rest and allowing him to catch his breath.

There was a pink glow to the morning sky. The large buildings of the city blocked the sun, but Ivan could see hints of its rays starting to light the streets.

"Dust." He dropped into the back of a flatbed truck as it sped east on Townsend Street, shoulder muscles aching. The best way to rest would be to retract his wings, but he had to keep them out if he wanted to stay invisible.

His eyes flicked upward. The streetlights were still on, but probably not for much longer. If they were off before Ivan made it to campus, he would be too late. The Gentlemen weren't likely to wait for him.

Ivan pulled his phone out of his pocket, hoping it hadn't died overnight. He pressed it and caught a glimpse of the time. *5:55 a.m.* That gave him five minutes before the Gentlemen closed the doors and refused to allow him in, knight's badge or not. It didn't look good.

Something else caught his eye. It was a barrage of missed calls, all from Daisy.

That was weird. His older sister never called.

The truck came to a stop at a traffic light before Ivan could check if there were any messages. He pushed the phone as deep into the pocket of his hoodie as he could get it, then jumped onto the roof of the car. He ran across, trying to pick up as much speed as he could before leaping into the sky and taking flight.

Fairies weren't fast flyers, a weakness that many of the other magical beings enjoyed throwing in their faces. But

Ivan had always been stubborn. He'd spent ages practicing as a child, absolutely refusing to believe that he couldn't reach the same speeds as a dragon. All he needed to do was to push himself enough.

I just need the right motivation.

It was 6:05 by the time Ivan's feet touched down on the doorstep of the Phi Eta Gentlemen.

He checked the time on his phone as he leaned against the door. The muscles in his back and abs were cramping now. Ivan felt like he was going to melt into a puddle, and all for what? He was still too late.

Ivan dropped his invisibility, twisting the tips of his wings and hiding them as fast as he could. After sustaining his magic for so long, the motion made his stomach turn. He leaned over and threw up into a large porcelain vase by the entrance. It had a pair of fighting griffins engraved on the front.

Probably some wealthy house's sigil. And now it was full of Ivan's puke.

He suddenly burst out laughing.

It was weird. Now that it was too late, Ivan didn't feel the immense disappointment that he'd expected. Instead, he felt relieved.

Who cared if any of the Gentlemen heard him cackling like a madman or discovered that he'd thrown up in their vase? Ivan didn't have to care about what they thought.

Fran's right. This is a hundred times easier.

Ivan wiped his mouth with the sleeve of his hoodie and let his head lean back onto one of the pillars.

His phone lit up in his hand. He glanced down. Another message from Daisy.

He sighed. What did she want? Did she need him to sub in for her at work? She'd promised never to ask again after he'd admitted to being tempted to steal sips of people's leftovers. Not that Ivan would have. He knew what people would've thought if they caught him chugging a half-finished drink. He just hated seeing perfectly good smoothie go to waste.

Although, maybe he would drink the leftovers if he subbed for Daisy now. This whole *not caring what people thought* thing was very freeing.

Ivan scanned Daisy's messages. There were way more than usual, spread out over the past fourteen hours that he'd been with Fran. His phone had been in his backpack, and he hadn't thought to check it the entire time.

You don't know anything more about that girl you met, right? People have been asking.

Call me. I saw Poppy buying a bag of meat.

If you've done something to upset Chase Hagen of all people, you're going to be dead. And it won't be me doing the killing.

I saw the file. This better be a huge misunderstanding! I can't keep saving your ass, Ivan.

Call me now!!!

The latest message had just come through.

Too late. He's here. There better not be anything to find.

Ivan's body went numb as he stared at his sister's words. What did Daisy mean? Where was she and who was she with?

"Dust!" Ivan's fingers trembled. He needed to call Daisy, right now.

"Finally." The door to the Gentleman's mansion opened. A tall figure stepped out wearing a silver mask with a long beak that should have disguised him, but the waves of blond hair spilling down to his shoulders gave Silvan away. He wore a black outfit that was what Ivan imagined a very wealthy army officer's uniform might look like. The shirt had silver embroidery in a crest over the chest and large buttons ran down the right. The pants fit as though they'd been tailored.

Ivan felt a pang of envy at the display of wealth, but he pushed it aside. He could forget about the Gentlemen. His only concern now was finding out what was going on with Daisy.

"I know. I'm too late," Ivan said before Silvan could chastise him. "Sorry, I'm heading out."

"Wait." Silvan's hand clasped around Ivan's wrist before he could leave. More figures, dressed in the same black military uniforms and silver masks stepped out from behind him. "You have the badge?"

Was that what they wanted? Ivan reached into his pocket, pulled it out, and tossed it to the Gentlemen. "Here."

The mask didn't hide Silvan's mouth, so Ivan saw the smile that flashed on his face. He caught the badge in his free hand and passed it to someone behind him.

"One of the new ones," someone said.

"Told you. He's the real deal." Silvan grinned. He was still holding Ivan's wrist. "He outsmarted one of the knights."

"Well, I guess." Ivan ran his free hand through his hair, a cautious smile growing on his face. Was he really being praised by the king's nephew?

So much for not caring what people think. He hadn't exactly tricked a knight to get the badge, just Fran, and that memory didn't make him feel all that clever, just mean.

"Thanks, Silvan, but I have to go. I have something to do."

"Yeah, you do." Silvan pulled him into the mass of masks.

Ivan felt his body jostled between them. Hands reached toward him. Someone took his phone.

"I need that." Ivan spun, trying to find the culprit.

"You'll get it back when we're done."

"Done with what?" Ivan turned trying to figure out who had spoken, but it was impossible to tell. And there was no guarantee the speaker was the one with his phone.

"Isn't it obvious?" Silvan said. "You, Ivan Dream, are about to become a Gentleman."

25
FRANCES

Fran's chest felt tight as she ran through the forest. For a change, it wasn't her anxiety. She just really needed to run more.

I've gone the wrong way. The dragon could've gone in any direction. The chances of Fran choosing correctly were so infinitesimally small, she couldn't believe she'd even bothered.

But she'd had to. The little dragon could be in danger. Someone might catch him and hurt him.

Fran's eyes skipped over the soft pockets of glowing pink that the sunrise painted on the forest floor, searching for a glint of gold in the darkness.

Something nudged her foot.

Fran's head snapped down, and a sigh escaped her. The little dragon stood, gold eyes glowing up at her, tail resting on her toes.

I went the right way.

The little creature turned and started scurrying away as if it were on a mission.

Not this time. Fran stumbled forward and threw herself

on top of the creature before it could gather too much speed. It grumbled in objection, but she wrapped her arms around it, holding it in place.

"You can't just wander off like that," Fran scolded. "You could get hurt."

The dragon opened its mouth, grumbling the way it did whenever it was hungry. Its nostrils twitched, it pressed its head to her cheek, then pushed it toward something in the distance.

"There's food back home." Fran struggled to stand while maintaining her hold on the dragon. It didn't fight against her, but she didn't dare loosen her grip all the same.

The dragon grumbled once more, still staring into the distance.

A moment later, a twig snapped. Fran froze, eyes darting toward the noise. The dragon's gaze followed in the same direction.

"I'm telling you, I smell something." It was a boy with a very familiar voice.

"Is it the girl you're looking for?" A woman asked. She sounded nervous, but familiar too.

A lump rose in Fran's throat. She hadn't met that many people since coming to Castor's Grove. There were only so many voices that she would recognize.

The boy didn't respond, but Fran could hear their footsteps getting closer. They were heading straight toward them.

They smell us. We need to get away.

Before Fran could compel her feet to move, the scent of raw meat suddenly filled the forest. The dragon stirred in her hands, hot saliva dripping onto her neck.

Shit.

"Come out, little one," the boy's voice said again.

Panic flooded through Fran. It stopped her from bolting long enough to realize that if the boy was trying to lure the dragon out, then he couldn't track it by scent alone. Maybe staying still was a safer option after all.

The dragon's stomach rumbled slightly. It wriggled in Fran's grip.

She got control of it, squeezing her eyes shut and praying as she pressed it to her body. If there was ever a time that a magical connection would come in handy, it would be now.

Please, stay quiet. We can't get the food. Just stay still.

To her surprise, the dragon settled, resting its head against her shoulder with a sulky acceptance. Even its stomach stopped grumbling.

"Just what do you think is here?" The woman sounded like she was gagging from the scent of the meat. Something about it made Fran think of Poppy, who pretended to be sick whenever Ivan tried to feed her vegetables.

It's their sister. Fran had only met her once when they'd tried to wipe her memory, but Ivan and Poppy talked about her often enough that the image of Daisy was fresh in Fran's memory.

Neither Ivan nor Poppy wanted their older sister to find out about Fran or the dragon, but both trusted her. It might not be so terrible if Daisy discovered them.

But who was she with?

Whoever it was, he didn't seem keen on answering Daisy's questions.

Afraid that even the slightest sound might give her away, Fran held her breath and peeped out from behind the trunk as fast as she dared.

Their backs were to her, but Fran recognized the boy with Daisy. Chase Hagen. The one who wanted her dead.

He wore a black outfit, but his visible white-scaled wings and tail gave him away. Chase waved a bag above his head. The scent of meat radiated from within.

"Look, Ivan wouldn't help someone like this. He's not that foolish," Daisy said. Her red hair was in a ponytail again, but she wore regular jeans and a long-sleeved white t-shirt. There was something in her hands, a beige file. She shook it before her as she spoke, and the light caught on a small red tab protruding from the top, making the letters flash in the air.

Buckler.

Fran held back a gasp. That file was about her family.

I have to get that somehow.

Maybe she could ask Ivan to steal it from his sister. That was his specialty after all.

Fran was so focused on the file that she didn't register the dragon squirming once more in her arms. Before she realized what it was doing, the little creature slipped free.

The sound of its wings beating against the wind caused both Chase and Daisy to turn. The red-haired girl shouted, leaping backward from the dragon. But Chase smiled. He lowered his backpack, managing to catch the flying creature inside of it.

There was a muffled grumble as the dragon realized that he'd been caught, then a delighted purr as he remembered there was food in the bag with him.

Fran's anxiety caused her to freeze, arms outstretched in a failed attempt to grab the dragon before he'd darted. She remained there, eyes flicking between the other two as they noticed her.

"Dust." Daisy stepped further away, eyeing Fran as though she were a dangerous creature. The redhead seemed

to be trying to position Chase between them. "Did she have
—I mean—was that—a dragon?"

"You got Starsong's egg to hatch." Chase stared at Fran,
pupils narrowing. His tongue snaked and flicked at her.

"Yes." There was no point denying it. Fran swallowed,
finding her mouth suddenly dry. She didn't like how Chase
was looking at her.

"How?" Chase passed the bag with the dragon to a startled looking Daisy. Then he slunk toward Fran, steps slow
and measured, eyes focused like a predator who'd spotted
its prey. "Did you coerce a witch into assisting you?"

Fran shook her head, hand lowering slowly toward the
knife that was still tucked in her waistband. "I just opened
the egg, and he was there."

"He has a name," Chase said, lowering his voice to a
feral growl. His mouth opened, revealing a row of teeth.
And suddenly, Fran understood why a being like Chase still
bore the name *dragon*. "Lostsong."

Even with her heart racing and legs trembling, Fran had
been managing to keep her anxiety at bay, managing to
keep herself moving, however slowly. But hearing the man
who she'd built up as pure evil in her mind say the name of
the dragon crushed Fran in a way she hadn't been
expecting.

She'd wanted so badly to belong with the dragon. But
Chase Hagen had known its name in less than a minute.

Fran felt numb.

Chase's hand around her neck changed that quickly.

He squeezed, and Fran felt what it truly meant to be
without air.

Chase was stronger than she would've guessed given
his frame. He picked Fran up with one hand, bashing her
into the tree. A sharp pain shot through the back of her

skull. She heard something whimper and then go quiet. Perhaps it was her.

"Who are the Order of the Egg working with? How have you managed to bypass all the enchantments that secure us?" He shook her, before loosening his grip on her neck, just enough to let some air in. "Tell me."

Fran had never imagined she'd do well under torture, and she stood by that assessment of herself. This was nothing compared to what other people went through, and she was ready to cave. She would have answered every one of Chase's questions. If she had a clue what he was talking about.

"I don't know," she said, gasping. trying to fill her lungs with air while she could. "I've never heard of any order."

"Don't lie." His hand tightened once again, claws shooting from his nails. They scratched at Fran's neck as he leaned closer, staring at her with his snake-like pupils. "Or these woods will be your grave, Knight."

"I—" Fran tried to insist that she wasn't lying, but spots were swimming before her vision. Had he just called her a knight?

"Too late." Chase opened his mouth. Fran stared at the darkness within, waiting for him to bite her. Instead, a bright white flame appeared within. It shot out, straight toward Fran.

And she found herself engulfed in the heat.

26

IVAN

The final step to becoming a Phi Eta Gentleman was thankfully faster than any of the others. With all the tasks and trials completed, Ivan had proven himself. All that was left to do was swear on a book before his new brothers, reciting an oath of loyalty.

Ivan rushed through the vows that were given to him, tripping over the words without care. There was a party waiting for him when he finished. The foyer had been set with a spread of food like nothing he had ever seen.

But all he could think about was his phone.

As soon as the oaths were finished, Silvan returned it to him along with the former knight's badge. It had been transformed now so that instead of the knights' sword, the Gentleman's black top hat shone on gold. Ivan only knew it was the same badge because the initials O.O.T.E remained engraved on the back.

He shoved it into his pocket, then dialed his sister.

Daisy didn't answer.

"Dust."

It might have been nothing. Daisy could be overdramatic when she was annoyed. But as the masks came off and the party began, Ivan couldn't help but notice that Chase Hagen was absent.

"This is amazing, Silvan, but I have to go," Ivan said, grabbing a handful of quiches and shoving them into his pocket with the badge.

"You're leaving your own welcome party early?"

Technically it was for Ivan and the other pledges who'd said their vows earlier, but either way, it was definitely rude.

"Unfortunately. I have somewhere I need to be."

"Huh." Silvan crossed his arms, a disappointed look on his face. "I hope it's important."

I don't.

Ivan shoved an extra quiche into his mouth and grabbed a cupcake that had yet to be offered off a tray on his way out the door. He'd never hoped that he was wrong so badly before in his life.

Ivan traveled the same way he had that morning, alternating between flying and hitching lifts. Every time he stopped, he took the opportunity to fuel himself with some of the stolen food and call his sister.

Daisy never answered. But Poppy did.

Ivan had never been more relieved to hear his younger sister's voice. Until he realized that she didn't sound as cheerful as usual.

The dragon had run off that morning, and Fran had gone looking for him. Poppy was waiting at the treehouse, only she couldn't stay because she had school and Mum and Dad were going to miss her soon and come looking. It was one more thing for Ivan to worry about.

"You wanted to tell me something about Daisy this morning. What was it?" Ivan tried to focus on his original concern. He leaped off a slow-moving bus and flew toward the woods as fast as he could manage. He kept the phone pressed to his ear.

"Oh. I think she knows about Fran. She was asking a lot of questions about her yesterday."

"Like what?" Ivan could see the trees rising from the Western Woodlands. He was close.

"Just if I'd seen her around. But she seemed really confused. I think she thinks Fran's a knight for some reason."

A chill went through Ivan. He hung up the phone.

He needed to find Daisy. Ivan tried calling her again. The phone was ringing in his ear when he first spotted the pale red dancing in the corner of his vision.

Fire.

The Western Woodlands were enchanted as best as possible to ensure that didn't happen, which meant this wasn't an accidental forest fire. This was something purposeful and magical in nature.

The dragon?

Ivan twisted, angling himself so that he was heading toward the flames. His back ached from the constant flying, and his pulse raced.

But as soon as he got low enough to see what was happening, a cold sense of dread numbed the pain. Ivan's body continued to move forward, but his mind was unable to accept what was happening before him.

Fran was in the flames.

Her frame, small without her characteristic jacket, shimmered before Ivan as though submerged. Her pale skin caught the colors, glowing with a strange pink light. The features of her face were obscured by the fire. Only the blackness of her hair stood out, defiant of the flames.

Fran's hands twitched at her sides. It looked like she was spasming for a moment. Then, her right hand slashed out toward Chase.

There was a grunt as the dragon stumbled backward. His grip loosened.

Fran dropped to the base of the tree and crawled out of the fire. Smoke trailed from the edges of her hair. But otherwise, she looked unharmed. By dragon fire.

Ivan didn't stop to think about the seeming impossibility of the situation.

Chase had already recovered and was lunging toward the retreating Fran.

Ivan grabbed the dragon before he could reach her, pulling him backward.

Chase stumbled but managed to catch his balance. Pupils narrow, the dragon looked around, trying to see who had pulled him. Seeing no one, his lips curled into a snarl. "Coward. If you want to fight, show yourself."

Ivan placed himself between the dragon and where Fran had stopped, still on the mud, but sitting against a tree with her knife out before her. He flicked his wings to reveal himself, raising his hands in a placating gesture as he did.

"I don't want to fight," he said. And even if he did, Ivan wasn't stupid enough to try to take on a dragon. Especially not one that had just shown he had no qualms about using his fire. Fran might have survived unscathed, but Ivan had no delusions about his own resistance. His best chance of making it out of this was to make Chase understand.

So, I'm definitely fucked.

"You claim peace, yet you protect the very enemy you know I hunt." Chase's lips curled back, revealing his fangs. "Move."

"Just listen to him, you idiot."

Ivan's head turned toward his sister. He'd been so focused on Fran that he hadn't noticed Daisy. She must've been hiding several feet away in the trees. But now that Ivan was visible, she marched forward. Daisy's eyes were wide, and she clung to something in her arms, but her jaw was set and her voice steady.

"She's a knight. I saw her file."

"Oh, he knows. He's the one who found it," Chase informed her. His tongue flicked between his lips, and he turned to Ivan with a sneer. "Though it begs the question why. I assumed at the time that you were looking for evidence to hand her over to the appropriate authorities and changed your mind when I informed you that my family would deal with the matter. But here you are now, protecting her."

"That's not what he's doing," Daisy insisted, stepping forward.

"Yes, it is," Ivan snapped at his sister before turning his attention back to Chase. "Because Fran's not a knight, okay? She's just an orphan who came looking for her family with no idea what kind of people they were. She didn't steal your egg, and she definitely doesn't deserve to be punished because the humans who abandoned her did."

"They're the sins of her blood."

"Yeah, I know." Ivan clenched his jaw shut before he said something he might regret in response to that statement. "And that matters with dragons, and maybe with fairies. But Fran is a human. They don't work that way."

"Yet her blood has been affected." Chase craned his neck, leaning around Ivan so that he could address Fran directly. "Your ancestors committed countless atrocities against our kind, all to protect the world against magic. Yet now your family taint themselves with the very thing they swore to destroy. It's the hypocrisy that wounds me."

He spat toward Fran, sending a spark of fire toward her.

The heat singed the air by Ivan's shoulder. He turned in time to see Fran catch it between the fingers of her left hand. She squashed it in her palm, like a fly.

"See?" Chase looked at Ivan once more. "A danger to us all. And you would have me leave her?"

"Fran's not a danger," Ivan insisted. The same worry had plagued him at first too, but that was before he'd gotten to know her. For all she tried to pretend otherwise, Fran was kind and caring. She wasn't the type to join the knights or go on a rampage against magic. Even if her parents were.

"And how can I know this?"

Ivan was about to say that she'd been taking care of the baby dragon for the past week, but Fran answered instead.

"Because I'm leaving the city," she said.

"What?" Ivan spun to Fran to find her standing, staring past him at Chase. He shook his head. "No, you can't. It won't be safe for the dragon outside of Castor's Grove."

"Oh, no one needs to worry about that," Chase said. He held his hand out toward Daisy. She passed the bag she was holding to him. "Lostsong will be living with his family, where he belongs. I'll accompany him myself this evening."

Lostsong? Ivan shook his head. Chase couldn't possibly be referring to the baby dragon. There was no way his name was Lostsong. Ivan had never heard anything so sad and depressing and less suited to the excitable little creature who purred whenever he managed to sneak a piece of food.

"And I'll be out of Castor's Grove, back where I belong," Fran said, pushing past Ivan.

He stared at her, unable to understand. This whole

week, she'd been insistent that she belonged with the baby dragon. She had to be bluffing. Was she going to swipe at Chase with her knife and run? That would be catastrophic. Fran was magic-proof, but she definitely didn't have the strength that would be required to defeat Chase.

Bur Fran closed the knife, pushing into the waistband of her jeans. She held her hand out toward Chase. "I leave. You keep Lostsong," she said the name as though it sent barbs through her throat. "Nobody hurts anyone. Deal?"

Chase's eyes flicked toward her outstretched hand. He didn't take it, but his pupils slowly began to look normal again. "Be gone by midnight. And understand I only offer you that kindness because against all odds, you managed to keep the egg alive."

Fran nodded, lowering her hand.

But Ivan didn't understand. *How could she agree to those terms?*

Before he could find the words to object, however, Chase stepped forward. He leaned in, rested a hand on Ivan's shoulder, and squeezed. Pain rippled through Ivan's already sore muscles. It was a friendly reminder of the dragon's strength.

"And you, I forgive only because Silvan likes you. But make no mistake, Gentleman or not, you and I are not brothers. And you only get one strike."

His lips curled upward in a tight, unfriendly smile. Then Chase adjusted the wriggling bag so that the strap was over his shoulder. He rested a hand on the creature within, trying to calm it before unfurling his wings and disappearing into the trees.

Ivan glared into the darkness after him.

He couldn't help but notice that despite Chase's

attempt, the baby dragon had kept wriggling. Almost as though it wanted to break free.

27
FRANCES

"We have to go after him," Ivan said, pointing toward where Chase had vanished. "We can't let him take your dragon—"

"He's not my dragon," Fran cut him off, staring at the grass beneath her toes. She couldn't bring herself to look at the red-headed boy beside her. Right now, Fran felt numb. But that wouldn't last. She knew it. As soon as she looked at Ivan, everything would become real, and the feelings would come rushing in.

My parents are knights. And Ivan knew.

"What are you talking about? How can you say that?" Ivan's voice rose as he spun toward her. "He hatched from your egg. You told me yourself that you belong with him."

"I was wrong." Fran twisted, blocking him with her shoulders and looking at his sister instead.

Daisy stood, holding the beige Buckler file before her like a shield, and staring at Fran as though she were a monster.

Maybe I am. Wouldn't that be just like Fran? To have been so focused on trying to figure out how best to survive in a horror movie that she'd forgotten to consider what character she was.

"Are you serious?" Ivan continued speaking to the back of her head. "If you were going to give up the dragon and agree to leave then why the hell did you hang out here this past week? We could've done that from the beginning."

"Can I have that?" Fran asked, ignoring the annoyed red-headed boy and focusing on his sister.

Despite the fear in her eyes, Daisy didn't meekly obey. She stepped backward, her jaw set in objection.

Fran didn't care. The file was hers by all rights. It had her name on it.

She grabbed the folder and snatched it away from Daisy. Ivan's sister didn't try to take it back.

"Fran, wait. You don't want to look in there," Ivan said, his voice suddenly softer. "It's not who you are."

Oh, and who is that?

Unable to resist anymore, Fran turned and met Ivan's gaze.

Just as she'd expected, her body began to tremble. Her eyes filled with water. She blinked it away as quickly as she could. She wouldn't cry. Not over this. Not over Ivan. He didn't deserve it.

She'd trusted him.

When he said there was no information on her family in The Archives, she'd believed him. She'd convinced herself that her initial distrust was just her usual anxiety. But she'd been right. This whole week, while she'd been starting to like Ivan, he'd been lying to her.

"What's in here, Ivan?" Fran asked, letting her anger swell her voice.

He winced. "Nothing."

"Nothing? Really? It's empty?" Fran flung the file open.

There were three pieces of paper. She held them up before him, letting the beige folder fall to the floor. "Funny. It looks like it contains information about my family to me."

"No, they're not your family," Ivan said, shaking his head. "They're the people who gave birth to you, but they're not your family. You're not like them."

Fran's stomach twisted. Ivan sounded just like her dads had when she'd confronted them about the letter from her mother that she'd never received. "So what? You were trying to protect me? Didn't think I could handle the truth? Thought I'd break down and never recover? What?"

"No, Fran, nothing like that. I didn't know you when I first found it. I thought, oh dust, I don't know, maybe that you could've been—" He was stumbling over his words, trying to avoid answering.

Yet again, trying to protect her from some truth he'd decided she couldn't handle. "What? A knight?"

"Yes," Ivan said, shoulders slumping as he admitted it. "And a dangerous one, capable of infiltrating all our defenses. But I don't think that now that I know you. You're not like that, Fran. You wouldn't go out of your way to hurt people. And you aren't going to be happy walking away from here and leaving your dragon behind."

His voice grew less frantic as he spoke, as though the admission made him feel better.

But it didn't make Fran feel better.

"You don't know me," she said.

"Of course I do. We've spent almost every waking hour together this week. You don't think that's enough time for me to know who you are?"

"No." Because it clearly hadn't been enough time for her to learn who he was. The thought made a sob rise in her throat. She swallowed it before it could escape, using her fury to quash the sadness. She shook the pages before her. "If you did, you'd have known how much this meant to me. That this was the only reason I was in this city."

"No, you came to find where you belong," Ivan said. "And you did. Fran, you can go places that no other human can. You belong here. With the magic."

It was everything she'd ever hoped to hear. And for a moment, Fran's emotions softened. She thought about how happy she'd been in the treehouse, curled up with Ivan, listening to the insects singing outside and feeling the warmth radiating from the little dragon.

But that was temporary. Those moments came and went. There were other times when she'd been anxious still or stressed. And the dragon had never told her his name.

"You don't know where I belong," Fran said, hating the way she choked on the words. Then, before she burst into tears and made a fool of herself, she turned and sprinted away.

Part of her hoped Ivan would follow. But a larger part of her was pleased that he didn't.

It meant she could stay angry.

Fran was relieved to see that Poppy had left when she returned to the treehouse. The last thing she wanted was to explain to the thirteen-year-old what had happened to the dragon. Having to tell her that Chase had come for him and learned his name in the first minute would have hurt Fran more than she wanted to admit.

Ivan is a liar. I don't care about him. And I don't belong here. She threw her few things into her backpack and shoved her feet into her boots. The pages from the Buckler file dangled from her hands, unread.

It was only when everything was packed and Fran was ready to leave that the weight of them became too much.

I have to read them.

Funny that it hadn't been the first thing she'd done. After all this time yearning for information on her birth family. And yet, now that she had it, her chest was tight, her palms sweating.

I might not like what I find.

But so what? Fran could handle it.

She stared down at the first page, eyes scanning a wall of text.

The Bucklers are believed to be the leaders of The Order of the Egg, a branch of knights that split from the original group... gained popularity to become the dominant order among the knights... believed to present a significant danger due to their willingness to use magic even as they attempt to destroy it...

Beneath was a list of crimes that the Bucklers were suspected of committing. Theft of magical items was one of the lesser offenses.

Fran's stomach turned, but she forced herself to read them all before going to the next page. Her breath caught at the sight of it. A family tree.

Her name was at the bottom with a line running up from it. Fran's heart stopped as she followed it to the words above.

There was no name for her father. He was listed only as "unknown knight." But for the first time, Fran learned her mother's name.

Noelle Buckler.

She traced it with her finger, a drop of water escaping the corner of her eye and splashing the page below.

Mrs. Franklin knows how to find her.

Fran intended to keep her agreement with Chase

Hagen. She was leaving Castor's Grove at midnight. But she'd come here for a purpose.

Forget the magic woods. Forget the baby dragon. Forget Ivan Dream.

They had all been distractions.

Fran was going to find her parents and learn the truth. Before she left the city, she would know who she was, why she had the abilities she did, and why her parents had abandoned her.

Even if she didn't like the answers.

28

IVAN

Ivan pressed his hand to his head, rubbing his temples as Fran ran off. Was he supposed to run after her or give her time to cool off? He had no idea. Maybe Fran was right, he didn't know her.

Dust. This wasn't at all how he'd wanted her to find out about her family. Admittedly, he hadn't wanted her to find out, period, because he hadn't seen how anything good could come of it. Hiding it made things easier. At least, for him. Maybe not for Fran. She hadn't mentioned her parents as much this past week, but she'd still been thinking about them. She'd still been longing for the truth.

Ivan groaned as it dawned on him just how selfish his decision had been. *I'm an asshole. And I didn't even say sorry, did I? Damn it, what's wrong with me?*

He needed to go after her.

"Don't you dare run off." Daisy's hand grabbed the back of his sweatshirt as though she could read his mind. "Do you have any idea what you've done?"

Ivan considered ignoring his older sister and running

off anyway. But one look at the tightness in her jaw made him forget that idea.

Fran might be calmer and more open to forgiving him after she'd had some time alone. Daisy's anger did not dissolve after leaving her to sit with it. Quite the opposite. Ivan knew from experience.

"I told you not to get involved with her, Ivan," Daisy said, releasing her grip on him only so that she could tighten both hands into fists. A vein near the base of her neck rose. "I told you she could be dangerous. But as always, you make the most reckless decision. I mean, what is it? Do you enjoy putting yourself at risk? What about me and Poppy?"

"That's not fair." Ivan's brow lowered as he turned to his older sister. "I never put you and Poppy at risk."

Daisy crossed her arms and threw her head back in a loud, hollow laugh. "Don't delude yourself, Ivan. You just made an enemy of the Hagens."

"That's nothing to do with you and Poppy," Ivan objected, though his gut twisted as he said it, Chase's words about blood repeating in his head. But he hadn't intended to get his family caught up in anything dangerous. He hadn't even meant to anger Chase. "You didn't have to get involved. If you'd stayed out of it, there wouldn't even be an issue."

"You're blaming this on me? Are you joking?" Daisy's jaw dropped. She pressed her hand to her chest. "Chase Hagen came to me asking questions about you. He wanted to know where you'd hide someone. Said he'd smelled her on you."

"So you just figured you'd show him? Gee, thanks, Dais."

"Do you have any idea how powerful the Hagens are?

And I'm sorry, Ivan, but I didn't think I needed to lie. Because prior to today, I actually had some slight modicum of faith in you."

Ouch. Ivan tried not to let that sting. His sister wasn't being completely honest though. She'd known something was going on. "Poppy told me you saw the meat in her bag."

"So what? I was supposed to assume that my idiot brother was hiding both a knight and a great dragon?"

Ivan clenched his jaw. Despite her profession of ignorance, Daisy wasn't stupid. She'd obviously suspected something, or she wouldn't have sent him all those messages. "I'll admit the dragon would've been a stretch, but you suspected Fran was in the treehouse, didn't you?"

"And I hoped I was wrong!"

Ivan shook his head. He couldn't believe it. "So talk to me about it. Don't agree to bring Chase Hagen in to find her. What did you think he was going to do to me?"

"I tried calling. You wouldn't answer," Daisy argued. "And you weren't in your room when I looked for you there either."

"You couldn't wait more than a day?"

"I didn't set the timeline. Chase did." Daisy covered her face with her hands, pulling at the skin. "Why am I defending myself? You're the one who brought a knight into the Western Woodlands."

"Fran's not a knight," Ivan objected.

"What if more of them find a way in? They could slaughter Mom, Dad, Poppy. Everyone we grew up with."

"Stop it! You're making crap up. Fran isn't dangerous, okay? She's been caring for a baby dragon for the past week, cuddling it in her sleep and letting it chew on her hair. Does that sound like the kind of person who's going to come in and murder people?"

"Oh my God." Daisy's eyebrows rose. "You like her, don't you? That's what this is about."

Ivan didn't see any point in objecting. His sister was going to be mad at him either way.

Daisy nodded, recognizing his silence as agreement. "That's why you weren't in your room last night. You were here with her. Brilliant. So you put everyone at risk so you could get your dick wet."

"Hey! It wasn't like that," Ivan snapped. "I like her, okay? But that's not why I brought her here. I did it because it was the right thing to do. Chase wanted to kill her. You think I should've just let that happen? Keep calling her a knight all you want, Daisy, but she's not. And even if she was, she wouldn't deserve to be just murdered in cold blood."

Daisy's lips pinched together. "You should've gotten her out of the city if you were that worried."

"She shouldn't have to leave because the Hagens are being unfair."

"Maybe not, but Chase is right to be afraid of her. A knight that's unaffected by magic is a knight that we can't beat. Not easily at least. We're all better with her leaving."

Ivan shook his head. "You didn't see her with that dragon. She fits here, with all the magic."

"Sounds like you just want to think she fits with you."

Ivan looked away. His sister was right. He did want that. But he also felt it.

"Look, did anything happen with you? Any deep professions of love?"

Ivan snorted. "You sound like Poppy."

A hint of a smile appeared before Daisy remembered to be angry and hide it. That was a good sign that she was thawing at least.

"Nothing happened."

"Then you need to forget about her. Maybe you're right, and she's a good person, but she made the decision to give the dragon to Chase. She made the decision to leave." Daisy stepped forward and wrapped her arm around his shoulder. "You need to accept it. For all our sakes, Ivan. Please."

A lump rose in Ivan's throat. He wanted to keep arguing, but now that Daisy was calm, it was difficult to hold onto his anger. His sister's concerns about Fran might've been wrong, but she wasn't the bad guy here. She was just looking out for her family the best way she knew how. Maybe she was right, and he needed to do the same.

Even if it meant letting Fran go.

29
FRANCES

Fran climbed over the painted fence that surrounded the Western Woodlands. Her chest felt tight as she glanced over her shoulder at the trees and the creatures on the mural beneath.

I'll never go there again.

The urge to turn back suddenly filled her. She'd grabbed her things and snuck off, not even saying goodbye. Even if Ivan didn't deserve it, she should've left a note for Poppy.

But if Fran turned around now, Ivan might be back at the treehouse. She was too angry to talk to him. At least that was what she told herself.

Deep down, she knew the real reason she couldn't bring herself to speak with him again was that he might convince her to stay. And then she might not feel as bold as she was feeling right now.

Fran focused on the road ahead and hurried away from the Western Woodlands. She hailed the first taxi she saw and jumped into the backseat. When the driver asked where she was going, she flashed the address on her phone.

Landed Knights Pub, on the corner of 95th and Knights Street. Not exactly subtle.

Fran's leg twitched. Her eyes flicked between the passing landscape of the city and her phone. Both her fathers were messaging her, one confirming that the tickets were booked and the other about what food they should order to celebrate her return.

When she'd called about returning that evening, they'd been so excited that they hadn't even asked what had caused the sudden change of heart. It was a good thing. Fran wouldn't have known how to explain. She was already going to have to come up with a story to explain the egg's absence. *It hatched a dragon* probably wouldn't fly.

Fran tried to focus on the excitement in the messages. She loved her fathers, and she of course wanted to see them. But the thought of returning to Lansing felt like a weight pressing against the back of her forehead. She couldn't resist stealing glances at the ever-changing variety of buildings as they drove further south. Castor's Grove truly did have a little bit of everything, something for everyone's taste.

Why was she only realizing how wonderful that was now?

———

The cab pulled to a stop outside of a three-story building. Its bricks had been painted gray and there were turrets at the top in imitation of a fortress. A pair of curved wooden doors opened to the street. Above them, a sign swung, suspended from a metal rod by a pair of chains. There was a familiar sword burned into it, and the name *The Knight's Tavern* shone in gold letters beneath.

Not subtle at all.

"Getting out?" the taxi driver asked, looking over his shoulder.

Fran found the cash in her pocket and passed it to him, then took a deep breath and exited the vehicle. She was still standing on the curb, staring into the building when the taxi sped off.

There was nothing ominous or ill-fated about the appearance of the tavern. Fran's eyes tried to find some potential danger, some reason to turn and run away. She would be well within her rights to do so. But she couldn't see any.

It was just a regular pub.

The bar ran along the left side of the wall. A few patrons sat on stools before it, heads turned toward a screen near the back where some sports game was on. There were tables and chairs on different levels to the right.

"Are you coming in?" A tall brunette stepped out from behind the door holding a menu. She wore her hair tied in braids behind her head and dressed in a Renaissance fair costume.

It's just a cheesy tavern.

Fran nodded. Her feet finally managed to move, carrying her inside.

"Sit wherever you like." The waitress waved to the mostly unoccupied tables on their right.

Fran was about to select one when a hand lighted on her shoulder. Her body froze with sudden fear.

"Thank you, dear, but she's with me," Mrs. Franklin said.

"Okay." The waitress shrugged as though this meant nothing to her. "Let me know when you're ready to order." She disappeared behind the bar and into the kitchen.

Mrs. Franklin wore a large pink dress in a similar style to the last one Fran had seen her in. Her long black hair was braided behind her head, revealing a pair of star-shaped silver earrings. Fran found herself oddly relieved that they weren't also swords.

Her former foster mother guided Fran to a table in the corner. But when they arrived, Mrs. Franklin remained standing. "Are you alone?"

Do you see anyone else here? Fran nodded, managing to hold her tongue.

"And you're certain you weren't followed?"

Fran's chest tightened. That was not a normal question. "You said my mother would meet us here. Is she coming?"

"She's waiting."

Fran's brows pulled together. What did that mean? Was her mother already in the tavern? Her heart began to race as she looked around the room.

"What happened when you left my house? You were with a fairy." Mrs. Franklin's voice wasn't unkind, but there was a definite downward tilt to her lips as though she didn't approve.

Fran hesitated. She hadn't considered that Mrs. Franklin would ask about Ivan. "We parted ways, and I went back to my apartment."

"He just let you go?"

"No." Fran chewed on the corner of her lip. "He tried to wipe my memory. It didn't work."

Mrs. Franklin smiled. "Your mother will be delighted to hear that."

"She will?" The excitement Fran had been missing began trembling in her chest.

"Oh yes. And what of the egg? Did you destroy it like I told you?"

Fran nodded, and Mrs. Franklin's smile grew broader.

"Wonderful. When I didn't hear from you for so long, I was worried something strange had happened. Those creatures, fairies and the like, they're dangerous you know. I can't imagine what that one was plotting, sneaking into my house in that manner. Nothing good, I'm sure."

Mrs. Franklin shuddered, making the sign of the cross before her as though warding an evil spirit. Fran didn't get the impression that it was for show. The woman truly believed Ivan was something wicked.

"Tell me, did he mistake you for one of their kind?" Mrs. Franklin asked, lowering her voice to a whisper as she leaned forward and grabbed Fran's hands. "Someone with magic?"

Fran nodded. At least at first that was what Ivan had thought. And Poppy.

And what I thought too.

The smile spread even further across Mrs. Franklin's face. She grabbed the sides of Fran's cheeks in excitement. Fran flinched, trying to pull away, afraid the other woman was going to suddenly kiss her. But Mrs. Franklin only kept beaming, her eyes shining with some sort of mad fervor that Fran didn't understand. "Come. You must meet your mother."

Fran's heart skipped a beat.

Finally.

Mrs. Franklin released Fran's face and walked away. She beckoned her toward the door with a crook of her hand.

"I don't understand. I thought my mother was meeting us here." Fran said, keeping her voice low. There seemed to be an air of secrecy about whatever was happening.

"Not exactly," Mrs. Franklin explained. "This tavern is a meeting spot only for the lower members of our rank. A distraction for any creatures that might wish to destroy us. The true meeting place is elsewhere in the city."

That made some sense. The tavern had seemed a tad too obvious, but Fran had just assumed the knights didn't care to hide. "There's a mark on your door as well."

"My husband and I used to be lower members. But then your mother entrusted you to our care." Mrs. Franklin's smile returned, and there was a hint of pride in her eyes as she glanced at Fran. "Kept you hidden until you were safely out of the city."

Mrs. Franklin looked to either side of the street, checking that no one was paying attention to the two of them. Then, she pulled Fran down a small alley between the tavern and the building beside it.

"But why wasn't I safe here?" Fran asked as she followed the older woman down the path. She kept glancing over her shoulder to check that this wasn't some sort of trap, so she didn't notice they'd come to a dead end until Mrs. Franklin stopped.

A short wall blocked their path.

Are we going to climb it? Somehow, Fran had a difficult time imagining Mrs. Franklin, in her large pink dress, engaging in any athletic endeavors.

"Castor's Grove is not like other cities. It's plagued by hordes of dangerous beings, vampires, and demons." Mrs. Franklin shuddered, making the sign of the cross yet again as though she were afraid that just speaking the words might summon them. "They hunt humans, these creatures, drink our blood, eat our flesh. And should they ever have learned the truth of you, they would never have allowed you to survive. You, Fran, represent a threat to them."

Because I can bypass their enchantments. Fran recalled the dread in Daisy's eyes when she'd looked at her in the woods earlier. *It's because she's worried about what I could do to harm them.*

But Fran hadn't encountered any vampires or demons in the Western Woodlands. The scariest creature she'd seen was Chase Hagen, but she assumed that had more to do with the individual than any inherent evil within his species. The baby great dragon had been lovely, after all.

"And then, of course, there's your father's people," Mrs. Franklin said, shaking her head. She wasn't looking at Fran, but staring down the alley, watching to see if anyone was coming.

"My father?" Fran's eyebrows rose. There hadn't been any information on him in the family tree in the Buckler file.

Mrs. Franklin waved her hand. "A former knight. Forget I mentioned him. He's long passed."

"He's dead?" Fran felt like she'd just walked straight into the wall before them. She pressed her hand to her chest, taking a few deep breaths. She'd never known him, so she didn't know why the news should upset her as much as it did.

"Killed in the line of duty," Mrs. Franklin said. Satisfied that no one had followed, she bent over beside a grate near the base of the wall. She tapped what Fran had initially mistaken for screws in a specific pattern, and the bars swung open.

There was a ladder below.

Mrs. Franklin wasted no time climbing down and disappearing into the darkness.

Fran stepped forward. Her head was still spinning, trying to process how she was supposed to feel about the loss of someone she'd never known, but she turned and put her foot on the first rung of the ladder.

Slowly, trying not to think about the fact that she was going into a dark, mysterious tunnel with a woman who had previously locked her in a house, Fran descended. Her anxiety flitted at the edges of her mind, tightening her chest, and turning her stomach. But Fran refused to let it stop her this time. She had less than twenty-four hours left in Castor's Grove, and no chance of meeting her birth father.

But her mother was still alive, and she was waiting.

30
IVAN

"She's really gone." Poppy hovered in the air where she'd just flown in through the window, head turning as she surveyed the tree house. "And the baby dragon too?"

The sound of the thirteen-year-old made Ivan jump. He wasn't normally skittish, but he'd assumed he was alone. Daisy had left after giving him a list of chores to tidy the treehouse. And Fran, well, he knew better than to hope she would reappear.

He'd messed up too badly for that.

"Why aren't you in school?" Ivan asked, raising his eyebrows at his sister.

"You thought I was going to stay?" Poppy narrowed her eyes, twisting her mouth in an expression that made it seem like he should have expected her arrival.

Perhaps, knowing how impulsive the thirteen-year-old could be, Ivan should've anticipated it. But he hadn't been thinking about how she might react when he'd informed her that Fran and the dragon were gone. He'd just wanted her to stop sending him a million questions.

His call earlier that morning had obviously set off his younger sister's anxiety. She'd sent him more messages in the space of an hour than Daisy had in a day. And when he hadn't responded, she'd begun trying to call. She'd only have ended up with her phone confiscated if he'd kept ignoring her.

And then when they had talked, she'd had a dozen concerns about Fran and the dragon, particularly in regard to Daisy. Ivan had gotten stressed and just told her the truth. That she didn't need to worry about it anymore because both Fran and the baby dragon were gone.

"Your coming home just doesn't make a difference," Ivan said, sighing and turning back to the jars. Daisy insisted that he take inventory of what food was there and get rid of all perishable items. "It's too late to change things. You're just skipping school."

"I'm not skipping," Poppy said, sounding annoyed as she landed on her feet. "I got sent home. Mom picked me up."

Ivan's brow furrowed. *Why would they—?* He slapped his palm against his forehead. Dust, he was a terrible brother.

"You had a panic attack," he guessed, turning around.

"Of course, I did. You said Fran was going home and that we'd never see her again. And the dragon too?" Poppy shook her head, mouth squeezed tight. "Ivan, I like them! I don't want them to just be gone."

"I'm sorry." Ivan stepped forward and wrapped his arms around his sister, forcing her blue and turquoise wings to fold behind her. "I don't want that either."

"Then why didn't you stop them?"

"I—" Ivan's voice caught. It was complicated. He wasn't sure how to explain to his sister.

Poppy pulled away, looking up at him with accusatory eyes. "You did something dumb, didn't you?"

"Why is that your first assumption?"

"Because Fran obviously liked you. She wouldn't just have left if you hadn't done something to mess that up."

"Fran didn't like me, Poppy. We were just..." Ivan couldn't bring himself to say *friends*. "... I was helping her out, giving her a place to lie low for a while. We all knew it was temporary."

"Bullshit," Poppy said, crossing her arms.

Ivan's eyebrows rose. Daisy would've commented on the thirteen-year-old cursing. But it wasn't unwarranted. Ivan was making stuff up.

"Just tell me the truth. Please. I can handle it."

Ivan winced at the words. Part of him wanted to argue that she couldn't because she was too young or because it would only upset her and make her anxious. But those were excuses. The truth was that he didn't want to tell her because he was afraid she would be angry with him. She'd either blame him for losing Fran and the dragon or for putting them in danger in the first place.

But he owed her the truth.

Just like I owed it to Fran.

"You're right. I did do something stupid. A lot of things actually."

Ivan explained everything to his younger sister, and Poppy stood, arms crossed, tongue moving under her lips as she ran it across her braces. It was impossible to tell what she was thinking, and by the time he'd finished, Ivan was experiencing his own anxiety. The muscles in his face twitched as he waited for her to speak, uncertain what attack he should be preparing to defend himself against.

Poppy remained silent, still licking her braces, eyes

staring at the jars on the wall behind Ivan as though he weren't even there.

Maybe he'd overestimated the thirteen-year-old's maturity level. "Did you hear anything I just said?"

Poppy nodded. "I'm thinking."

"Well, about what?"

"How you can fix it."

Clearly, she hadn't listened. "There's nothing to fix. Fran's gone, and the Hagens have their great dragon. No one's coming after us."

Poppy pursed her lips, finally bringing her gaze to her brother. "But that's exactly what you need to fix. He's Fran's dragon. He should be with her. And she should be here. With us."

"You want a knight and a dragon to live in the Western Woodlands?"

"She's not a knight. You said so yourself. She's just descended from one, but so what." Poppy shrugged, dismissing it as though it were the same as learning that Fran's mother wore glasses.

"So everyone is petrified that she's going to destroy us," Ivan pointed out.

"But you're not."

"No, I'm not." It wasn't a question, but Ivan felt it important to answer all the same. "And I think you're right. Fran does belong with the great dragon."

Poppy grinned, revealing the metal on her teeth for a second before she realized and closed her lips. She didn't stop smiling, however.

Ivan didn't see what there was to be so happy about. "But what I think doesn't matter."

"It will, to Fran. You need to tell her."

Ivan spread his arms, gesturing to the treehouse, devoid

of Fran's personal belongings that had been scattered around the room. "Bit late for that."

"Come on. You have no idea where we could find her?"

Ivan crossed his arms. He did have one idea. But this was ludicrous. "I promised Daisy that I wouldn't try to stop Fran from leaving. I can't keep putting you guys in danger."

Poppy pressed her lips together, mouth twisting. He could almost read the arguments she was trying to concoct from the furrows in her brow.

Or maybe they were arguments Ivan was making in his own mind. The conversation with Poppy might have pushed the thought to the forefront, but the truth was that Ivan had considered finding Fran the moment he'd realized she was missing.

Maybe it would be irresponsible to convince her to stay. But that didn't mean he couldn't at least see her one last time before she left, did it?

"Okay, you convinced me." Ivan nudged his sister and forced a smile. "Let's find Fran. She owes you a goodbye at least."

And I owe her an apology.

———

They took the bus downtown and walked the rest of the way to Stone's Throw Apartments. The squat tower looked like Ivan recalled, a beige urban apartment building that stood out in Castor's Grove on account of its mundanity.

"Should we duck down an alley?" Poppy asked, flicking her eyes toward a narrow passage a few buildings down.

The corner of Ivan's lip quirked upward. It was good to hear his sister talking in code. Not too long ago, she would've just blurted out *Should we turn invisible?* in the middle of a crowded bus.

"Yeah, okay."

Ivan checked no one was looking before he pulled his wings out. He rotated the top two clockwise and the bottom two counterclockwise twice, feeling them twinge as he did. His sprints to and from the university that morning had exhausted him.

The human education system didn't teach much about how magic worked, but Ivan had always understood his own to be a kind of muscle. He could push its limits and often did, but it would spasm and cramp if he pushed too hard, and eventually refuse to work until it was rested.

I should probably take it easy the rest of the day.

Ivan grabbed his sister's hand and felt another twinge of pain as his magic worked to hide her as well.

There was a keypad on the outside of the apartment building. Management clearly thought that the visual security it provided was sufficient because it didn't work, as Ivan had learned. The door swung open without any need for a key.

The small space was designed to be reminiscent of a hotel's lobby. There was a reception desk and a vending machine squashed against the wall to Ivan and Poppy's right. However, unlike a hotel, there was no security guard or clerk sitting there to see when people entered. He didn't even see security cameras.

For someone so focused on surviving a horror movie, she really chose a shitty place to stay.

Ivan dropped their invisibility once they got to the stairway, and he was confident there were no recording devices. The tension eased from his body.

"She was staying on the third floor. Apartment B."

"You know the exact room number?" Poppy giggled as she skipped after him.

Ivan shrugged, not sure why the thirteen-year-old would find that at all notable. "She mentioned it."

"Yeah, but you remembered."

Because he'd thought about making a joke that B stood for Beautiful. A lot of the girls he'd dated before would've loved a line like that. But Fran would've mocked him mercilessly had he said something that cheesy, so he'd commented that three was a lucky number instead. Fran had taken the comment a bit too seriously and begun asking if numerology was real too.

"Bet you don't remember what class I'm in at school." There was a smug little smirk on Poppy's face.

Ivan scowled at her. But she was right. He didn't have a clue. And answering wrong would only make her giggle more.

"Here." They reached the third floor and found apartment 3B. Ivan knocked on the door. There was no response, but he thought he heard something within.

"Fran?" Poppy called to her through the door. "Are you there? It's us. We need to talk to you." She jiggled the handle on the door. It was locked. A new, high-tech digital keypad twinkled at them from above it. Evidently, the individual units had better security than the building itself.

Ivan sighed and leaned against the wall, a sudden sinking feeling going through him. "We might be too late. She may have already gotten her stuff and left."

"One way to find out," Poppy muttered. She glanced down the short hallway. Seeing no one there, she pulled her wings out.

"Whoa, what're you doing?"

"Using my magic. Like you do all the time." Poppy fluttered her wings, not looking at him.

Ivan opened his mouth to scold her and explain why it was different, but maybe she had a point. After all, it wasn't like he was invisible when he took his wings out. There was always the risk of being spotted.

Poppy's wings flitted up and down. To Ivan, it looked like a purposeless frenzy, but there was a pattern and a rhythm to the movements.

And with every quick movement, a bead of water fell above the electronic lock, so that it had its own personal rain cloud above it.

Eventually, it sizzled and popped.

"Not going to lie. That was pretty great." Ivan grinned at his sister. "We could eke out quite a living if we ever decide to become thieves."

Poppy blocked her teeth with her hand while she laughed. "Just don't tell Daisy."

"Definitely not," Ivan said, continuing the joke as he opened the door. "She's the good one. She'd turn us into the police."

Poppy kept laughing as she followed him into the room.

The door swung shut behind her. Ivan scanned, seeing Fran's things here. They were in disarray. "Wow. I knew Fran was a bit messy, but this is crazy."

It looked like someone had ransacked the room.

Because someone had.

"Ivan!" Poppy squeaked.

He spun around and his heart froze. His little sister had been lifted into the air, a knife to her throat.

Holding her was the man in shades and a trench coat.

31
FRANCES

Fran lost track of the direction they were walking as she followed her former foster mother through the dark underground tunnels. At first, she'd done the intelligent thing and kept track of the route in her head. *Third right, fourth right, second left* – but the longer they walked and the more tunnels they encountered, the more challenging it became.

They'd started off heading east, but had they tracked back west again? Or were they going south? Fran had no idea, and she was starting to think that Mrs. Franklin didn't either. Maybe the woman was insane. She probably had no idea who Fran's birth parents were. This was just a setup to lure her into the tunnels and murder her.

Fran gripped her pocketknife, praying she had the guts to stab the woman and run if it came to it.

The tunnels began to narrow. The smooth concrete on the sides turned to jagged stone, and the scent of salt filled Fran's nostrils. Were they by the beach?

Mrs. Franklin brought her to a long flight of stairs.

"That's your family's house up there. The ancestral

home of the Bucklers." Her voice quivered with a strange sort of reverence.

"Right." Fran's stomach tightened. She waited for the woman to ascend, but Mrs. Franklin only kept staring at her, a slight smile on her face. "You're not coming with me?"

"No, I've done my part."

Fran wasn't certain if losing the peculiar woman relieved or stressed her. Mrs. Franklin did have an energy about her that put Fran on edge, but she was at least somewhat familiar.

The woman she was about to meet was a complete stranger.

No, she's not. She's my mother.

"Thanks, Mrs. Franklin. I'll tell her you did a good job."

Fran left the older woman smiling at the bottom of the steps.

There was a metal door at the top of the stairs. It was solid silver, unmarked by any sword.

Fran had to push it with the full force of her shoulder to get it to open.

She stepped through into a large living space with hardwood floors and cream-colored walls. Bookshelves, full of a variety of trinkets lined the wall to her left, and to her right, there was a large glass window through which Fran could see the ocean, deep blue water sparkling beyond the edge of a cliff.

The room itself contained a seating area full of plush couches. A low coffee table stood atop a large rug woven with different shades of seaside blue. Flames flickered in a stone fireplace on the far wall. Above it, a painting depicted the view from the window, but how it might look at night during a storm, moon hanging in a dark sky above, waves crashing toward the cliff.

This is my family's house?

Before coming to Castor's Grove, whenever Fran had thought of her birth parents, she'd always imagined them poor, lacking the resources to care for her. This past week, she'd thought of them as renegade magical creatures, Robin Hood-styled thieves with hearts of gold and a vision.

It hadn't occurred to her that her mother might be wealthy.

"Is that my Frances?" A woman's voice, high and powerful, came from one of the couches. Tall cushions hid the speaker from view, but it could only have been one person.

That's my mother's voice.

It made Fran think of an opera singer.

"Yes, it's me." Fran's voice sounded high, even to herself. She licked her lips, expecting her mother to rise any moment and rush to her. The moment she'd been dreaming of since she was a little girl danced before her eyes.

Her mother would wrap Fran in her arms, tell her how much she'd missed her, and explain why she'd had to give her up. Fran would sink into her mother's embrace. And finally, she'd understand who she was, her place in the world.

But Fran's mother didn't stand.

She does want to meet me, doesn't' she?

"Come on then." A slender hand rose from behind the large cushion. Silver bracelets shone on the pale wrist. "Let us see you."

Us?

Fran chewed the edge of her lip as she approached.

There were indeed two people on the couch.

My mother and my grandfather.

Was it some innate kinship that she knew this without being told? Or perhaps it was just the facial features? That was Fran's nose on the old man's face, small with a slight turn at the tip. And those were her lips on her mother, thin, narrow, but with a little cupid's bow at the top. They all shared the same flat green eyes and narrow jaw.

Yet, despite the recognition, Fran couldn't help but feel that three more different people had never assembled in the same room.

The old man, her grandfather, had a leathery face furrowed with wrinkles that suggested he'd spent most of his life scowling the way he was doing now, hunched against the side of the couch, head propped up by a calloused hand. He wore a large, loose, long-sleeved shirt that hid his frame. Fran might have assumed he was old and frail beneath were it not for muscles that popped around his neck and the square set of his shoulders. His eyes flicked over Fran with a lack of curiosity that edged on boredom.

Noelle Buckler was a different story. The sight of her made Fran's breath catch, and it wasn't just because she finally had a face for her mother. A sense of beauty clung to the very air about Noelle, which had less to do with her features than her general demeanor. She wore a striking red beach dress that fell in waves across her legs. One arm rested on the couch, and she stretched in such a manner that, had Fran not been intent on studying every detail of her mother's person, she might have mistaken her for a runway model.

Fran stopped before the beautiful woman and shoved her hands into her pockets. She twisted pieces of paper she'd ripped from her notebook, uncertain what to do next.

"My daughter." Noelle's rose red lips blossomed into a smile. Finally, she stood, spread her arms, and pulled Fran into the hug she'd longed for.

They were the same height and both small. Fran couldn't sink into Noelle and feel safe the way she'd imagined as a child. But that didn't matter. This was her mother. And she was embracing her.

Before Fran could raise her arms and return the gesture, Noelle stepped back.

"Didn't I tell you she'd find us?" She swatted a hand affectionately at the old man. His scowl deepened in response. She looked back at Fran. "And my goodness, I'm glad you did. We could have gone to your house and never recognized you. I mean, your hair. Did your fathers never tell you that men prefer blondes?"

Ivan liked my hair.

Fran didn't know why that was the first response that came to her. She hadn't dyed her hair thinking, or much caring, about what men might think. And her dads wouldn't have wanted her to conform to someone else's idea of beauty, even if they'd had a clue what heterosexual men preferred.

"You don't care though, do you?" Noelle smiled again. "You're one of those individuals. I can tell. I've always admired an individual."

The change from what she'd thought was an insult into a compliment caught Fran off guard. Why was she being so quick to assume the worst of her mother? Noelle was being nice, trying to get to know her.

"Thank you," Fran said.

"Your grandfather's an individual too." Noelle smiled and tapped her father's shoulder again. "He went against everyone to create a new order. Didn't you, Dad?"

The old man grunted. "Ask her about the egg."

Why doesn't he ask me himself? Fran might have commented on how rude it was to speak as though she couldn't hear them, but the thought of the baby dragon filled her with a sudden sense of sadness. She pulled her arms tighter around herself.

"I hatched it like you wanted," she said, staring up at the ceiling, afraid she might cry now that she was being forced to say it aloud. "But I lost the dragon. The Hagens took him back."

There was a loud, deep laugh from the couch.

Confused, Fran looked at the old man. His body shook with the sound, veins pulsing on his massive neck like drums providing the rhythm.

"I'm sorry." Noelle's smile stretched across her face as though it had frozen in position. Her jaw clenched tight. "Did you not get my message to destroy the egg?"

Fran's brow pulled together. "I did. That's how I hatched it."

The old man's laugh grew so loud the couch beneath him started shaking. "I told you not to trust him. West always had his own purpose."

The name made the hair rise on the back of Fran's neck. "West?"

"Your father," Noelle said, the skin on her cheeks threatening to crack from her constant smile. "He and your grandfather had their differences."

"He was barely human," said the old man. He spat onto the expensive cream carpet. "Always knew he wanted to bring them back. Traitor."

Fran barely registered the old man's words. Her father's name was West? What were the chances of that?

"My last name is West," Fran said.

"Yes, I always thought that was poignant." Noelle said, resting a hand on Fran's shoulder. Her nails glimmered with painted red polish as she squeezed.

It was just the right amount of pressure to feel comforting. Yet there was no warmth, no matter how hard Fran tried to feel it. A single thought stuck in her head, spinning around. Noelle had said something about fathers before. *Fathers*, plural. Not singular. And the name connection didn't surprise her.

Perhaps if Noelle had been paying attention, she would have noticed Fran's distress and said something reassuring. But Noelle's focus had shifted to her father.

She turned to the old man, and her smile finally failed. Her thin lips pulled together so tightly that they might have disappeared were it not for the bright red.

"What?" the old man barked. "Don't tell me you're still defending him. You made a mistake, Noelle. I've told you—"

"I did not!" Her voice was shrill and childlike. She pulled her hand away from Fran, crossed her arms and stomped her foot. The rug muffled the sound. "West wasn't a traitor. He simply wasn't strong enough when it came down to it. But Fran will be. She kept that egg for years, never mind if it hatched unexplainably."

"West's hand through the grave."

"Forget about West," Noelle snapped. "Fran is here now. She's your granddaughter. She'll understand. She'll help us."

They turned to Fran with such synchronicity, it was as though they were a single beast with two heads. Their eyes bored into hers, and Fran's stomach tightened into a knot.

"What do you know about magic?" the old man asked,

leaning forward, elbows on his knees and arms clasped before him.

Fran's hands twisted tighter in her pockets, aware that this was the first time her grandfather had addressed her directly. Her throat felt dry. It took her longer than it should have to respond. "Not much. Just that it exists."

"Aye. And the creatures that possess it? Have you encountered any of them?" He raised an eyebrow.

Fran started to shake her head then remembered that Mrs. Franklin had likely already told them about Ivan. "Just a fairy."

"Worst of the lot." Her grandfather stood. He was steady on his feet, walking toward her with the confident strides of a much younger man. "What do you consider yourself?"

Fran shook her head. She didn't understand what he meant.

"Are you human?"

"Yes."

"Then you're prey. Understand? You're nothing to those creatures. That fairy you met wouldn't hesitate to let a demon devour you. They don't protect us, they protect *one another*. They have magic and humans don't, and in their view that makes us less than them. They rule over this city, using their powers to subjugate us humans without most of us ever even realizing that we're under their thumb. Do you believe that being born without magic makes you less deserving, Frances?"

She shook her head.

Noelle clapped her hands together. She wrapped an arm around Fran's shoulders. "See? I knew you'd understand. You are my daughter, after all."

Finally, there was a wave of the warmth Fran had

craved, that sense of belonging. A smile spread across her face. When her mother hugged her this time, she reciprocated, wrapping her arms around the slender blonde and pressing her cheek against Noelle's neck.

But the feeling was short-lived before Fran's thoughts began spinning again.

That's not true. Ivan and Poppy didn't think you were beneath them.

Or had they? Ivan had kept her family a secret from her. And Poppy, well she was only a child, and even she'd clearly thought Fran was incapable of caring for the dragon.

The image of the sweet little creature with its big gold eyes sent another stab of pain through Fran.

You belonged with him. These people don't love you. They're not your family.

But yes. They were! Frances was a Buckler. She wasn't really a West.

Fran's stomach felt as twisted and crumpled as the bits of paper in her pockets. She pulled away from Noelle. "Did you know where I was? This whole time?"

"Of course," Noelle said, smoothing a strand of hair behind Fran's ear. "We had to keep track of where you went."

Because you love me or because you need me?

Fran desperately wanted to believe it was the first. That it was just her anxiety making her question her mother's motivations.

"What do you want my help with?"

"Oh, it's a small thing," her mother reassured her, continuing to smooth Fran's hair. "It's just your blood is special, see? You have a natural resistance to magic. Isn't that incredible? And if we all had that ability, it would make us much safer from the creatures in the city. It would make us their equals, allow us humans to protect ourselves."

A knight with the ability to withstand magic.

Fran recalled the terror that chilled her blood when Chase Hagen had opened his mouth and blasted her with fire.

"We wouldn't need to hide in the shadows or cower in fear from their powers," her grandfather said, standing on the other side of Fran, his deep voice a booming whisper. "We could stand up for ourselves, root them from the city. Make it safe for humans again."

A knight with the ability to bypass the enchantments that the creatures of Castor's Grove placed.

Daisy's eyes, wide with fear, flashed through Fran's mind. Only this time, she saw what was reflected in them. The Western Woodlands ablaze, its harmless creatures killed, and its other inhabitants slaughtered by humans who wanted to eradicate the possibility of danger that flickered on the edges of the unfamiliar.

"We have a spell," Noelle continued, "that would allow us to transfer your resistance to more people. And all we need from you is a bit of blood."

Fran thought of Ivan and his sisters, of what the people before her might do to them.

And the truth that she'd sensed from the moment she'd first entered the room, but had been trying to push away and ignore, slapped her across the face. It was a sharp pain, followed by a bright clarity.

I came all the way to find my mother, but this isn't my family. I don't belong here.

And she didn't want to.

She wanted to belong with the dragon and Ivan in an enchanted wood.

It was too late to hope for that, but at least she knew. With complete certainty, Fran knew.

Suddenly, Ivan's lie didn't seem so cruel. Fran hoped she'd have the chance to tell him that one day. To tell him that he was right and that she regretted letting Chase take the dragon. Her little hatched egg with his big gold eyes. Fran closed her eyes and wished for him to be okay.

I'll never do anything that might hurt you.

But Fran got the sense that it was going to be difficult to explain that to the Bucklers.

"I'd be happy to give you some blood," she lied, trying to keep her face calm as she stepped away. "But I always get very faint at the sight, or even just the thought. So, I need a bit of time to mentally prepare, if that's okay? Just a day or so. I'm sure I'll feel able tomorrow."

By which point Fran should be long gone from Castor's Grove, but she kept that part to herself.

Noelle's smile faltered for a moment, before becoming even broader and more cheerful. "Of course, that would be fine. And since you're family, you can stay here until then."

"Oh, no. I'd feel like I was imposing." Fran raised her hands and shook her head. "And my dads are expecting me to video call them this afternoon. They'll ask questions if the background is different."

"We insist," Noelle said, leaning forward and grabbing Fran's hands. She clasped them in hers, pulling them close to her chest.

Fran resisted the urge to pull away, her chest growing tight. How was she supposed to leave without raising their suspicions? "Well, okay. I'll just have to get my stuff from my apartment."

Noelle nodded, and Fran felt a flicker of hope that she'd

said the right thing. She was going to get out of here without making everything worse.

The old man grunted. "Your way is too tedious, Noelle. It always has been. Just hold her still."

"Oh, Dad, you'll scare her," Noelle said. But her hands were tight around Fran's, holding them in a vice grip.

Fran tried to pull free, but it was useless. For all the magical resistance of her blood, she didn't have any natural strength.

And the sight of the old man pulling a syringe full of a strange liquid from the pocket of his shirt didn't help things.

Fran's eyes went wide. Instead of the boost of adrenaline she needed to escape, her body did what it did best whenever there was an emergency. It froze, leaving Fran useless to do anything as he plunged the needle into the vein on her neck.

She whimpered.

And the world went black.

32
IVAN

Ivan's heart pounded in his chest as he stared at his little sister, gasping for breath as she stared down at the steel against her throat. His body itched to do something, but what? Any move he made, and Poppy could get hurt.

I'm such an idiot! Why did I drop my invisibility? Tiredness was a poor excuse. He should've known better.

The man who held Poppy captive was the same one who'd attacked Fran. Though the tan trench coat and shades hid his features, Ivan recognized the dark, shaved head and slightly flared nostrils.

What does he want?

The man didn't work for the Hagens. Ivan felt certain of that. But who else would have been after Fran?

He had one theory, but he really didn't want it to be true.

Because Poppy's wings were out. Instead of hiding them immediately after using her magic to short circuit the lock, the thirteen-year-old had left them out, folding them behind her back instead. Now, they were crushed against the man's body.

The fact that he wasn't asking about them only confirmed Ivan's theory. And it made the situation a hundred times worse because they couldn't deny what they were.

Elbows bent, Ivan raised his hands in the air in the universal sign for surrender. Not that it was a very good one for most magical creatures. Their hands were seldom their most dangerous weapon. With a fairy, it was the wings that should've given people pause.

But even if Ivan pulled his own out and worked his magic, it would still be useless. He'd always liked being able to turn invisible, but he suddenly wished he was one of those fairies who could summon fire or wind. He could've attacked their mysterious assailant from a distance.

Unfortunately, Ivan didn't have anything to fight with. They were stuck. He just needed to find a way to get his sister out of this.

"Let her go, and you can have my wings instead," Ivan said.

"Your what?" The man's voice was neither as deep nor as menacing as it should have been given his general demeanor and the knife he was holding against a thirteen-year-old's neck.

"My wings." Ivan paused. Was the knight stupid? "I'm a fairy too."

"I don't want your wings." The man lowered the knife from Poppy's throat, though he kept his grip around her waist. "I want information. I'm looking for the girl who was in this room."

"Why?" Ivan exchanged a nervous glance with his sister. Poppy's face was pale, but at least she was managing to breathe now that the threat of the blade was temporarily gone. "Do you work for the Bucklers?"

"You think I'm a knight?" The man laughed as though it was a ridiculous assumption.

Ivan's ears felt hot. It had seemed like a pretty good guess to him. After all, other than the Hagens, Fran's family seemed the most likely to want to find her. And the man hadn't reacted to seeing Poppy's wings. What humans knew about magical creatures other than knights?

Wait.

"You're not human?"

The man's mouth twisted into a scowl. "I'm troublingly human."

Ivan had no idea what that meant.

"Why're you looking for Fran?" Poppy asked, looking up at the man. "Did the Hagens send you?"

The man's brow furrowed as if he were searching in a dusty corner of his memory for the name. "Human-dragon hybrids?" he guessed once he'd found it. "They're more likely to skin me alive."

Ivan and Poppy exchanged another look. Not the Bucklers. Not the Hagens. So, who was the man working for?

He must have read the question on their faces.

"Flies with honey," he muttered under his breath. With a sigh, he took his hand off Poppy. It took her a moment to notice, by which point Ivan had already stepped forward and pulled her over to him.

Not that it did much good. The man was still blocking the door.

Ivan's eyes scanned the room, searching for another exit. *The window.*

It would be a squeeze, but they could fit. The more

pressing issue would be getting it open before the man grabbed them again.

"Name's Mac. I was a friend of Frances' father," the man in the trench coat—Mac, since they were suddenly on a first name basis— explained, pushing his shades onto his shaved head.

The action drew Ivan's attention away from the window. He'd been expecting something strange and secret under the dark shades. The reveal of a pair of normal, brown eyes surprised him in a different way.

"Was?" Poppy asked, sticking her head out from behind Ivan's arm where he'd tucked her safely behind him.

Is she seriously expecting that we're about to have a nice, casual conversation with a man who just had a knife at her throat?

It seemed mad. But Ivan had to admit, he was curious.

"He died," Mac said. "Bucklers killed him. I'm worried they might try to do the same thing to Frances."

Ivan's eyebrows jumped almost to his hairline. That was a lot of information at once. He wasn't certain how to process it.

"You're saying that Fran's mum killed her dad?" Poppy gasped, hand covering her mouth like the viewer of a bad soap opera. "Why?"

"His blood. They have this spell that they're trying to perform. Think they can make themselves immune to magic." The man sat down on the bed, his head bowed toward his chest and his shoulders slumped. "I warned him it was madness. But West wouldn't listen. They really brainwashed him. He was barely himself by the end."

Ivan flicked his eyes between the door and the man on the bed. There was nothing stopping him from grabbing

Poppy and escaping. They could turn invisible and wait for Fran outside the building.

But was Mac a threat? He didn't look like one now, but perhaps he was just a very good actor. After all, if he'd been trying to protect Fran, he'd gone about it in a strange way, stalking her dressed like the hero from a 90s sci-fi action movie.

Then again, who was Ivan to judge? *I made some pretty horrible choices when it came to Fran too.*

And friend or foe, Mac had answers.

Gesturing for Poppy to stay against the wall, Ivan dared to take a step closer to the man in the trench coat. "Fran's dad, your friend, he had an immunity to magic?"

Mac's gaze snapped to Ivan. His eyes, ordinary as they were, made the fairy freeze, unable to look away.

Some magical beings had a talent for reading a person's character by their eyes. Ivan had never considered himself skilled in the area. But he thought he caught a glimpse of Mac. Tired, bitter, and more affected by the world than he wished to be. He was a man who had cloaked his losses in a trench coat of stubborn solitude.

Mac lowered his shades, hiding his eyes and breaking the hold they'd momentarily had on the fairy. "By the end, West had a slight immunity, but it's nothing compared to what Frances might have if she kept the egg."

Ivan's eyebrows twitched as his brain tried to fit the little snippets of information into the puzzle in his head. Fran's natural resistance had never made sense to him. The source had to be something magical.

Why hadn't he thought of the egg?

Because that's not a thing.

"Humans don't get magical resistance from dragon eggs," Ivan's voice was more confident than he felt.

"They don't." A smile flashed across Mac's face. "But after spending enough time with the egg, I doubt Fran's human anymore."

"I knew it." Poppy squealed and leaped forward, catching her excitement just enough to stop in line with her brother. "What is she?"

Ivan and Poppy stared at Mac, desperate for the answer.

"Our people used to call themselves dragon tamers, though I understand that term is quite offensive in your world."

"Because dragons are intelligent beings. You can't tame them like a cat or a dog." Poppy found herself speaking to Mac like an elementary school teacher might to one of their students.

"No, you can't," Ivan agreed, a wild smile spreading across his face as he realized what Fran had done. "But you can bond with one."

33
IVAN

The group of humans who had first developed their affinity for the great dragons simply hadn't had the right words to describe it. But bonding with an animal was a well-understood concept among the magical inhabitants of Castor's Grove. It was most commonly seen with witches and their familiars, but any creature was capable of it.

Evidently, that included humans.

As he stood in the room, listening to Mac, Ivan's mind flittered between learning the story of the Bucklers and trying to piece together how Fran's bond with the little dragon must work.

Witches' familiars were more intelligent than regular animals; they also carried uniquely magical properties. The theory had always been that they took on the abilities of their partner.

Did that make Fran the dragon's familiar?

Ivan was no expert on the topic. But he knew enough to know that separating a familiar from its witch could have a devastating effect on both parties. Bad luck, illness, and in some terrible cases, death.

Fran couldn't leave Castor's Grove.

The realization made Ivan's heart flutter with excitement before he forced himself back to reality. Just because Fran needed to stay didn't mean she'd forgive him.

She might never speak to me again.

The thought only half sobered him. He liked the idea of Fran being nearby, even if she ignored him. At least he might catch sight of her downtown, walking around with her backpack across her chest like an absolute weirdo, and he'd know that she was happy and safe.

But Chase has her dragon.

It was that realization that finally got Ivan to stop feeling giddy. Just being in the city wasn't sufficient.

"We have to get the dragon back to Fran."

"Duh," Poppy said. "But we also need to get Fran back to us. Why hasn't she come for her suitcase yet? You don't think she left without her stuff, do you?"

"From the timeline you've given me, she can't have made it on the morning train," Mac said. At some point, though it was impossible for Ivan to pinpoint precisely when this nonverbal agreement occurred, the three of them had become a team. "We should be able to catch her at the station if we wait there."

Ivan doubted Fran would leave without her belongings. She wasn't materialistic necessarily, but he'd spent enough time with her during the past week to hear her complain about a variety of clothing options that she'd left behind. He'd even been contemplating sneaking back to steal some to surprise her with.

Despite his sister's objection, the real problem wasn't finding Fran. It was retrieving the dragon.

Chase had mentioned returning with the dragon at sundown. Ivan had no doubt that he'd been referring to the Hagen's Manse. The massive estate was somewhere in the Northeast of the city, where the majority of wealthy dragons had their homes. Finding it wouldn't be a problem, but infiltrating it would be near impossible.

Turning invisible and sneaking in would be doomed to failure. The Hagens would have the best security. They'd probably have enchantments that would block Ivan's magic. He'd be caught and then who knew what they would do to him.

"We have to get the dragon today," Ivan insisted. "We can't wait until Fran's about to board the train. Don't you want the dragon back?"

"Of course I do! How could you suggest I don't?"

"Frances and her dragon will seek one another out," Mac explained. "They'll find one another. We just need Frances to stay long enough for that to happen."

"But it won't be possible if the dragon is being safe-guarded in an enchanted mansion."

A short argument broke out amongst the three of them before Poppy, of all people, came to the obvious conclusion.

"We have to split up."

Ivan objected, partly because Poppy was too young to stay alone and partly because he was annoyed it was his little sister's idea in the first place. But ultimately, he knew she was right.

And so, after exchanging numbers and arranging details, the three parted ways. Poppy stayed in the apart-ment in case Fran returned. Mac went to the train station in case she didn't. And Ivan took the subway from downtown to the Castor's Grove University campus.

He was about to steal a dragon.

34
FRANCES

Fran's limbs felt strange, heavy almost as though someone had tied weights to them. Her head spun with an achy dizziness. Her eyes felt as though someone had glued them shut.

Where am I?

Fran shuddered, trying to force her body into action.

"Shh." Something soft stroked her hair. "You're okay. We're not going to hurt you."

"She can't hear you, Noelle. She'll be out cold for another few hours. Come help me with the rest of the ingredients. You know I've never had the taste for this magic stuff."

The Bucklers.

The image of her beautiful blonde mother and muscular old grandfather flitted across the back of Fran's eyelids. *What did they do to me?*

The scent of salt water filled her nostrils, Fran shuddered again, and her consciousness slipped away.

35
IVAN

The party was still going on back at the Phi Eta Gentlemen's House. The five other new pledges were still in the large entryway, giggling and toasting with dark drinks in their glasses. Their new brothers regaled them and one another with stories of their own trials.

Ivan caught the end of a vampire's story about how he'd gotten his knight's badge. The tall, dark-haired boy claimed to have stolen it from a young female knight who'd secretly had an obsession with all things vampire related. If his story was to be believed then the woman in question had made an odd choice joining the knights. They were supposed to kill vampires, not kiss them.

There were a few other details that seemed shaky. Ivan heard enough to notice that the knight in the story changed from a brunette to a redhead and then back again. Another time, Ivan would've enjoyed catching the wealthy vampire in a lie, or at least a gross exaggeration. But at the moment, Ivan's focus was elsewhere.

He was studying doors.

When Silvan had fetched Chase for him, it hadn't occurred to Ivan that he needed to memorize the exact location of the dragon's room. Now, he wished he'd paid a bit more attention.

It was the third floor. Ivan was quite certain he recalled that much. And somewhere to the right if he flew straight up from the entrance.

Ivan's eyes flitted between two adjacent doors. How close to the back was Chase's room?

"So, you returned." A hand slapped down on Ivan's shoulder as Silvan approached him. The blond still wore the black uniform from that morning, but he'd taken off the mask. Unlike most of the Gentlemen in the room, there was no whiff of alcohol on his clothes and his voice sounded steady. "Excellent. We've all been dying to learn more about how you got your badge."

"It's not a very good story," Ivan said, brushing Silvan off. He stepped away, eyes going back to the doors.

"Curious to know which one will be yours? The ones higher up get taken quickly. Pledges tend to room together on the second floor."

"So that one's taken." Ivan pointed at the door he thought most likely to be Chase's.

Silvan nodded. Unfortunately, he didn't say whose it was as Ivan had hoped.

Dust.

But this could be an opening.

"You know, it actually is kind of interesting how I got my badge," Ivan said. "But I don't know if I should tell it without Chase around. He was a big part of it."

One of Silvan's eyebrows rose. "Gentlemen aren't supposed to help pledges obtain their badges."

"I thought most people just bought them."

"No." Silvan's brow lowered, darkening his expression. The sternness aged him, but it also gave him a regal impression that reminded Ivan that he was talking to the King's nephew. "Where did you get that idea?"

Is he pulling my leg? He had to be. Because Ivan didn't think Chase had been lying. Which meant that either Silvan was joking, or he was too naive to realize how most of his brothers had gotten into their elite fraternity.

There was no flicker of a smile or sudden laugh. Silvan continued to stare at Ivan, awaiting an answer.

"Maybe I misunderstood," Ivan said, clearing his throat and wiping his hands on his sweatshirt despite the fact that they were clean.

"What role did Chase play in your obtaining of the badge?" Silvan put a hand on Ivan's shoulder. The movement had an air of authority to it, so that, while Ivan doubted Silvan would try to physically stop him, walking away didn't seem like an option. "Did he purchase it for you? I'm aware you two are friends."

Friends? Him and Chase Hagen. It took a great deal of effort for Ivan to keep himself from laughing in Silvan's face.

"We're acquaintances," he said. "But I don't think I'd say friends."

"He spoke highly of you. Told me how you obtained your badge. I wonder if his story matches yours." Silvan's tone was polite, but there was a clear edge to his tone.

"Uh..." Ivan wracked his brain, trying to think what Chase Hagen was likely to have said. "I got it from one of the Bucklers, you know, the leaders of the Order of The Egg."

"I'm familiar with the order," Silvan said as though such knowledge was implied.

Dust, maybe I should've just come to Silvan when I was looking for information.

"Well, she was a girl about our age, and she had it. I traded her a favor in exchange for it." Then Ivan quickly added, "Not that I delivered on my end of the bargain, obviously."

"You would make yourself ignoble in your story?" Silvan raised an eyebrow. The smile hadn't returned to his face.

"No, no. I just mean, I wouldn't help a knight," Ivan said. He had a feeling that he was very much putting his foot in his mouth. "Is Chase here? I think I should speak with him. Just can't remember which is his room."

"Your stories match," Silvan said, his mouth narrowing as his eyes peered into Ivan's. "That should calm you, but it doesn't. Why are you so agitated, Ivan? You're not acting like a normal pledge."

Damn it. Silvan liked him. Maybe Ivan could risk telling him the truth.

"Chase took something from a friend of mine. I need it back."

"The dragon."

Ivan's eyes widened. So Silvan did know what was going on. The boy was just a better actor than Ivan had realized.

"I must say, it doesn't sound like you're giving up on your end of the bargain to this knight. What did you promise her?"

"That I'd help her find out who her family is."

Silvan lowered his hand. It had been so unobtrusive on Ivan's shoulder that he'd almost forgotten it was there. "And who are they?"

"Her mother's a Buckler with the Order of the Egg." That was safe to say. Silvan would already know that. But

Ivan was taking a massive risk by telling him more. "Her father was a human who came from a lineage of dragon bonders."

A quick flutter of his lashes was the only giveaway that the news surprised Silvan. "I thought they were all dead."

"Almost. A few still exist." Like Fran and Mac. "So, now that you know the truth, will you help me?"

"I like you, Ivan. You're as bold as I thought when I first met you." Silvan smiled. "But you're asking me to intercede in a dragon matter. We're fairies. This is beyond either of us."

"But you're the king's nephew," Ivan pointed out.

"And my uncle would be furious if I forced myself into a situation that doesn't concern me. Perhaps you don't realize, Ivan, but the balance in Castor's Grove is tenuous. There are boundaries on us all, imposed by the humans as much as by one another. The King is allowed supreme power precisely because he knows when not to exercise it."

But surely, this wasn't one of those times. "I just told you that Chase stole a dragon."

"Which was originally stolen from his family."

Ivan opened his mouth to object. The two cases were clearly different. An egg didn't get a say where it went, but a great dragon should, baby or not.

But Silvan knows that. He just doesn't care.

Ivan couldn't believe it. He'd wanted so badly to join the Gentlemen, thought that once he was part of the elite fraternity, he'd be able to control things. But here was the King's own nephew insisting that he was powerless to use any of his connections to stop an action that he knew was wrong.

"I think you're the one who's ignoble in this story," Ivan said, stepping away from Silvan. He looked up at the doors again. He could maybe get one guess before Silvan stopped him.

"Perhaps," Silvan agreed, his tone almost sad in a way Ivan hadn't expected. "You're the one who's too late though. Chase isn't here. He left only a few minutes before you arrived. His chauffeur picked him up."

"Dust." Ivan spun his head away from the doors. "What's the car look like?"

"Black Audi. You'll know it when you see it. Custom license plate with their name. Probably find them on Xanthus."

"Perfect." Ivan was almost out the door when Silvan's hand landed on his shoulder again.

"Gentlemen don't act against one another, Ivan. You go after Chase now, and you lose your membership here. Do you understand?"

Ivan nodded. He did.

And it was the easiest decision he'd made in his life.

Ivan whipped his wings out, turning invisible before hurrying through the door. Behind him, he thought he heard Silvan wish him luck.

But perhaps it was just his imagination.

36
FRANCES

Someone was humming a children's lullaby. The melody quivered at the corner of Fran's consciousness as she became aware of the fingers in her hair, twisting strands into small braids.

She pried her eyes open.

Fran blinked, trying to adjust to the dim light of the room. The first thing that came into focus was the massive shield on the wall before her. The silver had been engraved with the Knight's Sword. There was a banner floating around the top and bottom. Beneath the sword's point were the words:

"By my honor, I vow to bring light into the darkness."

Above it read:

Order of the Egg.

Apart from the shield, there was little ornamentation. An old photograph taped near the corner of one wall showed a man with a shaved head and thick beard. A pair of heavy curtains blocked everything but a sliver of white sunlight. It shimmered on something silver near Fran's wrist.

Her eyes flicked downward, and a gasp stuck in her throat.

There were straps around her wrists and ankles, and above her knees and elbows.

Fran tried to pull her right arm free. The movement made her muscles burn. The restraints wouldn't loosen.

"Conserve your energy. You'll need it for tonight."

It was Noelle, sitting on a chair to Fran's left. The blonde had changed into a long blue gown, the color of the sky. Matching silver jewelry hung from her neck and ears, accentuated by aquamarine gemstones. Her hair was now woven in braids behind her head.

She seemed to be styling Fran's to match.

Fran jerked her head away, messing up what her mother was doing. She'd never been a fan of braids. They pulled at her scalp.

Noelle clicked her tongue in a disapproving manner. "Don't you want to look pretty for the ceremony this evening? When we tried it with your father, I dressed him in the nicest pair of cotton blue pants. They matched perfectly with the ocean. I have a dress set out for you too. It'll match mine."

"Ceremony?" Fran's voice was hoarse, and just speaking made her throat burn. She wondered what the old man had injected her with.

"Where you'll share your resistance with us." Noelle's fingernails scraped Fran's scalp as she resumed her braiding. "Once we baptize ourselves with your blood, we'll rise from the ocean with the same abilities that you have." She licked her thumb, wiped a smudge of mascara from beneath Fran's eye, then smiled at the result. "Isn't that positively wonderful?"

No. Fran needed to find a way out of here. Her eyes darted around the room. There were no weapons other than the shield, nothing she could use.

Her only chance of escape was to trick her mother into releasing her.

"I can't stay for your ceremony," Fran said, trying desperately to sound sorry about missing out on having her blood stolen by a madman and his daughter. "My fathers will call the police if I'm not home tonight."

"Oh no, we'll call and explain everything to them. After all, you're back with your real family. This is your home now. There." Noelle tapped the side of Fran's head, pleased with the braid. She stuck a hairpin in, sealing it in place and stabbing her daughter's scalp.

Fran winced.

"You'll love it here. I know your grandfather can be a bit tough, but he'll melt once he sees that your blood works. He thought I was crazy when I married your father, you know. He thought that his ability made him practically another creature, but I saw it for what it was. Just another example of magic that we could harness."

"Is that why you were with him? For his blood?" It hardly mattered now, but curiosity and fear crept into the practical part of Fran's brain that was focused on escape. *Is that the only reason I exist?*

Noelle's lips pressed together in a pout for a moment as though she'd never considered it. "A bit. And of course, West loved me. You should only give your heart to a man who adores you."

But shouldn't you adore him too?

An image of Ivan rose from Fran's memories. He stood in the treehouse in a tight white shirt that showed his muscles, wings shining sky blue and fire red. He smiled at her and whispered, *this is where you belong, Fran. With the magic. With me.*

Fran's face grew hot. In the real memory, Ivan had asked if she wanted to try juggling oranges. Her mind was inventing things she wished had happened.

How stupid am I to blush about Ivan at a time like this?

The fairy had probably long forgotten about her, but Fran could only imagine how much he'd laugh at her if she ever admitted to thinking about him while tied to a bed.

Ivan was the last thing that should've been on her mind.

"I'm the reason West joined the order," Noelle continued, her voice rising with pride. "I mean, not initially. At first, he was trying to steal the egg. But then he fell for me, and everything changed. He became a true believer. He realized how dangerous those creatures are. I suppose he always knew, of course. His ancestors were almost hunted to their deaths by dragons. He wanted them all dead."

That's not true. He saved my dragon.

But, of course, Noelle couldn't see the inherent contradiction. Her ego blinded her, refusing to entertain anything that might suggest West hadn't been as infatuated with her as she believed.

That's it. That's how I escape.

"The Hagens were hunting me too. They were absolutely awful." Fran closed her eyes, pretending to sob as she tried to think of the right words. "Horrible creatures! The humans of this city are so lucky that people like you exist, mom."

The last word tasted bitter on her tongue.

She sniffed and blinked, giving Noelle her most adoring look and hoping that her mother wouldn't notice that her eyes were dry. Fran never had been much of an actress.

Noelle pressed her hands to her chest, beaming in delight. "Oh, isn't it? And with your blood, Fran, the good we'll be able to do. We can destroy all of them. Every magical being. We can put an end to their tyranny."

There was the image of Ivan again.

"That's incredible. I'm so happy that I'll be able to help you." Fran stressed all the wrong words. It must have been obvious she was faking.

Noelle pushed another pin into her hair, a little gentler this time, still smiling.

Fran chewed the corner of her lip. Was her mother really buying this? "Where's my dress for the ceremony? I'd love to see it."

"Oh?" Noelle's eyes lit up. "Of course. I'll show it to you! You'll just love it. It's so bright and the frills are gorgeous."

Frills? Just the word made Fran recoil.

"Sounds beautiful! Can I try it on?"

"Of course!" Noelle smiled. "I suppose I'll have to untie you first."

Fran couldn't believe it was that easy. She fought to stay calm as Noelle undid the restraints.

The moment the final strap fell from her left ankle, Fran kicked her mother away and leaped off the bed. Chest tight and heart racing, she ran toward the window, not stopping to check if Noelle was attempting to catch her.

They couldn't be that high up. She could jump out and onto the ground beneath and hopefully run from there. Fran just had to hope she didn't break anything.

Please, let me be lucky for once.

But when Fran pushed the curtain back, she froze.

What she'd mistaken for a window was actually a hole in the wall. And the light coming through wasn't sunlight, it was coming from a bright clinical light that hung above a white sterile chair.

Her grandfather stood before it, a syringe in his hand. He looked up at her and their eyes met.

Oh crap.

Fran tried to turn to head back to the door, but Noelle blocked her path.

"Such a pity." Her mother frowned. "I really thought you wanted to be part of the family. But maybe you'll come around when you understand."

The old man's footsteps were heavy as he approached. "You are of monumental importance to our cause, Frances. Like it or not, you will be giving us your blood."

37
IVAN

Silvan was right. The Hagens' vehicle proved easy to identify, traveling east on Xanthus Road. Luckily, it had been slowed by the afterwork traffic, and Ivan only had to fly thirty blocks.

His muscles ached as he lighted on the top of the car, careful to land softly so as not to notify the driver that anything was amiss. Ivan lay down, spreading his wings and back against the top of the car. He'd hoped it would be cool and soothing. Instead, the metal had been roasting in the sun.

Why does anyone paint cars black?

It was almost like they didn't stop to consider that there might be an overheated invisible fairy hoping to hitch a ride.

The traffic lights turned green, and the car lurched forward. Ivan sprang up, clinging to the side to keep himself steady.

It was all well and good to catch a car, but what was he supposed to do now?

Ivan was certain once the car went through the gates to

the Hagens' manse that there would be some enchantment that would block his magic, or worse, it might block him entirely. He might find himself knocked off the car and lying on the road outside of a massive iron gate.

Which meant he needed to get to the dragon now, while the car was on the road. But how?

He could break the window.

It was a terrible idea. Destruction of property was illegal. Destruction of a wealthy person's property was probably punishable by death.

But Chase would retaliate the moment Ivan took back the dragon. So, what was there to lose?

He can't kill me twice!

Ivan kicked his heel against the tinted screen at the back of the car. A sharp pain shot through his foot.

Dust that glass is strong.

A second kick proved just as painful. Ivan wasn't stupid enough to try a third time.

This was the Hagens' vehicle. He couldn't kick the glass loose. It was probably both bullet proof and magic proof.

What if there's nothing I can do? What if I can't get the dragon back?

Just because some familiars died when separated from their witches, didn't mean Fran's life was at risk. She might just languish emotionally instead of physically, lose all sense of happiness, stop eating, and starve to death.

No.

Ivan wouldn't let that happen.

He was going to find a way into the Hagens' car. If he couldn't get in from the outside, then... *I'll have to get them to open it from the inside.*

The next time the car stopped at a light, Ivan jumped from the top. He might have been kicked out of the Gentlemen, but he still had the shiny pin they'd given him in exchange for the Knights' badge. Ivan pulled the back out and jabbed it at the tire.

The sharp metal bent against the rubber. Obviously, the Hagens' hadn't forgotten to enchant their tires.

It was a pity, but not unexpected.

Sorry to involve the rest of you in this. Ivan apologized as he ran to the cars in front.

The next two stops, Ivan busied himself with poking holes into the tires of all the nearby cars. By the third traffic light, his plan was paying off.

Xanthus Road was one of the smaller ones in the city. Two lanes headed east, and another two west. However, the ones closest to the sidewalk were used for parking, forcing the traffic to flow in single file. One car with a flat tire might be able to find a nearby empty space and pull over. But ten?

Vehicles pulled to a stop in the center of the road, frustrated drivers getting out and apologizing profusely to the people behind them, only to discover that they weren't the only ones with flats. Clearly, there was something in the road.

The cars going west couldn't stop to allow them to pass either. They had their own block only a bit further ahead for similar reasons. Ivan had been generous with his pin.

But would it work?

If he'd found himself in this situation, Ivan would have gotten out his car to try assist the other people. But would Chase's conscience compel him to help humans?

No. But, his chauffeur's conscience did.

As Ivan had hoped, the driver's door opened. The man's sleek brown hair parted in the center to frame a pair of dark sunken eyes above high cheekbones. He leaped from the car like a cat pouncing toward a mouse, pushing the door behind him with a swiftness that almost ruined Ivan's plan.

Luckily, Ivan had already slipped his hand inside. He swallowed a yelp of pain as the edge of the door slammed into his fingers. That would leave a mark.

But it was worth it. Because it meant that the door didn't close and lock, and as soon as the man was gone, Ivan managed to pull it open and climb in the front. The lock clicked as soon as he was in.

There was a partition between the driver's seat and the back of the car. Ivan found the button to bring it down and pressed it.

"Did you fix the problem?" Chase didn't look up. He was too focused on the bag writhing beside him. Growls came from within. "We need to get him home."

I couldn't agree more.

"There's something wrong with him, Eddie," Chase continued, still not realizing that his driver wasn't there. "I don't know what they did to him. He's acting distressed. It's like he's got Stockholm syndrome or something. Why isn't he happy to be back with us?"

Ivan hesitated as he studied the boy before him, grappling with the baby great dragon. There was nothing of his usual smug arrogance in his expression. Instead, the twist in Chase's mouth looked like he was closer to crying than insulting someone.

"My parents are going to think it's my fault. You know they will. What should we do? Eddie?"

Chase looked up, finally realizing that his driver wasn't responding. His brow furrowed as he searched for some sign of his driver behind the seat. Then a look of panic spread across his face.

At that moment, Ivan's muscles spasmed with the weight of prolonged magic use. He flashed into visibility.

The fear on Chase's face was replaced by an annoyed scowl. "Dream? Is that you? I thought you'd learned to keep your nose out of this."

Ivan got his magic under control, hiding from sight again, but it was too late. Chase knew it was him. Any deniability was gone. There was a chance his whole family was going to have to go into hiding.

But quitting now wouldn't change that.

Ivan lunged forward and grabbed the bag.

Chase held tight to the other side.

It turned into a tug-of-war, fairy against dragon. Ivan knew how that would end. So he did the only thing he could think to do.

He unzipped the bag.

The baby great dragon shot out in an explosion of smoke. It sprayed a jet of fire into the air, which Ivan had to duck behind the chair to avoid.

"You imbecile," Chase spat in the direction of the front seat. "Lostsong, please, settle. You're safe now. I'm taking you home. I'm your family."

He pressed a button, and the partition began to rise again. The baby great dragon zipped into the front before it closed.

Perfect.

This was Ivan's chance to catch it. Once he had the baby dragon, he would message Mac and Poppy. Fran must've been with one of them by now.

Maybe she'll forgive me when she realizes I've gotten her dragon back.

Only, he hadn't.

Another muscle spasm turned Ivan visible as he

reached forward. He planned to coax the baby dragon to him. He wasn't anticipating the return of Chase's driver.

The front door opened, and the little dragon shot through it like a bolt of purple lightning.

"What the—?" The driver's confusion at seeing a fairy sitting in his seat was immediately replaced with a look of horror. His head snapped to the street as he realized what had happened.

From beyond, Ivan heard a chorus of gasps from the humans watching.

A great dragon had just gotten loose on a very public street.

Ivan scrambled through the passenger door and out into the middle of the road. Chase was already on the street.

"Can't you see what you've done?" Chase shouted over his shoulder as he ran in the direction the great dragon had gone.

South.

"You won't catch it by foot, sir," The driver, Eddie, called after him.

Eddie was right.

Ivan's wings were still out, but none of the humans were looking at him. They were all too fascinated by the unexplained flying object. He squeezed his eyes shut and summoned his strength. Somehow, he managed to turn invisible again and leap into the air.

Dragons were faster than fairies. It was a known fact. But Fran's great dragon was only a little baby. Surely, Ivan could out fly it.

"Fuck it," Chase muttered, glancing behind him. He was a foot in front of Ivan. "They'll have to wipe their memories anyway."

Suddenly, a massive pair of white scaled wings unfurled, scratching the metal of the stopped cars. A white lizard-like tail swiped at the tires. There was a loud shout from the crowd, and then Chase took off into the sky.

It would be a race to Fran's dragon.

Somehow, Ivan—with his tired, fluttering fairy wings —had to win.

38
FRANCES

"Trying to figure out how many things you can strap me to?" Fran asked, glaring at the new restraints that tied her to the chair. Despite trying to sound tough, her voice shook with fear, and her chest felt tight.

Deep breaths. Do not give these people the satisfaction of giving you a panic attack.

"We have a number of means of keeping prisoners," the old man said, deep voice matter-of-fact as though Fran had asked a genuine question instead of trying to make a catty remark. "I believe you'll find they work against creatures much stronger than yourself."

Her grandfather leaned toward her. He was in a large black chair beside a wooden table that was covered in an assortment of bottles and tubes. Noelle remained in the other room, fussing over the bed sheets.

The old man grabbed Fran's right arm, tied another band above her elbow, and flicked her vein. He grabbed a needle from beside him and ripped the package open with his teeth before pressing the point to her skin.

It looked sharp.

"Do I have your permission?" the old man asked.

As if it matters.

Fran shook her head, a lump rising in her throat as she looked at the long, pointed needle.

Focus on something else.

Fran's eyes darted around the room looking for something comforting. They landed on a small purple oval with gold details on one of the shelves.

"Is that my egg?"

Her grandfather's face blocked her view of the replica. "*My* egg. The one that you lost."

His green eyes locked with Fran's. They burned with a strange sort of intensity. It was intimidating. Just the sight made Fran's chest tighten.

But her grandfather was wrong.

I didn't lose it. It hatched and then my dragon was stolen.

Not his egg, not his dragon. Hers.

No, that's not right. No matter how much she loved the tiny purple creature with its big liquid gold eyes, the dragon belonged with the Hagens. *Lostsong.*

It seemed a tragic name for such a cheerful creature.

But I guess I didn't know him that well.

The old man grunted, a satisfied glint in his eyes that suggested he'd mistaken Fran's averted gaze for acquiescence. He leaned back, still holding the large syringe in one hand. "That was the first magical item I ever stole, you know. It's how my new order of knights got their name."

"Never would have guessed."

He didn't notice the sarcasm, or perhaps he didn't hear her at all, for the old man was no longer looking at Fran. Instead, his eyes saw through her as though he were staring into the past. The hint of a smile quivered on his thin lips.

"A dragon egg. Guarded by some of the most dangerous of their kind. Said to possess immunities that we could only dream of," he said. "The other knights were afraid of magic. But I understood. You can't fight guns with knives."

Fran's eyes went to the needle, dangling in his hand. Why wasn't he taking her blood? Did he just want to deliver a villain monologue first?

Suddenly, he reached out and pressed his thumb to her wrist. His eyes became focused once more. "Your mother thinks you grew attached to the fairy you were with." He paused, then nodded. "Yes, I can feel you did from the way your blood pounded. You wouldn't be the first young girl to fall in love with one of these creatures. But you need to understand, Frances. We bear no malice toward any individual fairy. It is the system of magic at large that is the problem. Every atrocity, every act of oppression has at its root an imbalance of power to blame. And magic is the ultimate imbalance. The Order of the Egg only seeks to destroy it so that we might make the world a happier place. Do you understand?"

"Yes." A smile spread across Fran's face, and she stared back at the old man, suddenly less afraid. He wasn't telling her all that just to be friendly. "You need me to agree to give you my blood in order for your plan to work, don't you?"

The old man's expression hardened. His grip tightened around her wrist.

It was probably going to bruise. But Fran didn't care. She had the upper hand after all. "I'll never give it to you if you hold me captive like this. I'll—"

The needle stabbed into her vein.

Fran gasped half from pain and half from shock.

"Don't overestimate your power," the old man told her.

"Blood willingly given may be better, but I'll take it unwillingly too."

39
IVAN

On seeing that it was being pursued, the baby dragon darted upward, away from the crowded streets and into the clouds above.

Chase followed without effort. Dragons' wings were made for soaring at high altitudes in the open air.

Ivan followed with a great deal of effort. The wind battered him either side, threatening to snap his wings in half. He had no choice but to drop his invisibility though it didn't matter now that they were so high. A thick layer of white cloud masked them from any onlookers in the city below, and darkness was slowly setting in, providing further cover.

Both dragons, great and bipedal, were getting away from Ivan. If he didn't catch them soon, he never would.

Ivan gritted his teeth and barreled toward them, arms outstretched. His muscles burned, but he refused to slow down.

I have to do this. For Fran.

He focused on the image of her, black hair pulled to the side of her head so that he could see her face. He remembered the sound of her, trying not to laugh and failing, every time he jumped during the horror movie. He saw the little dragon purring on her thigh, her body leaning toward its heat instead of away from it.

With a final push, Ivan caught up to Chase.

The baby dragon was still a good distance ahead. Ivan had never seen it fly so far or so long. He'd always assumed it was beyond its capabilities, but maybe the little creature had just always gotten distracted. Its attention could flit from an exciting twig to a plastic wrapper to a curious beetle in a matter of seconds.

But now it flew straight, not stopping to play in the damp air of the clouds.

Because he has a purpose.

"You can't keep up that speed, Dream," Chase snarled, swooping closer in an attempt to push Ivan off course with his white scaled wing. "Quit now and maybe I'll go back to forgetting about you."

"You're right," Ivan shouted back, dodging the attack. "But I don't have to."

Ivan slipped underneath Chase's wing, allowing the dragon to inch ahead of him. He stopped fighting the wind, letting it push him back, leaning his body to the side.

He reached his hands up and latched his fingers around Chase's tail.

The dragon whipped Ivan in the air, trying to throw him off. The fairy's left hand, crushed by the door, cramped and burned and spasmed until he had no choice but to let it fall limp at his side.

But his right hand remained strong, fingers wrapping around the tail, burrowing under the white scales, and refusing to budge.

"Let go of me, or we'll both lose Lostsong!" Chase

snapped; his words carried to Ivan on the wind "He's a baby with no idea where he's going. He'll get himself injured or lost."

"You're wrong. He's flying to Fran," Ivan shouted, white blurring his vision and water droplets forcing him to close his eyes as they flew through a cloud.

"What?"

Ivan wasn't sure if Chase didn't believe him or if he just hadn't heard. But he had to hope that talking might slow the bipedal dragon down, and give the little creature a chance to get away and find Fran.

"They're bonded," Ivan shouted louder, and a bug flew into his mouth.

"Are those the lies you've been feeding him?" Chase snarled and lashed his tail and Ivan. The fairy gritted his teeth, muscles in his arm burning as he strained to keep his grip. The bug slipped down his throat.

Ivan shuddered at the strange, acidic tang. Another insect hit against his cheek as they flew. But he needed to talk if he was going to distract Chase. "It's true. Fran's father was from a special line of dragon tamers."

From the way Chase tail stiffened, Ivan knew he was familiar with them.

"You're lying. They were killed centuries ago."

Ivan took a deep breath. He wished Chase would pull him closer so that he could stop shouting. His throat was going to burn as badly as his arm tomorrow.

"Not all of them. Fran's bonded to Lostsong." *Dust, what an awful name.* "You can throw all your wealth and threats at the problem. But he'll always try to find her."

Chase tucked his head under, and for a moment, Ivan thought he'd gotten through to the dragon. *This could be the start of a productive conversation.*

A jet of fire streamed from Chase's mouth, barreling toward the fairy that was dangling from his tail. Somehow, they continued to rocket forward.

Dust! Ivan had tucked his wings in to protect them from the wind, but he flung them out now, using them for leverage as he swung out of the way of the fireball.

His ear burned as the flames hissed past.

Maybe I should keep my mouth shut after all.

Ivan managed to hitch another five minutes of ride on the back of the dragon's tail. Then, something snapped beneath his fingers.

The dragon's scales fell loose.

So did Ivan.

A gust caught his wings, pushing him toward the Earth. He managed to right himself just before he fell below the clouds, but both dragons were way ahead of him now.

Dust!

Wings too weak to ascend on his own, Ivan flew below and behind, craning his neck backward to follow. Lucky that Chase's white scales stood out against the darkening sky.

There was a hint of salt in the air. Ivan could taste it on his tongue.

When they'd flown past downtown and Stone's Throw Apartments, Ivan had assumed the baby dragon was heading to the train station. But it wasn't so close to the beach, was it?

He flicked his gaze down just long enough to spot the ocean in the distance before them. A shiver ran down the back of his neck. *Where are you, Fran?*

A few miles ahead, Chase darted toward the ground.

He must have been chasing the great dragon.

If it was heading to the ground Fran was close.

Last push, Ivan reassured himself as he forced his wings to beat faster. And in one final burst of speed, the fairy barreled toward where he thought the dragons had gone.

Ivan's landing was not graceful. He stumbled onto an empty gravel avenue between two large seaside houses. To his right, Azure Road ran parallel to the city's southern coast. Beyond it were the cliffs of Bride's Bay. The waves washed against them like a steady heartbeat.

To his left, also on the gravel, Chase had hidden his wings and tail. Their race was finished, and he had won. The baby dragon wriggled in his arms, snapping its teeth at his chin.

Damn it. Ivan was too tired to hide his own wings, so he folded them instead, the muscles sighing in relief. Hopefully, it was just dark enough that any of the wealthy humans who lived in the area would mistake them for a pattern on a shirt if they looked out the window.

Ivan stumbled closer to Chase. He couldn't accept his defeat. There had to be a way still to get Fran's dragon back to her. He just needed to keep Chase there until he could figure it out.

"You know fairies are supposed to be useless fliers." Chase's eyes were on the little creature, still trying to break free of his grip, but it was obvious that he was talking to Ivan. "Can't you even do that right?"

Is that a compliment? Ivan leaned against the fence of the house beside him, trying to catch his breath and think of a witty retort in case it wasn't. A sharp pain ran through his arm, like electricity shooting through him. He pulled his hand away.

"It's enchanted." Chase scoffed as he flicked his eyes toward Ivan. The baby dragon took the opportunity to send a trail of fire up into his face.

It didn't do anything more than make Chase wrinkle his nose in annoyance, but Ivan smiled all the same. "Looks real happy to be with you."

"He's not." Chase's mouth twisted in a snarl. He turned his body away from the house and toward Ivan. "You were right. I can smell her in there. This is one of their houses. I'm sure of it."

"Whose?" Ivan flicked his eyes to the fenced property. A tall house, made of limestone bricks, rose proudly from a field of grass that its owners must have spent a fortune to keep green despite the constant salt spray.

"Your girlfriend's family," Chase suggested with a sneer.

"She's not—" Ivan ran a hand through his hair and swallowed an uncomfortable laugh. Now wasn't the time to worry about the specifics of his relationship with Fran. "This property belongs to the Knights?"

"The Order of the Egg," Chase spat the name. The dragon growled in his arms. Ivan wasn't certain if it was in agreement or objection. "They've enchanted their property to block us. Clever."

Ivan glanced at the fence, recalling the strange jolt that had shot through him when he touched it. *Magic.*

He studied the house again, looking for a sign that it belonged to the Knights. They loved stamping their sword on things, or even their motto. Something about honor, though Ivan didn't think he'd ever learned the precise words.

But there was nothing to mark it.

The hairs rose on the back of Ivan's neck. "Are you—?"

He turned to Chase to ask if he was certain that the property belonged to the Order of the Egg. But the words died on his lips when he caught sight of the boy beside him.

Although his jaw was clenched tight and his teeth were bared in a sneer, there were tears running down his cheeks as he stared at the baby dragon, still hissing and writhing in his arms.

Dust. Chase Hagen is crying.

Ivan had been prepared to keep fighting him for the dragon. He'd even been ready to trade insults or try to latch onto his tail again if he tried to fly. But tears?

What the hell was Ivan supposed to do?

"Are you scared?" Ivan reached his hand out, resting it tentatively on Chase's shoulder.

"Oh fuck off." Chase shoved his shoulder against Ivan's arm, almost knocking him down. "You're the one who should be afraid. Getting mixed up with knights, angering my family. I could have you killed, you know. Your sisters too. I'd probably never get caught."

The truth of the statement stabbed into Ivan's heart like a sharp pinprick, making him freeze for a moment.

But Chase was posturing. His threats weren't coming from a place of psychotic hatred or even the *laissez-faire* indifference of the wealthy. Somewhere, beneath his callous scoffs and condescending sneers, he was a regular person with feelings.

"You're right," Ivan said, losing at least a portion of the disdain he'd had for the boy before him. "I'm nothing in the grand scheme of things compared to you. I don't matter, so just explain it to me. Why are you crying?"

There was a flash of sharp canines in Chase's mouth. Ivan thought he might scream again, but to his surprise, the dark-haired boy lowered his head with a deep sigh.

"His name isn't Lostsong."

40

IVAN

Of course it wasn't. Ivan had known that the moment he'd heard it. "What made you think it was?"

"It was the name his mother gave him," Chase said, eyes filling with water. He squeezed them shut. "Before she died, she called her egg her Lostsong. But he's rejecting her name. By some sliver of luck, he survived his capture. He should be returned to his family, with us. But you're right. He fights me at every turn, and now he's flown to her. I can smell her in there, even through their enchantments."

Chase and the baby dragon in his arms turned to stare at the house before them, their noses raised in the air. The scent of Fran must have mingled with the salt to them.

"He rejects us for the people who stole him." The scowl returned to Chase's face, but now Ivan recognized the sadness that lurked behind it.

And to his utter shock, he understood Chase Hagen.

His whole life, he had known of the stolen egg, the baby ripped from his family. He'd grown up loathing the people who'd committed such a crime, viewing them as evil. Now the baby dragon had hatched and been recovered, but instead of solace, his return brought pain as Chase struggled between what he'd always assumed best and what the creature itself wanted.

Ivan stepped closer, putting his hand on Chase's shoulder. This time, the fairy didn't let the dragon push him away.

"He's not rejecting you, Chase. He's telling you where he belongs."

"With his captor?"

"Fran didn't steal him. Her family abandoned her. She was as much an orphan as him. And they bonded to each other. I think they became the family each other lacked."

"But we're his actual family," Chase said, sadness breaking through the mask of anger. "We're dragons. He should be with us."

He sounded desperate, pleading. And he stared at Ivan with his pupils large and circular, begging him to agree with him.

But Ivan couldn't. "Sometimes, what we are isn't who we are. He's bonded to her. You know I'm not lying. Let him go. He wants to be with her."

The dragon stopped wriggling in Chase's grip. It curved its long neck so that its head faced the dark-haired boy's. The creature stared at him with his big golden eyes, curling wisps of smoke blowing from its nostrils

Chase squeezed his eyes tight. Ivan suspected he was trying not to cry again.

Then, the dark-haired boy extended his arms to Ivan. "Here. Take him before I change my mind. He wants to be with you. He says you're her person too."

I'm Fran's person? A cautious smile rose on Ivan's face as he accepted the little creature. His hands were ripped and bloody from clinging to Chase's tail, but the heat from the baby dragon was surprisingly soothing.

The creature allowed itself to be transferred to Ivan without fuss, settling in his hands with its wings folded at its sides. It opened its mouth and breathed a ring of fire at Chase.

Evidently it was an affectionate gesture, because the dark-haired boy smiled for a moment, a genuinely happy expression that softened the hardness of his features. But he wiped it away faster than he had his tears.

"Don't go onto the property by yourself. They'll kill you if they catch you, and you're not as fast as you think." Chase held up a finger cautioning the baby dragon, who grumbled in what Ivan was fairly certain was a reluctant yes.

Chase looked up at Ivan. There was an odd expression on his face. Was he about to apologize for threatening to murder Ivan and his entire family? Maybe thank Ivan for helping him see the truth?

"You should know, he thinks she's in danger."

Ivan's head snapped to the house. The muscles in his arms clenched, fear making them forget their exhaustion. "Why does he think that?"

"He says she's fading. But don't do anything rash. They won't harm her."

"Because she's their family," Ivan guessed.

"Because she's the best weapon a group hellbent on destroying magic could hope for," Chase said. His lips curled upward in a condescending smile that suggested he thought the answer was obvious. It was both annoying and reassuring to know that his one moment of kindness hadn't erased his usual pompous persona. "Think smarter, Dream. Because I will kill you if you let anything happen to my cousin."

He rested his hand on the baby dragon's head in farewell.

"You could stay and help us," Ivan suggested. But Chase had already spread his wings and jumped into the sky.

How any humans who happened to spot him would explain that to themselves, Ivan had no idea. A reverse shooting star?

"Guess it's just you and me then," Ivan said, scratching behind the baby dragon's ears. The creature purred in response, its head swiveling to the house beside them.

Ivan turned to face it as well. He took a deep breath, filling his muscles with all the strength he could muster.

He would need it all.

Because despite Chase's certainty that Fran was safe, Ivan wasn't taking any chances. If she was fading, they needed to get her to safety as soon as possible.

Which meant that this had just become a rescue mission.

41
FRANCES

Fran's vision spun as she stared at the Bucklers. The two were hunched like a pair of conspirators in the corner of the gloom, speaking in whispers that drifted to her on occasion. They were arguing about her, whether she'd come around. They had to postpone the ceremony.

It was a small win. Fran clung to that as her mind threatened to shut down. Her limbs were stiff and achy from being stuck in the chair, and the skin at the back of her elbow burned from where the needle had stolen her blood.

So much blood. Too much.

Or Fran wouldn't have been so ill.

I need something. They gave people cookies after giving blood, didn't they? Fran needed sugar, electrolytes, at least some water. Her throat was dry. She imagined she could feel her skin shriveling from dehydration.

But she wouldn't give the Bucklers the satisfaction of asking.

A loud bell rang throughout the room. The sound

seemed to seep down from the ceiling. Fran would have frozen in terror, but she was too exhausted to panic.

That's one way to beat my anxiety.

The Bucklers looked up toward the sound. Through the fog of her vision, Fran thought she saw Noelle look at her and smile.

The old man muttered a curse and pulled a large tablet from within his shirt. His daughter leaned in, watching the screen with her father, and a moment later, her smile grew larger again.

"I told you so," she sang, voice loud and clear enough that she must have intended Fran to hear.

But why? *What did she tell me?*

The Bucklers exchanged another whispered exchange. Fran strained her ears trying to listen. Did the alarm signal a good thing? A bad thing? They weren't in agreement, judging from their tones.

Fran's eyes fluttered, the effort of listening weighing on her. She began to dream about a glass of cold iced tea with a spoonful of sugar.

The old man's heavy footsteps pounded against the side of her head before growing distant. A soft hand stroked her cheekbone.

"Don't fall asleep, my baby," Noelle said. "We have to get you ready."

42
IVAN

Bypassing the knights' security proved easy. It encircled the property, extending a good ten feet above the fence, but whoever had set the enchantment for them had been lax. They'd forgotten to secure the house from the sky.

There was a strange ringing sound in his ear for a moment as he flew down. His invisibility flickered, and the hair on Ivan's body rose, waiting for the shock of magic that would repel him.

But it never came, and he landed on the unnaturally green grass without an issue. The baby dragon chirped, sticking its head out the large pocket of Ivan's sweatshirt that it had somehow squeezed into.

You're as tired as I am, aren't you? Ivan smiled as he tickled under its chin. The little creature had flown further today than it had in the rest of its existence. It must have been longing for a nap. But it squirmed in his pocket, eyes alert whenever it poked its head out.

Ivan understood. He suspected that he felt the same as the dragon.

"We'll rest when she's safe," Ivan said, looking up at the house. There were no knights with their faces pressed to the windows. *Good.*

Ivan forced the tips of his wings to turn. They fought against the motion, but he insisted, and eventually he turned invisible.

Now it was just a matter of finding a weak point.

The front door was locked, which was unfortunate but expected. He did a loop of the house, scanning for open windows. He'd sworn that he'd seen a few on the second and third floors earlier, but all were slammed shut now.

Still, there was a single open window on the first floor, beside the door.

The little dragon tapped its tail against Ivan's stomach. Its nose pointed toward it.

How did I miss that?

Ivan hurried toward it, but as he rested his hand on the ledge, he hesitated.

There was something strangely familiar about the situation. Sneaking into a knight's house through a window? Fran somewhere within?

It was like a replay of his first attempt to get the badge.

And look how well that had gone. If it weren't for Fran, the knights might've sawed off Ivan's wings and chucked him in one of their prisons somewhere.

He couldn't risk entering. There could easily be a net waiting for him within.

But Ivan couldn't ignore the open window either. It was the only entrance he'd seen. And he couldn't pass up the opportunity.

The little dragon was agitated for a reason. Ivan could feel it starting to claw at the fabric of his sweatshirt. Fran needed their help.

The thought of her, hurt or injured in some creepy knight chamber within made Ivan's muscles tense. What would she do in this situation?

Think like she was in a horror movie.

The thought made Ivan smile for a second, but it didn't help him. He hadn't watched enough horror movies.

So, what do we do? Ivan looked down at the little dragon, hoping it might have the answer.

43
FRANCES

"Don't you look beautiful," Noelle crooned, holding up the mirror for her daughter.

I look like you.

Fran didn't have the energy to speak the thought aloud. The best she could manage was to glare at her reflection.

Not only was Fran's braided updo the dark version of her mother's, but Noelle had also taken advantage of her father's absence to resume styling her daughter. She'd pulled a palette from who knew where and painted Fran's eyes with blue eyeshadow and brushed her cheeks pink with rouge. Only Fran's lips still looked like hers, cracked and dry and black.

"Red would be overpowering on you," Noelle had said.

If she'd had the energy, Fran might've pointed out that they had the same complexion. But she was happier with the fading black anyway.

Noelle laid the mirror down on the table of vials and test tubes. She clapped her hands together and beamed at her daughter. "You're going to look just like a little mini-me once we get you in your dress."

Fran's eyes flicked through the open curtain to the other room where the blue frilled dress hung from the door. That had to be the dress her mother meant, but hadn't she said that it was for the ceremony? Noelle couldn't expect that stealing pints of her blood had made Fran change her mind.

She leaned forward, lips finding the straw to the cup of juice that Noelle had placed in her hand. Fran took a sip and wet her lips.

"I won't help you," she said, throat burning as she spoke. "You already took my blood. I'm not participating in your spell."

"Ceremony," Noelle corrected her, smiling and holding up a finger. "That's a very important distinction within the order. You can't make mistakes like that when you're talking to our followers, or there'll be consequences, understood? They'll see you as an authority figure, given that you're a Buckler."

Fran would've laughed if her throat would let her. "What makes you think I want to talk to any of your people?"

"Because you won't have a choice. Or, rather you will, but I'm quite certain I know which one you'll make." The calculated smile returned to Noelle's face. "You'll play the part of a good daughter, and give us your blood, and say whatever we tell you to say."

Fran snorted. She was giving the blonde too much credit. She was as delusional as she seemed.

"Your fairy friend is quite handsome. I can see why you like him," Noelle said, still smiling as she stood and turned away. "Redheads have never been my type personally, but there's something about the way his hair seems to match his wings that is quite captivating."

A chill crept from Fran's chest, out to the rest of her body, spreading with every word her mother said.

How does she know what Ivan looks like?

Noelle took the tablet that the old man had left behind off the table. She turned, holding it before Fran, beaming once more. "Do you want to see why I'm so certain you're going to do as we say?"

44
IVAN

I van held his breath as he rested his foot against the floor. He paused, eyes scanning the room, waiting for a trap.

No net flew out. Everything remained still.

He released a sigh. Maybe he was being overly cautious for nothing. The enchantment on the property had been its protection, and he'd already passed that, so why was he so worried?

Ivan turned around to tap the window, but it slammed shut behind him.

Dust.

He pushed it, muscles straining. The effort was more than he could handle with his magic, and he flashed into view.

"Don't move."

Ivan's head snapped backward. Had the voice come from the ceiling?

Yes. His eyes landed on a black box. It was some sort of PA system.

A lump rose in Ivan's throat. He slammed his fist

against the window and felt the pain ripple through his arm. It was the same crap the Hagens' car had been protected with.

There was a noise behind him, like something clicking into position.

"I said, don't move."

The voice wasn't coming from the PA system anymore.

Ivan raised his hands and risked turning his head.

There was an old man, pointing a shotgun straight at Ivan.

45
FRANCES

Fran stared at the screen. In an unfamiliar room, her grandfather held a shotgun to Ivan's head, marching him out of view.

It didn't make sense. Was this some kind of trick? They couldn't have Ivan. What would he even have been doing here?

"I knew there was something there." Noelle laughed in delight, tapping the tip of Fran's nose with her finger as she pulled the tablet away. "Deny it all you want, but it's plain on your face. You're your father's daughter after all. So, let's see? You keep fighting us and we kill him. Or you sacrifice yourself to save the boy you love, and we'll keep him alive. Wings intact and everything."

Fran stared down at her lap where the tablet had been a moment earlier. Her body trembled, and it wasn't from loss of blood.

As much as she hated it, her mother was right. Ivan had protected her even when he learned the truth about her family. He'd saved her more than once, given her a place to stay, helped her care for her dragon.

Fran couldn't let the Bucklers hurt him.

46
IVAN

The old man threw him into a dark cell in the basement of the house. A ripple of pain went through Ivan as he was pushed through. The little energy that he'd managed to summon leached toward the floor, and the fairy fell to his knees.

So the window had been a trap after all. And Ivan had climbed straight into it. Just like at the Franklins' house.

No, not quite.

At least this time, he had something of a backup plan.

"Tobias Buckler?" Ivan guessed, managing to turn his head just enough to look at the old man who'd caught him. The name had been on the family tree in The Archives, and his captor resembled Fran too closely to be of no relation.

The old man grunted. Ivan wasn't fluent in grunts, but he took it as affirmative.

Tobias flicked his eyes over Ivan with an expression of disdain that was surprisingly similar to Chase's.

They'd be great friends in another lifetime.

"I wouldn't try to escape from there," the old man said, his tone matter-of-fact. "The more you try, the worse you'll feel. Paid a very clever witch to make it. Was almost a pity I had to kill her after."

Ivan's stomach churned, threatening to be sick. Tobias talked about murder as though it were no more upsetting than breaking a glass.

"My granddaughter will be a lot less complacent if you die," the old man continued. "So, I'd advise you to listen to me. We both want you to survive. For now, at least."

Oh good.

The old man went through another door, leaving Ivan alone on the floor of the cell. Did he trust Tobias' advice?

Every enchantment has a weak point. Brilliant as the poor murdered witch might have been, the cell would be no exception. He could find its weak point.

But getting the energy to do so was a different matter.

Every time he attempted to touch and examine the bars, they repelled him with such force that Ivan was knocked backward onto the floor.

His lungs burned in his chest. His head spun.

Tobias was telling the truth.

Dust.

Ivan lay on the floor, gasping for air. The more he accepted his defeat, the less his body felt like it was on fire.

I can't escape.

Ivan would be trapped here for the rest of his life, and one day, he'd probably die on the floor of the cell. Just like the witch who'd made it.

But at least Fran still had a chance.

Ivan may have doomed himself, but no one else. *I actually did think about everyone else. See, Daisy? I'm not as selfish as you think.*

He hoped someone would point that out to his older sister one day.

The door swung open. Ivan turned his head. Was Tobias back to taunt him about his fast failure to escape? Funny. The old man hadn't seemed the type to gloat.

But it wasn't Tobias.

It was Fran.

Her black hair was twisted into a knot behind her head, four thin braids swooping above her ears before joining the rest. Her face was beautiful, but in an eerie way that made Ivan blink when he first saw it. Her eyes were too bright, her cheeks too pink. But those were Fran's lips, small and black with the little cupid bow at the top.

She wore a long blue dress with layers of fabric spreading from her waist to her feet like waves crashing to the shore. She pulled it up as she entered, fists grabbing at the front of the skirt to allow her to run without tripping.

Ivan pushed himself up and went as close to the bars as he dared, studying her through the iron. From the corner of his eye, he saw a blonde hovering just behind the door. But he didn't try to get a better look.

His focus was on Fran.

She's okay. A smile started to spread across Ivan's face, but it vanished as he noticed what the makeup hid. Thin red veins ran through her eyes. Her lips were cracked and dry, the cut on the corner visible beyond the black paint. Her body trembled as though she might faint.

Fran wrapped her hands around the bars, immune to whatever magic repelled Ivan. Her face poked through the center, staring at him with wild bloodshot eyes.

She didn't look happy to see him.

Why would she be? A spark of fear rose in Ivan suddenly as he recalled the last time they'd spoken. He'd been an ass.

"I'm sorry," he said. The words felt insufficient. They were too small to hold the many things he was apologizing for. *Sorry I lied to you. Sorry I ever thought you could've been a knight. Sorry I've gotten caught trying to save you.*

"You're so stupid." Fran's eyes filled with tears. She leaned closer, lowering her voice. "I'm going to get you out of here."

Ivan smiled. "That's supposed to be my line."

"One minute, Frances, remember, that's the deal," a woman's voice called from the door.

Fran's jaw clenched for a second, then she leaned closer. Her body was almost small enough to fit through the bars.

"I have to do something, but then I promise, I'm coming back for you. How do I get you out?"

Ivan's head fell. He stared down at his feet. "You can't. This cell is enchanted. I'd need your blood to escape it anytime soon."

Her eyebrows rose.

That's right. She doesn't know. "Fran, you're special. Your father was a dragon tamer. You've bonded with your dragon, he's—"

"That must be a minute, Frances." The blonde swept into the room. "Come on now, or I'll worry you're plotting something."

"Shit," Fran muttered. She closed her eyes and winced. Then, before the other woman could grab her and before Ivan fully understood what was happening, she reached through the bars.

Fran's hands wrapped around his head, fingers grabbing his hair and pulling his face down toward her. Ivan was too surprised to resist.

Her lips found his, crashing against them, hot and feverish. There was a sense of desperation in the kiss.

Ivan didn't understand. This was the last thing he'd been expecting.

But it might also be his only chance to kiss Fran.

Ivan's eyes closed. He forgot where he was, forgot about the bars that trapped him, forgot about the enchantment that continued to steal his strength. Fran was the only thing that was real.

His hand pressed against the side of her cheek, fingers brushing the braids above her ear. Her tongue knocked on his lips, seeking entry, and Ivan complied almost at once.

He wasn't sure how long they stayed like that before the woman pulled Fran away.

"Quite enough," the blonde said, an amused lilt to her voice. "Your grandfather will have both our heads if he knows I'm encouraging your relationship with a fairy."

And before Ivan could say anything else, Fran was being dragged away.

She turned her head and their eyes met just before she vanished from sight. She mouthed something to him. *Willingly given.*

There was the taste of something hot and metallic in Ivan's mouth.

47
FRANCES

Fran's tongue throbbed as she followed her mother out of the house.

She stepped outside to find that night had fallen at some point while she'd been in the Buckler's house. A crescent moon smiled from the sky, a thousand twinkling stars for eyes. A cool breeze rose from the ocean and whistled across the cliffs, accompanied by the occasional crash of a wave against the rocks.

Alongside the Bucklers' property were other large seaside homes with varying degrees of ostentation. Even the humbler homes made it clear that this was an affluent area of the city.

This was not at all the right setting for the dark spell that the Bucklers had planned.

Noelle could disguise it as a ceremony as much as she wished, but now Fran understood what it really was. *A blood baptism.*

She shuddered at the image of what her mother had described. Fran would bathe them in her blood, letting it seep into the skin of their faces, through their nostrils, and into their lips. Then, Noelle would baptize them both in the ocean, repeating magic words they'd learned from a witch. And the Bucklers would rise with Fran's immunity.

They shouldn't be allowed to complain about vampires.

Her grandfather waited for them outside the door. His eyes scanned the bushes of his property, a shotgun at the ready in his hands. Fran recognized it from the tablet. It was the same one he'd had to the back of Ivan's head when he marched him to the basement.

A lump rose in Fran's throat.

"She's not going to give us any trouble," Noelle said, batting her hand at her father as though there was something amusing about the old man with the shotgun. "Not so long as we have the fairy."

The old man turned his gaze to them, though thankfully, he kept the shotgun focused near the ground. "Thought I heard something."

"Trust your own defenses." Noelle laughed, but she slipped her arm through her daughter's, linking them together and holding Fran close. "Now, come on. Let's not waste time."

The old man grunted, but he repositioned his shotgun so that it leaned against his shoulder and led the way out of the property.

It was a short walk across the street from the Bucklers' house to the cliff. Fran glanced over her shoulder back at the house. She couldn't go through with this twisted ritual. Somehow, she needed to get back to Ivan and escape.

But if she timed things wrong, he might still be trapped. The Bucklers would catch up to her, then punish Ivan for her disobedience.

Patience. Give him as much time as possible.

The bushes on the sides of the road trembled as they reached the edge. Almost like there really was something following them.

A long flight of stairs, carved into the rock, wound from the top of the cliff to a small sandy cove below. Those would make Fran's plan difficult. After she got rid of the blood that her grandfather had stolen, she needed to run. But she still felt weak and just going down the stairs had her feeling winded.

At least she was barefoot. Fran had no idea how her mother managed in the silver pointed stilettos that peeked out under the hem of her gown. But it might let her outrun Noelle.

Her grandfather, with his shotgun, was a significantly larger problem.

About halfway down the steps, Fran gasped and grabbed her mother's arm. Something had run underneath her dress.

"It's a bit late to develop a fear of heights," Noelle said, smiling and patting Fran's hand with faked affection.

But that wasn't it.

Something warm and hard wrapped around Fran's ankle. Claws scratched the top of her foot.

It was impossible. It couldn't be—but Fran knew with absolute certainty that it was.

My dragon.

That's who Ivan had meant: *He'll find you.*

"Just general anxiety," Fran said, hiding her smile by tucking her head down. "I suffer with it sometimes."

"Well, you'll need to get that sorted now that you're going to be a Buckler." Noelle leaned over and kissed her cheek before forcing her to continue.

The little dragon ran alongside her feet, hidden by the frills of Fran's dress. He blew warm puffs of air onto her ground beside her, tail tapping against her foot, and she understood what he was trying to say.

I'm here to help. Tell me what I can do.

48

IVAN

*S*he gave me her blood.

Ivan could taste it still on his tongue. He was careful not to swallow, uncertain how long it would last, but for now, it was enough.

He touched the bars of the cell. Nothing happened.

Fran was a genius.

Probably should've guessed she was up to something when she kissed me.

The back of Ivan's neck felt hot as he recalled. He'd been a bit too enthusiastic in hindsight. Perhaps he could claim that he'd guessed what she was up to the entire time.

Though it would've been a definite lie. It hadn't even occurred to Ivan that drinking Fran's blood would grant him temporary magical immunity. He was a fairy, not a vampire after all.

But her plan had worked, and now Ivan could plan his escape without having the cell leach his strength.

He just had to make sure he found a way out before his immunity wore off.

The bars were too close together for Ivan to fit through.

Even turned on his side, his shoulders and back were too broad.

He couldn't fly out. The bars reached to the roof. And the floor below him was concrete. Digging wasn't an option.

So where was the weak spot?

The door.

Ivan's head snapped to where he'd entered the cell. If he hadn't known where to look, he might not have noticed the hinges on the outside.

Could it be that simple?

Heart pounding in his chest, Ivan hurried toward them. He slipped his hands through the bars. His fingers felt for the grooves. *Bingo!*

A smile spread across his face.

Screws. Regular, normal, mundane screws held the door to the rest of the cell.

Ivan could deal with those.

With no time to lose, Ivan pulled the Gentlemen's badge out of his pocket. He fit the edge into the groove and began to turn.

49
FRANCES

Fran's feet sank into the wet sand. The dark waves lapped at the edges of her dress. The little dragon bounced around in them beneath her, splashing water up the sides of her legs.

Noelle was already up to her knees in the ocean, her dress spreading around her in a perfect circle. She held a piece of paper before her in one hand and a lighter in the other. The light shone on her red lips, mouthing the words as she practiced reciting the spell that the witch had given her.

The old man blocked Fran's path to the steps. He'd leaned his shotgun against a boulder and was slowly approaching. As he drew nearer, he reached into his pocket and produced two vials. The red liquid within seemed to absorb the moonlight.

My blood.

The sight made Fran stiffen.

He'd had no right to steal it, but at least she would get it back now. And once she did, and it had been disposed of, she and the little dragon could run free.

Her grandfather held the vials out. Fran reached for them.

A bell sounded from his pocket.

The old man snapped his arm back, latching his fingers tight around the vials of blood. His body went rigid, and his head snapped toward the house.

Something was happening.

There were soft splashes as Noelle hurried out of the ocean with the small flickering fire of her lighter. "Someone coming to save him?"

"Not likely he broke free himself," the old man snarled.

Fran's chest trembled as she glanced up toward where the house was beyond the top of the cliff. Ivan had managed to escape, which meant she needed to do the same.

Run! She hoped the little dragon understood.

Fran pushed past her grandfather, trying to get to the stairs.

His hand dug into her arm as he grabbed her. The pain made her wince.

"Hold her. I'll check—" the old man started to bark orders at his daughter, but a moment later, he screamed and dropped Fran's arm.

Hanging from his wrist, with its sharp teeth latched into his skin, was the baby great dragon.

"My God!" Noelle exclaimed, covering her mouth with her hands as she stared at it.

The old man whipped his arm around, attempting to shake the creature off. When that failed, he dropped the vials of Fran's blood onto the sand and began to fully pry it off.

Noelle caught sight of them and dropped to her knees, reaching to collect them.

Fran stomped the glass before she could get to them, slicing the bottom of her bare foot. Fresh blood mingled with the old.

But Fran didn't care. It was worth it to see the look of horror on Noelle's face.

"You little bitch," her mother said, her mad, red-lipped grin spreading across her face as she stared up at Fran. "Do you think we won't take more today?"

No, Fran had delusions that the Bucklers cared about how much blood was safe to take in a single day.

They'd kill her if it served their purpose.

Fran whistled, and the little dragon flew to her shoulder. She lifted up her dress and ran toward the stairs.

Spots danced before her vision as she ran, but she couldn't risk stopping. Noelle was just behind her.

She stumbled, scraping her knees on the stone. Which proved lucky, for there was a sharp crack as the shotgun went off. The bullet sailed over her head, and a wave of terror knifed through Fran.

This is how I die, isn't it? The thought paralyzed her. She couldn't even turn her head. Her eyes remained frozen, staring down at the little purple dragon that had been knocked from her shoulder.

The Bucklers' footsteps drew closer.

"Go! Fly! Get out of here!" Fran managed to whisper.

The little dragon whimpered, tucked his head under her neck, and curled in a tight ball beneath her.

Fran recognized the position. It was how Ivan had found her when he'd saved her from the man in the trench coat.

It's my fear. It's affecting him.

Fran couldn't let anything happen to him.

She spun around and faced the Bucklers. Chest tight

and head still spinning, Fran raised her hand. "Stop," she shouted. "I'm warning you."

The shock of being ordered was enough to make both the blonde and the old man hesitate.

Fran doubted they'd keep listening though, and she didn't have much more of a plan.

"There, by her feet!" Noelle exclaimed, pointing down to where the little dragon had dared to peep its head from behind the safety of Fran's dress.

A fraction of a second later, Fran realized why she'd shouted it. The crack of the shotgun echoed again.

No.

Fran immediately fell to the floor, curling her body into a ball to block the bullet from reaching the dragon.

The pain burned through her shoulder, and Fran screamed.

Behind her the dragon howled as well.

There was another shot.

The little dragon, now more furious than scared, flapped its wings and rose above Fran's head before opening its mouth and releasing a wave of flame, stronger and more intense than Fran had seen it before.

The bullet didn't reach Fran this time. It didn't reach anywhere, because it ran into a small wall of dragon fire and burned up in the air.

50
IVAN

Ivan's magic refused to work, so he remained visible as he wandered up the stairs from the basement. He walked on the tips of his toes, too tired to flutter, trying to visualize a map of the house in his head. The front door should be in the next room to his right.

He entered it and found a large sitting room. Against the far wall was a white double door with seashells painted along the bottom.

Brilliant.

Ivan's pride in navigating the unfamiliar house was short-lived. A moment later, the door flew open.

Dust!

A wide-eyed Fran raced in, her braids falling and unraveling alongside her face. Cradled in her arms was the baby dragon.

She smiled when she saw him.

"Come on." Fran slammed the door closed behind her and ran to Ivan, grabbing his arm and pulling him further into the house.

Ivan didn't fight her, but he couldn't help but turn back to look at the door. "Wrong way, isn't it?"

"Noelle's burnt, but my grandfather's still following." Fran pulled him up a flight of stairs, head turning as she looked around. "There's an exit on the third floor. I don't know where."

There was a pounding on the door near the bottom, then a loud noise as it flew in. Tobias was in the house.

And they'd be easy to find. Fran was leaving a trail of blood.

"Your arm." Ivan's eyes widened as he saw it.

"It's nothing."

But it wasn't. Fran kept stumbling, her eyes closing for too long every so often. Even the makeup couldn't hide how pale her skin was.

Ivan wrapped an arm around her waist, supporting her. She didn't object to the help.

They opened the door to a room with a large bed. A silver shield hung alongside the wall.

The little dragon flew from Fran. He tapped it with his tail.

"That's not really what we're looking for," Ivan said, trying to call him back, but the little creature was insistent. He kept tapping against the engraved shield, using his tail to bang against each word in turn, like a teacher using a pointer to show their students: Order of the Egg.

"Fine, we'll take it." Ivan let Fran support herself against the wall while he grabbed the shield.

To his surprise, as he held it, a wave of strength washed through him, rejuvenating him.

Of course. Might've guessed it was enchanted.

Ivan passed it to Fran, but of course, it didn't have any

effect on her. Magical immunity could be both a blessing and a curse.

Still, at least he had his powers back.

He ripped a piece of fabric from Fran's dress and tied it around her arm to stop the bleeding. The little dragon hovered in the air beside her, inspecting Ivan's work. He glanced at the little creature. "How'd you know the shield was enchanted?"

The little creature blinked its golden eyes in response.

"He didn't." A weak laugh escaped Fran. Despite the fact that she looked like she might pass out at any moment, there was a smile spreading across her face. "He was trying to tell me his name."

51

FRANCES

Fran managed to remain conscious just long enough to guide Ivan to the secret tunnels below.

The noise of Ivan forcing the door open brought her grandfather to the study. He fired his shotgun down the passage after them.

Fran had a vague memory of Ivan blocking the bullets with the stolen shield as they ran through the tunnels. After that, everything went blurry.

When she awoke, she was in a small unfamiliar bedroom, tucked under a set of blue sheets. A nearby shelf displayed a collection of trophies with runners on top, a row of books that looked mostly unopened and a pile of games near the bottom. On top of them was a familiar badge, a downward-facing sword glinting in the light.

Something warm snuggled against her neck and head, sharing her pillow. Her dragon.

Fran smiled and reached up to tickle his spine.

The door opened and Poppy appeared carrying a tray with bandages. Her eyes widened and she squealed. "You're awake! I can't believe it."

The thirteen-year-old hurried into the room and put the tray down on the side table by Fran's head. Her auburn hair was pulled up in a bun near the top of her head. It bounced, threatening to fall loose with every step. She had her mouth open in a wide grin, too excited to hide her braces.

"Ivan is going to be so annoyed that I'm the first to see you. He's basically spent the last twelve hours sitting beside you."

"Really?" The thought that Ivan had been that concerned about her made Fran's heart flutter. She smiled as she pushed herself up. A pain went through her arm.

Poppy nodded. "He'd still be here if Mum hadn't insisted he go shower. Daisy claimed he was starting to smell."

It suddenly clicked on Fran where she was. "This is your house." *And this is Ivan's room.*

Fran's eyes flicked around it once more, now more curious about the items on the shelf. She should've guessed when she'd seen the badge.

"Mmhm. Ivan didn't want to take you to the hospital since magic doesn't work on you anyway, and they were bound to ask questions. But the treehouse isn't sterile enough. And obviously, our parents didn't mind now that they know you're basically one of us. But, oh my God, you should've heard the questions Mum asked him when she found out he'd been hiding you in the treehouse. As soon as you're up, she's going to ask if you're his girlfriend."

Fran felt her face grow hot. She was struggling to keep up with everything Poppy was saying, but she understood that last bit.

"Poppy." Ivan opened the door in time to hear the end

of his younger sister's story. Fran's eyes went to him and got stuck.

He was shirtless. With only a towel wrapped around him.

If she hadn't been blushing before, she definitely was now.

Ivan held the white towel with his hand as he crossed to the shelves across from Fran. The muscles along his arms tensed and flexed as he opened a drawer. "Get out and give her a minute. She's only just woken up."

"No way! I want—"

Ivan tossed a pair of shorts out and flung them over his sister's head. She grumbled in protest beneath, but her brother ignored her and sat at the foot of the bed, still wearing just a towel.

Fran realized a moment later that she was still staring at his arms. She pulled her eyes up to his own, feeling self-conscious.

He raised his eyebrows. She waited for him to call her out on staring, but all he said was, "How're you feeling?"

"Better than I think I should be," Fran admitted, running her hand through her hair and finding that someone had taken out the braids.

"Good." Ivan gave her his characteristic grin. Then he turned to his sister. Poppy had thrown his shorts onto the floor and was now glaring at him with her arms crossed. "Get out. I need to change."

"With Fran in here?"

"She'll close her eyes."

Would she? *Yes, obviously. If he asks me to.* Though Fran was moderately curious about what was underneath Ivan's towel.

As if he sensed her thoughts, the little dragon opened

an eye and raised his head, turning his face in the direction of the fairy. A wisp of smoke curled from his nostrils.

"Want me to burn it?" His posture asked.

"No," Fran answered quickly, resting her hand over his mouth just in case. But a smile was spreading on her face. She'd understood him.

"Oh, he's up too!" Poppy squealed with delight and jumped onto the bed beside Fran, leaning over to scratch his head.

"What part of *out* do you not understand?" Ivan groaned, trying to shove his sister off.

Poppy stuck her tongue out at him. "Not until I hear his name. He keeps trying to tell us. But he just keeps tapping the shield, and he says it's not Shield or Silver or Sword so what is it?"

The baby dragon gave an annoyed snort, but his tongue flicked out and licked the thirteen-year-old's hands affectionately.

Fran laughed, imagining the little creature hitting the letters of the shield over and over and growing increasingly exasperated as no one understood him. But it had made perfect sense to Fran. After all, the Order of the Egg, vile as its members were, had only come into existence because of him.

"His name," she explained to the waiting fairies, "is Oote."

52
IVAN

After Poppy cooed over the little dragon, hooting his name at him like it made him an owl, Ivan finally managed to kick his younger sister out his room. He locked the door behind her.

"Should I close my eyes now?"

Ivan rubbed the back of his neck, feeling it grow hot. He turned back around and gave Fran an apologetic smile. "I was joking."

"So, I can watch?"

Ivan's eyebrows rose. Was Fran flirting with him? Or was this leading to a joke where she reminded him that he wasn't her type? "I just needed Poppy to leave. Listen, there's something I need to tell you."

Fran frowned, her expression growing serious. She shuffled under the sheets until she was sitting straight up, the pillows behind her back. Oote crawled onto her lap, resting his long neck down her thigh and watching Ivan as well.

The fairy took a deep breath. He'd been preparing for this conversation for the past few hours. Whenever he'd imagined it, he'd been wearing clothes. But that didn't matter. He was just thinking of excuses because he was nervous.

But he'd promised Fran that he'd help her find out about her parents. He'd broken it already. It wouldn't happen again. He needed to be the one to tell her this time.

"It's about your father."

"Okay."

Ivan started off by explaining how he and Poppy had met Mac at Stone's Throw Apartments. Fran looked surprised to learn that the man in the trench coat was actually a friend of her father's, but she remained silent as Ivan relayed the tale he'd heard the previous day.

West Bishop was one of the few humans still alive capable of bonding with a great dragon, but it had been more than a century since anyone had. The bipedal dragons had taken most of the eggs and closed ranks around their cousins, hunting and killing any humans who claimed to have the ability to tame their cousins. Which was why West and Mac were so intrigued by rumors that a new order of Knights had stolen a dragon egg.

So, they hatched a plan. The bolder of the two, West, would infiltrate the Knights to steal the egg for himself. Mac would help him when the time came to act.

Only, that time never came. West fell in love with Noelle Buckler and changed his mind. He and Mac fought, but West was too far gone. He'd fallen for the Knights' diatribe about magical creatures being evil. He became a true believer, performing every horrible task the Bucklers assigned him until their final request killed him.

"I suspected." Fran cut him off, finally speaking. "I think they wanted his blood to obtain his magical resistance. Only he didn't have enough because he wasn't bonded."

She stared at the badge, lying on the corner of Ivan's shelves, a far off look in her eye.

He reached over and rested his hand on top of hers.

She didn't freeze or push him away. Instead, Fran intertwined her fingers with his.

"But you've got part of it wrong," Fran said, turning her gaze to him finally. "My father didn't forget his purpose. He's the one who convinced the Bucklers to send me off with the egg. He tricked them into giving me instructions for how to hatch it. He's the reason I have Oote."

The little dragon purred in agreement.

The sound made Ivan feel happy. "You'd know better than me."

Fran smiled back at him. Their hands were still intertwined. It made Ivan recall the way her fingers had locked around his hair when she'd pulled him in to kiss him.

"So, what now?" Ivan kept grinning, hoping it would hide how tight his chest felt, waiting to hear what she'd say. This was the second bit of what he needed to discuss with her. "What's next for Frances West?"

"What do you mean?" Fran's eyes narrowed, watching him like she was waiting for the punchline to a joke.

"You've gotten everything you came here for. Answers about your parents. Your very own dragon." Ivan's eyes flicked to Oote and saw the creature was watching him as closely as Fran. "So, what now? I mean, your dads have been messaging you. Poppy responded and said you'd had an accident and missed your train, but they really want to see you."

"You want me to go home?"

"No, well, I mean, not that I don't want you to go home." Ivan had never considered himself bad with words, but he felt like he was fumbling them all now. "But Oote will be a lot safer in Castor's Grove. There's more magical enchantments and stuff to protect him. And..." Ivan paused, taking a deep breath. This was what he really didn't want to tell her, but he had to. "Mac lives in Castor's Woods, to the north of the city. He says you and Oote could go and live with him. He says it's the right place for a great dragon, far from people, lots to hunt."

Fran's grip on his hand tightened, and her lips pulled together so that they were barely visible. "You want me to go and live with a man I've never met in a cabin in the woods?"

"I don't know that it's a cabin," Ivan said. A lump rose in his throat, and the back of his neck grew hot.

Dust, it's not that hard to say, is it?

"Well, as long as it's not a cabin," Fran said, rolling her eyes. "Then it totally doesn't sound like the start of a horror movie. Honestly, Ivan, I'm sure this Mac dude is nice, but Oote and I can find our own place." She started to withdraw her hand from his own.

Ivan held it so that she couldn't. "Stay here."

"Your parents' house?"

"Maybe. Or the treehouse. Somewhere in the Western Woodlands." *Somewhere close to me.*

"Oote eats meat."

"Is that why I kept having to buy it? Wow, that makes so much more sense now."

Fran grinned and pushed his shoulder with her free hand. Her fingers seemed to linger on his skin for a moment.

On her lap, the little dragon blew a few coils of smoke from his nose. He wiggled his tail and pounced a few times.

Ivan tilted his head as he studied Oote's movements. He'd seen the dragon make them before.

"Wait a minute. Is he saying he could try eating insects?"

"I think he is."

The little dragon looked up at them and nodded his head. He opened his mouth and breathed a ring of smoke toward Ivan. It looked like a heart.

"He really loves it here," Fran said, her cheeks pink. "That's what he's trying to say."

Ivan didn't think that was what the dragon was saying at all. He smiled and raised his eyebrows, confidence returning. "In my bed?"

Fran's cheeks turned a shade darker. "I meant the woodlands, obviously."

"I know." But she'd set him up for the joke. "I think the woodlands love Oote being here too."

A small smile flickered on Fran's face, but it looked like she was holding it back. "That makes no sense."

"Would it make more sense if I said I love having you here?"

The smile she'd been holding back won, spreading across Fran's face. "I love being here too."

Oote grumbled and tapped his tail against her chest.

"And you being here is maybe a nice bonus." Oote thwacked his tail on her again. "Okay, definitely a nice bonus."

"You know, you're being really shy for a girl who kissed me less than twenty-four hours ago."

Fran's mouth opened, cheeks still pink. "I was trying to save— That didn't count!"

"I know." Ivan smiled. Her lips pouting in objection danced at the bottom of his vision. He focused on her eyes and leaned toward her.

Oote slipped off her lap, disappearing to a different

corner of the room as though he sensed it was his time to exit. Fran sat up, bringing her face closer to Ivan's until their noses almost touched. He could hear when her breath stopped.

"Would it count if I kissed you now?"

There was a pause. "Yes."

Ivan closed the small space between them. His lips brushed against hers.

It was gentler than when she'd kissed him at Bucklers' house. Ivan took his time, tracing her lips with his tongue, sliding his fingers through her hair, enjoying the feel of her hands pressed against his chest. Her fingers traced the grooves of his muscles, light and feathery on his skin. It made him shiver.

A noise came from the other side of the door. It sounded like Poppy on her way back.

Fran pulled her lips away from him, though her hands remained on his chest. Her cheeks were pink.

"You're cute when you blush."

Fran's mouth closed in a pout, but it looked like she was holding back a smile. "I don't blush."

There was a knock at the door and Oote chirped.

Either Poppy didn't understand how knocking worked, or she thought that was the dragon's way of telling her to come in. She pushed the door open.

Fran pulled her hands away from Ivan's chest, cheeks ridiculously red for someone who claimed that she didn't blush.

Ivan was slower to turn around.

"How're you still not dressed?" Poppy sounded annoyed, then her eyes widened, and her mouth opened. "Wait. Were you guys doing something?"

Oote gave a little bark, nodding his head as he fluttered around the thirteen-year-old's shoulder.

Traitor.

"I'm so sorry." Poppy put her hand over her mouth, but Ivan had a feeling she was smiling behind it, not looking contrite. "I didn't think you guys would be—I mean, you haven't even gone on a date or anything yet or like defined anything or—"

"We weren't doing anything," Fran said, leaning around Ivan so that she could see the thirteen-year-old. The look on her face was not convincing. Poppy probably assumed she'd interrupted way more than just a kiss.

Maybe it could've been.

Best not to think about that now. Ivan sighed and looked at his younger sister and the overexcited dragon still spinning by her head. "Did you want something?"

"Yes!" the thirteen-year-old snapped her fingers as if suddenly remembering why she'd returned. "Mac is here. He wants to talk to Fran."

Right. Poppy must have messaged and told him that Fran was awake. The tamer had been staying close by just in case.

Ivan glanced at her. This was it. The moment of truth. Despite their earlier jokes about Oote eating insects, and the kiss they'd just had, Ivan felt his stomach tighten. What would Fran really choose when the opportunity was presented to her?

53
FRANCES

Fran crossed her arms as she looked out the window toward the city beneath.

She stood in a small, single-bedroom apartment in the northeast of the city. The place she'd rented was on the sixth floor. Considering the view, it was surprisingly cheap, but then, not many humans wanted to be this close to Castor's Forest. There were rumors about strange things living in the woods.

Because those rumors were true.

Oote landed on her shoulder. His weight caught her off guard, and she had to throw her hand out to catch herself on the wall.

The dragon chirped and hung his head down, looking up at her with big, guilty, golden eyes.

"Yes, you are getting too big for this," Fran said, smiling as she adjusted to his weight and got her balance back. She rubbed under his neck, enjoying feeling his stomach tremble as he purred. "But I guess we should take advantage of it while you still can."

Almost two months had passed since Oote had hatched,

and the dragon had grown substantially, going from the size of a newborn kitten to a medium-sized dog.

"Don't mind," Mac's voice said from behind her. "You'll be sitting on him instead soon."

Oote let out a peal of fire in excitement at the idea. Fran caught the flame in her hand, squashing it before it reached the curtain. She couldn't afford to set the apartment on fire.

"How's the saddle design coming?" Fran asked, somehow managing to turn without toppling both her and Oote to the floor.

She looked at Mac, sitting on the brown couch with his ankle crossed over his knee. He wore a woolen red jumper and a pair of warm gray pants. He'd pushed his sunglasses onto his head, and his trench coat hung behind the door. Without them, he looked like a typical friendly human.

It was strange remembering how petrified she'd been during their first encounter.

"Oh, it'll be ready before him. Assuming this accelerated growth is just a phase. Just have to make sure the straps can keep adjusting," Mac said, eyes flicking between Fran, the door, and the watch on his wrist. He bounced his foot against his knee. "We're going to be late if we don't leave soon."

Oote flew off Fran's shoulder and landed on the couch beside him. The dragon patted his shoulder with its tail.

Mac had been warning them of that for the past half an hour, and he was probably right by now.

"Should I message the others and see where they are?" Fran offered.

"It won't get them here any faster. Why don't they just meet us at the restaurant?"

"Because Poppy has Oote's collar." And truthfully, Fran didn't want to leave without Ivan.

"How did you get him here?" Mac asked, eyebrows rising in concern. Then he snorted, and it looked like he was holding back a smile. "Ivan turned him invisible I suppose."

"He helped bring over a few things." Fran glanced at the origami swans on a nearby shelf, then to a stack of horror-themed books on the table. Ivan had also offered to buy a black vase with some dead flowers to really make it look like she lived there. He'd been teasing. The fairies all considered Fran terrible with plants.

The memory of him made Fran start to smile. She caught herself quick and surveyed the small apartment for flaws instead. The walls were too yellow. The appliances in the kitchen looked too used. The welcome mat seemed too cheerful.

A stray piece of hair tickled her cheek. Fran tried to shove it back into the ponytail with the rest as she crossed to the mat. Her heart pounded in her chest.

Fran hated her anxiety for acting up now. Her dads were coming to visit. She should be happy.

And she was, really. She couldn't wait to see them next week when they arrived. But her stupid brain kept obsessing.

What if they notice something's off?

Fran had sublet this apartment for the month, but the space wasn't hers. She needed to convince her dads other-wise. She couldn't repaint the walls or buy new kitchen appliances. But Fran could do something about that bright, sunflower covered mat.

Just as she went to roll it up, someone knocked. Fran opened the door instead.

The sight of the two fairies, wings hidden and looking

like regular human teens in sweaters and jeans, eased some of the tension from Fran's chest.

"Sorry we took so long," Poppy said, skipping past Fran to get to Oote and Mac. She held a shiny gold collar in her hand. "Ivan kept changing his shirt."

Her brother coughed and shook his head as if to suggest Poppy was inventing that. But he smoothed the gray sweater down with his hands, and spun around, modeling. "Looks good though, right?"

It did. The color brought out the striking, fiery reds in his hair and the bright blue of his eyes. He smiled, and Fran's heart skipped. For once it wasn't due to anxiety. Ivan was far too handsome.

"Looks like a sweater," Mac complained, standing up at once while Poppy dealt with Oote. "We're going to be late for our reservation. Honestly, if I'd known how late you two would be, I'd have insisted we strategize here instead of offering to pay for dinner."

"Someone's more anxious about your dads' visit than you," Ivan whispered to Fran as she grabbed her coat.

She elbowed him. "Are you not anxious?"

"I get to meet them?"

Fran's cheeks heated. Ivan must have known he did, otherwise why would he be coming to strategize with her and Mac. "Obviously, you do."

"Oote, put your wings away! You're in disguise," Mac barked before turning to Ivan. "What kind of half-baked collar did you get that lets him do that?"

Fran turned to see a brown-and-white boxer puppy with big gold eyes and a massive pair of purple wings extending from its back. Oote folded them, and they vanished from sight, leaving no sign that the dog walking out the door behind them was actually a dragon.

"That's incredible." Fran wasn't certain if she would ever get used to magic. She couldn't believe the collar had managed to disguise him so completely. "My dads will never guess."

Oote chirped in agreement as he jumped off the couch. That sound alone might make them ask some questions.

Mac rubbed his forehead. "Dogs bark, Oote. Remember you're disguised as a *dog*. We'll go through it all at dinner. Luckily I found somewhere pet friendly. Come on." He tried to usher the rest of them toward the door.

"I have to go to the bathroom first," Poppy said.

Mac's eyes narrowed. He groaned and stomped off. "I'm going to get the car started anyways. Meet me outside the building. Coming, Oote?"

Looking like a boxer puppy, the dragon wagged his tail and bounded toward the tall man. For all his gruffness, Mac waited and walked alongside Oote.

"So who do your dads think Mac is?" Ivan asked, stepping out into the hallway and watching the two as they walked off.

"My godfather," Fran said, taking the opportunity to roll up the welcome mat and stuff it in a nearby cupboard. "It seemed less complicated than *former friend of my bio-dad's due to their shared magical bloodline*."

"And who are you going to tell them I am?"

"My friend," Fran said, cheeks heating again as she stepped into the hallway with him.

When she'd made the decision to stay and live in the Western Woodlands, the possibility of something happening between her and Ivan had obviously been on her mind. But it was too much pressure to declare anything official. Fran's move had been for her and Oote. She didn't want to complicate things by also making it about a boy.

The past couple months had been a transition period. The inhabitants of the Western Woodlands had never allowed a human to live there before. Or a dragon. They had mixed feelings about Oote's growth spurts. But Fran had never loved any place more. And once things settled, then maybe she and Ivan could—

"That's it?" Ivan asked, interrupting Fran's thoughts. He sounded a bit upset, but he had the same smirk he got whenever he teased her.

Fran's heart skipped again. "Would you like me to introduce you as something else?"

"Your *best* friend, obviously." Ivan grinned.

Fran rolled her eyes and shoved him away. She'd thought he was going to ask her out. Not that she'd have been quite ready for that yet.

"Oote is my best friend," Fran said. "Then Poppy, then Mac, then Daisy—"

"Ouch! Are you going to put my parents ahead of me too?"

"Friends don't kiss each other!" Poppy shouted, skipping through the door. Her sudden return startled Fran. How long had the thirteen-year-old been listening?

Fran crossed her arms, suddenly unable to meet Ivan's eyes. Poppy knew not to make comments like that in front of her dads right? They'd already picked up on how often Fran mentioned Ivan when they talked on the phone and grown suspicious.

"What's the cod to lock it, Fran?" Poppy asked, studying the pin pad outside of the apartment's door.

"I don't have it memorized." Fran slapped her palm to her forehead and pulled out her phone. The code was saved with the rest of the information about the rental. "What are my dads going if I don't know the code to my own apartment?"

"Probably not that you're really living in an enchanted forest with a bunch of magical creatures," Ivan reassured her. He rested his hand on her shoulder, reminding Fran to breathe. "It's seventeen-twenty-three."

Poppy typed it in.

Fran stared at Ivan. "You memorized it."

"Not for any nefarious reason," Ivan said, looking abashed and perhaps misunderstanding her tone. "But I unlocked it when I helped bring Oote over."

"And he probably has nefarious plans too," Poppy said, slipping between them and grabbing both their arms. "Now let's run before we get left behind and lose our free dinner."

She dragged them both through the corridors and down to the first floor where Mac waited in the car.

"Shotgun!" Poppy called, climbing into the front seat. Neither Fran nor Ivan tried to stop her.

They sat in the back with Oote half between them. The disguised dragon had placed his front paws in the center console, so he could stare out the windshield.

Together, they drove down the streets of Castor's Grove. And somehow on the drive, between Poppy's excited chatter, Mac's instructions, Oote's incorrect dog noises, and Ivan's smile whenever she caught his eye, Fran's anxiety vanished.

She appreciated Mac wanting to strategize prior to her dads' arrival, but there was no reason to worry. A small oddity here or there wouldn't matter. Her dads wouldn't be looking for flaws in Fran's new life, because they'd see her and they'd know, the same way that she did.

Fran had finally found where she belonged.

NOTE FROM A.J. RENWICK

Thank you so much for exploring the magical city of Castor's Grove!

If you enjoyed *Orphan's Egg*, please tell your friends, or leave a review in the place where you purchased it. It would mean so much to me!

Please visit Plotworks Publishing to explore more of the Castor's Grove universe. Sign up for my newsletter and get a discount!

You can also follow me on Instagram: @aj.renwick

While my initial intention was to keep all of the novels in The Castor's Grove Universe as stand-alones, I'm making an exception. *Orphan's Egg* is getting a sequel. Fran hasn't escaped the crosshairs of the Knights' schemes, and there's more to explore about her bond with Oote and her relationship with Ivan. If this story is something that interests you, definitely sign up for our Plotworks Publishing newsletter!

In the meantime, you can discover more about the many magical species in the city of Castor's Grove. Learn about the Blackwell witches' coven in *Banshee's Breath*, see more of Tobias' villainy in *Changeling's Dagger*, or check out *Dragon's Wisp* for more—well, you can guess which type of creature!

Or read *Angel's Feather*, which features different characters, but does have a surprise cameo from a familiar face (and might offer a hint at where Ivan and Fran's relationship will go)! You'll get to learn about the romance between Eva, a reluctant guardian angel, and Nathan, the boy who has no interest in accepting her assistance. Turn the page now for a preview—

CASTOR'S  GROVE

ANGEL'S FEATHER

a young adult
paranormal
romance

A.J. RENWICK

ANGEL'S FEATHER

Most people would be annoyed about transferring schools at the start of their senior year. Eva preferred to think of it as an opportunity to make new friends.

The crowded parking lot and narrow halls of Dashmoor High School possessed a unique charm. The building's gray and brown color-scheme wasn't drab, but reminiscent of the earth and clouds on a rainy day.

Eva forced a smile as she walked down the hallway. Several of the boys returned it, but their eyes swept toward the hem of her dress. Eva tugged it lower. She tried not to miss the purple plaid skirt and white button-down of her old uniform. Or her friends. Leah would've smiled back at a stranger, and Max never leered at girls and—.

No, stop it. Don't think about them.

Otherwise, Eva's thoughts would turn to her brother. She needed to keep her composure and stay positive.

With that in mind, Eva took a seat near the front of the classroom. She smiled at a pair of girls as they walked past her. One nudged the other and whispered something. Both girls snickered. They kept glancing at Eva as they made their way to the back of the classroom.

That couldn't be good.

Eva reached over her shoulder. The only feathers she felt belonged to her dress.

Phew.

"Interesting outfit for your first day of school." A large girl with gorgeous brown hair stopped beside the desk. She studied Eva's notebook with a pair of bright green eyes. "That your name?"

The brunette tapped the pink swirly letters at the top, which read *Evangelina Heaven.*

"Yes!" Eva responded a bit too quickly. But she couldn't help it. The brunette was the first girl to speak to her. "Everyone calls me Eva though. It's much shorter."

"Huh."

"What's your—?" Before Eva could learn the brunette's name, their teacher stormed in and ordered everyone to their seats.

Mr. Harris was a short man with a bald spot on the back of his head. He taught Grade 12 Advanced Functions and AP Calculus. Unfortunately, Eva had been forced to take the latter. Her math grades had been artificially inflated by Cassel's lax standards for the subject. Teachers at Dashmoor would care a lot more about numbers.

Eva struggled to keep up as Mr. Harris launched a slideshow providing the definitions and explanations of limits. She wasn't used to taking her own notes. Her penmanship looked like chicken scratch.

With more than a little envy, she eyed the tablets of her classmates. Maybe she should ask her parents for one. It could help her blend in. And taking photographs seemed a lot easier than writing by hand. Before the end of the period, Eva's fingers had started to cramp.

The door swung open. A tall boy with long limbs strolled into the room. He kept one hand in his pocket while the other pushed back the black waves of hair falling in his face.

Wow.

Eva forgot about the slideshow. Judging from the whispers, the rest of the class did too.

The boy could've been a model. He had the height, the long limbs, and near perfect features, almost like an artist's sketch come to life. His smooth, golden-brown skin held a natural glow. Just talking to Mr. Harris, the boy's movements displayed an easy casualness that a camera would've loved. Perhaps he thought he'd walked into a photoshoot now because—though he looked about Eva's age—he couldn't be a student. Otherwise, he'd be over thirty minutes late!

"Welcome back, Nathan. So pleased you could join us," Mr. Harris said with obvious annoyance. He pointed to an empty seat near the front.

"Of course," the boy, Nathan, responded in a deep voice that carried the same sense of relaxed wryness as his posture. "Figure if I'm around for at least half the classes, I'll have a full year of work under my belt."

The other students laughed. Eva didn't understand the joke. But she decided to join in.

Unfortunately, she was a beat too late.

The class fell silent, and Eva's giggle hung awkwardly in the air.

From his place in the row ahead, Nathan turned to consider her.

Eva's breath caught. Viewing him in profile at the front

of the class, she'd hadn't noticed his eyes. But they might've been his most striking feature: warm and dark with thick lashes. They reminded Eva of a deer: sweet and almost shy, at odds with his angular feature and aloof demeanor.

Hope flickered in Eva's chest. Maybe Nathan was nice. Maybe they could be friends.

She smiled and raised her hand in a wave.

Nathan snorted and turned away. Not so sweet after all.

Mildly embarrassed, Eva checked her shoulders. Still just her dress. Good. Eva relaxed for a second before realizing that she'd missed several slides.

———

Despite the spasms in her fingers, Eva felt a flutter of excitement as fourth period began. She'd never taken a French class before. But Dashmoor insisted that she needed a language credit.

Eva spotted a vacant seat at the back of the room. A freckle-faced boy in a backward blue baseball cap sat beside it. He leaned against the wall, eyes already closed.

"Mind if I sit here?" Eva inquired as she approached. Asking might've been the wrong move. She'd have been mortified if he said no. But so far, the boys at Dashmoor seemed nicer than the girls.

Baseball Cap opened one eye and grinned. "Not at all. But what're you doing in the back with us slackers?"

Us?

Eva glanced around, expecting another student to materialize in one of the vacant chairs. But of course, no one did.

"Don't you talk?"

"Oh. Yes!" Eva nodded quickly, feeling embarrassed. She should know better than to look for someone invisible hiding in a chair at Dashmoor. "I need a break from taking notes." As evidence, Eva lifted her hand, showing him the way her fingers had cramped, tightening and bending into a claw.

"Yikes. That's why you should never work too hard." He grinned. "My name's Chris by the way."

"I'm Evangelina, but you can call me—"

He snapped his fingers before she could finish. "Blue eyes."

"I was going to say Eva, but sure." Nicknames were a sign of friendship, right? And *Blue Eyes* was still fewer syllables than *Evangelina*.

Ms. Lyle, their French teacher arrived. She was a tall, thin woman with her lips downturned in a perpetual frown. She greeted the class, connected her laptop to a cable on the desk, and projected a slideshow onto the board.

"They're not very creative in their teaching style here, are they?" Eva whispered to Chris.

He gave her another grin. "Now you're getting it."

But Eva had been too hasty in her judgment. Ms. Lyle deviated from the typical slideshow after a few minutes, instructing them to pair up and practice the reviewed vocabulary in conversation.

"That assignment's not for us slackers, Blue Eyes," Chris informed Eva, turning toward her. Still speaking English, he asked, "So, where'd you transfer from?"

"Nowhere interesting," Eva said. It bordered on a lie, but people in the city considered Cassel snobbish and elite. Eva didn't blame them. The school catered to a narrow selection of the population.

"Mysterious," Chris said, rubbing the end of his rather pointed nose. "What do you think of Castor's Grove so far?"

Eva had lived in the city all her life, so her answer was technically the truth. "I love it!"

"Ahem." Ms. Lyle cleared her throat.

Eva jumped. She hadn't noticed the teacher approach, but Ms. Lyle now stood beside them, staring down her nose.

"That doesn't sound like French."

"Aw come on, ma'am," Chris said, rocking his chair as he shrugged. "It's the first day. Let us just chat for once, *sill-vooz-plate*." He butchered the pronunciation so badly that it could only have been intentional.

Ms. Lyle smiled. She clapped her hands and turned toward the rest of the class. "Everyone, focus your attention here. Christopher and his new friend want to chat. Let's listen."

Eva took a deep breath as almost thirty chairs turned toward her.

Don't panic.

Ms. Lyle started with Chris. She asked him several questions about his family and hobbies, but Chris must not have understood. In a phony French accent, he proceeded to tell her about how he'd spent his summer perfecting his skills in a racing game. Other than *oui, oui* and *mademoiselle*, he spoke in English.

Eva laughed along with the rest of the class until Ms. Lyle silenced them.

"Charming. But you'll impress a lot more girls if you can speak the language. Right now, they're simply laughing at you." Ms. Lyle turned to Eva next. "*Ou alors êtes-vous impressionné par les garçons qui échouent en cours de français?*"

Eva stopped laughing. The question seemed like a trap,

but she did her best to answer. *"Non, mademoiselle. Mais Chris a l'air sympa, et je suis hereux de me faire un ami."*

Ms. Lyle's eyebrows rose. Her frown grew more pronounced.

Perhaps Eva should've thrown in an apology. Her response had clearly displeased the teacher.

Ms. Lyle fired off question after question. First about Eva's family, then pets, then books, then movies. Eva had no idea why the French teacher kept changing topic, but she continued to answer until the bell rang signaling the start of lunch.

No one in Room 4B moved.

"I'm sorry, what did you say your name was?" Ms. Lyle asked, switching back to English.

"Evangelina Heaven," Eva responded, shuffling in her chair and wishing the rest of the class would stop staring.

Ms. Lyle's eyes narrowed in immediate dislike. "You're the transfer from Cassel."

A lump rose in Eva's throat. She avoided looking at Chris, but she heard him whistle. Whispers broke out among the rest of the class.

"Your French is quite advanced." Ms. Lyle did not sound impressed. "Perhaps you should challenge yourself with a new language. Spanish perhaps? Or German?"

Eva hesitated. But skirting the truth hadn't helped her before, so she admitted, "I'm fluent in those too."

The class grew louder. Snippets of conversation reached Eva's ears.

"...you really think..."

"...she's such a showoff..."

"...Why is she even here?"

Eva's throat tightened. She didn't know where to look. Her classmates stabbed her with glares or gaped with undeserved awe. They were right to question her presence. Eva shouldn't be there.

Except that my brother got arrested, and now my family are pariahs, and— oh no!

Eva felt it at once. No need to reach over her shoulder and check. She pressed her back further against the seat, heart pounding.

Ms. Lyle's nostrils flared before she forced a tight-lipped smile. "My, my, I do hope we here at Dashmoor can find something to teach you, Evangelina. Class dismissed."

She didn't notice. No one has.

At least, they hadn't yet.

Eva grabbed her bag, slung it over her back, and bolted for the door. Her limbs bumped at least a dozen people as she ran down the hallway. Eva shouted apologies, but she didn't dare stop.

She needed to get to the bathroom before someone realized: Eva's wings had popped out.

PLOTWORKS PUBLISHING

And now turn the page for a peek at another A.J. Renwick series, *The Warlock's Homeowners Association*, a comedic suburban fantasy!

the

WARLOCK'S HOMEOWNERS ASSOCIATION

presents...

BOOK ONE

SUB DIVISION BATTLES OF THE DEAD AND UNDEAD

A.J. RENWICK

SUBDIVISION BATTLES OF
THE DEAD AND UNDEAD

On a cold night in the middle of June, at exactly 10:57 pm (though when the story was retold, the time would be changed to midnight for dramatic purposes), a dead man strode into The Clover Motel.

A brown messenger bag hung from his shoulder, and beneath his arm, he clutched a black chrysalis. It shimmered with iridescent light and radiated with the heavy heat of the underworld.

Bartholomew Whitlock wasn't dead in the traditional sense, or even the untraditional sense. His heart still beat. His breath was steady. He had no desire to moan, hold his arms stiff before him, or eat brains. His death was a metaphorical one.

Gone was Bartholomew Whitlock, exalted among the Acquisitions Department of The Bearded Syndicate, in his place was—

"Bartholomew Bartlow?"

Rebecca Willis, the woman stuck working the night shift at the motel's front desk, peered at the identification card through a pair of pink-rimmed spectacles. Had she looked closely, she might have noticed a curious sheen on the plastic, like it was turning brown in a pattern of lines and dots. But the news was reporting on a plane crash, and Rebecca took a morbid delight in listening to tragic stories, even if only so she could inform her husband the next day and chide him for his lack of empathy when he remained indifferent. She was eager to get this new guest checked in so that she could get back to the television.

Still, she attempted to make what she considered polite conversation as she typed Bartholomew's information into the old computer. "I'll bet school was tough for you."

Rebecca cracked a sympathetic smile and looked at the man before her desk.

He stared back, dark eyes serious beneath a pair of thick black brows that matched the curls on his head. His lips were drawn in a tight thin line. "No," he said, "I was an excellent student."

Rebecca stared at him. There was something unsettling about his voice. In the moment, she couldn't place what it was, but when she recounted the meeting later, she'd realize. Though Bartholomew's face was smooth, not a day over thirty, he spoke like a radio-announcer who was pushing seventy.

"No, I meant— Right, well..." Rebecca waved her hand in dismissal and continued entering the information. "And do you know how long you'll be staying with us, Mr. Bartlow?"

"Who? Oh that's me." He nodded. "No, not yet. But I'll need a pet-friendly room. I'm about to get a cat." For some reason, he shifted the black chrysalis in his arm as he spoke. An arc of light shimmered around it, as though it were wrapped in a rainbow.

Rebecca blinked. She'd never seen anything like it,

which wasn't surprising. Most people, even magical and undead ones, hadn't.

"Very good, Mr. Bartlow. Pets are only allowed in rooms on the first floor. We have one still available." The Clover Motel in fact was mostly empty, but Rebecca had been instructed to say otherwise by her boss, who was under the mistaken assumption that the lie gave the establishment an air of desirability. "We'll keep your credit card information on file until then. Wi-Fi password and information are in a binder on the side table when you go in. Room is right down the hall, second on the left. Here's the key."

She dropped it into Bartholomew's waiting hand. Like the rest of his body, his fingers were long and thin. Unlike the rest of him, they had a tendency to twitch like the limbs of a dying spider. They curled around the key with a snap.

He turned, took two steps toward the hall, and stopped. His fingers flitted into his pocket and retrieved a green bill.

As a habit, Rebecca's interest in guests ended the moment the room key was exchanged. She'd already begun switching the computer tab back to the news. However, the glint of green caught her eye.

It wasn't often that guests bothered to tip her.

And it wasn't a one-, or five-, or even a ten-dollar bill that Bartholomew was crinkling in his fingers. Rebecca recognized Benjamin Franklin's shiny forehead, and even if she hadn't, the two zeros beside it could have only meant one thing.

Bartholomew had her interest once more.

He rested the hundred-dollar bill on the desk. "If someone with a beard shows up, tell me."

"Absolutely!" Rebecca grabbed the money before Bartholomew could change his mind. She would have responded just as eagerly to a ten.

Of course, she would have been just as inefficient if he'd given her a thousand.

Two bearded men would visit the motel in the next week, and Rebecca would inform Bartholomew about neither. Not due to malice, but because the entire encounter slipped from her mind, replaced instead with facts about the night's disaster.

The private plane had exploded mid-air, killing three individuals: the pilot, co-pilot, and a single unnamed passenger. His face flashed across the screen: a man in his thirties with a black beard, long, slicked back hair, and dark eyes that seemed strangely familiar.

I bet he'd be handsome if he shaved, Rebecca thought, and then immediately imagined a new, and incorrect, face for the deceased passenger, which drew more than a little inspiration from the hero on the cover of a romance novel that currently waited beside her bed.

It would be years before she realized that she'd rented a room to a dead man, or even remembered Bartholomew's request. And even then, it would be only for a second before a bearded man plucked the memory from her mind.

PLOTWORKS PUBLISHING

Visit Plotworks Publishing to to continue exploring the Castor's Grove universe—and find many other titles too!

ABOUT THE AUTHOR

A.J. Renwick is a lover of all things fantasy, from mermaids and unicorns to vampires and dragons. She writes young adult paranormal romance with strong plots, dual points of view, and happily ever afters. *Orphan's Egg* is her debut novel.

When she's not writing, A.J. Renwick enjoys reading (duh!), baking (some things more successfully than others), and spending time with her three dogs (the Dragon Squad).

You can find out more about her at Plotworks Publishing.

www.ingramcontent.com/pod-product-compliance
Lightning Source LLC
Chambersburg PA
CBHW031205020726
47499CB00002B/488